CELLARS
OF THE DEAD

Other Five Star Titles
by Marilyn Ross:

Don't Look Behind You

CELLARS
OF THE DEAD

The Stewarts of Stormhaven-2

Marilyn Ross

Five Star • Waterville, Maine

Published in 2004 in conjunction with Maureen Moran
Agency.

The text of this edition is unabridged.

Set in 11 pt. Plantin by Ramona Watson.

Printed in the United States on permanent paper.

Library of Congress Cataloging-in-Publication Data

Ross, Marilyn, 1912–
    Cellars of the dead / Marilyn Ross.
       p. cm.—(The Stewarts of Stormhaven ; 2)
     ISBN 1-59414-173-8 (hc : alk. paper)
     1. Scotland—Fiction.   2. Physicians' spouses—Fiction.
   3. Human experimentation in medicine—Fiction.   I. Title.
PR9199.3.R5996C45 2004
    813'.54—dc22   2004043324

To Irving Fields, pianist, band leader and composer, who I am privileged to call my friend.

Prologue

The Stewarts of Stormhaven!

In a majestic castle of gray stone overlooking the city of Edinburgh the banking dynasty of the Stewarts had lived for the better part of a century. In 1775 the eldest son of the family married Flora Murray, the lovely daughter of a Glasgow doctor. Although the marriage was a happy one, it brought a time of torment to the young bride. Flora was suddenly faced with a set of cool, disapproving in-laws and a weird, hidden secret of the grim Stormhaven. A secret so frightening and dangerous that it threatened her life!

Back in Glasgow, before she considered marrying Ian Stewart, she had been a witness in court against a murderous highwayman, Black Charlie. As a result of her evidence, the burly highwayman was convicted and hung for murder. And from the lips of his witch-like mother a curse was hurled at Flora! It was the Curse of Black Charlie and it followed her to Edinburgh and came to shadow her marriage to the handsome banker, Ian Stewart.

Flora courageously fought the threats, both real and supernatural, which were made against her. Life at the great stone mansion on a hill above the famous Scotch city became a nightmare for her. But she would not give in! And so she survived a period of crisis which might have sent the average young woman to the dark depths of madness.

Flora was determined to solve the mystery of the ancient mansion and become a wife and mother of whom her banker husband could be proud. Within the first ten years of their marriage five children blessed their union.

Flora and Ian also raised Billy, the child of Ian's dead sister. In the period between their marriage in 1775 and the year 1801, the time in which the present story is laid, there were many changes in the Stewart family. Ian Stewart, Sr. and his wife, Flora, found themselves in middle-age, with two grandchildren by their young banker son, Walter, and his wife, Heather Rae.

The eldest of their sons, Ian, Jr., had become a doctor, following in the footsteps of Dr. Jock Gregory, a close friend of the family and a bachelor. In the days before Flora married Ian Stewart, Sr., the young Jock Gregory had courted her. Now he is in his late forties, bald, and one of Edinburgh's most respected physicians.

The present story deals with Dr. Ian Stewart and his wife, Ann. Having chosen to spurn the banking career which was his inheritance, Dr. Ian Stewart is determined to become a noted surgeon. Medicine as we know it today was still in its infancy in 1801. Surgery, especially, was a primitive affair with far too little known about the human anatomy.

Doctors like Ian Stewart who wished to further investigate the human body and needed cadavers to experiment upon were in bad repute. To dissect a human body was considered the height of evil. A sacrilegious act which the ignorant and superstitious felt could bring all manner of horror upon the head of those conducting such experiments. Thus it was that the cellars of the ancient house Dr. Ian Stewart and his wife purchased and which adjoined Mercy Cemetery became known as the "Cellars Of The Dead!"

One

Was her newly-wedded husband insane?

Ann Stewart stared up into the forbidding darkness of her bedroom and debated this terrifying possibility. Only a few minutes earlier she had wakened to find her husband gone from the bed. She lay there with the bedclothes drawn up tightly around her and now she could hear the murmuring of rough male voices from outside.

Her fears increased and she raised herself up from her pillow and stared in the direction of the partly-opened window from which the voices had come. Too many times lately this had happened. Mysterious strangers presented themselves at the house at all odd hours of the night to see her husband. And Ian would tell her little or nothing about these callers and why he was so willing to accommodate them.

Ann slid out of bed and lit the candle in the pewter holder on the bedside table. Then she picked it up and went across the big bedroom to the window which had been raised a little to let in the fresh air. Her winsome, oval face framed by shoulder length auburn tresses was pale. Her lovely blue eyes were glazed with fear. As she came to a halt by the window her slim body, in a nightgown of pink muslin with pretty blue ribbons at neckline and sleeves, was tense.

She gazed out into the black night and strained to see who might be standing down there by the side door to the cellars. The voices were deep and coarse and came to her so blurred she could not tell what was being said. She could recognize her husband's more cultured tones now and then in what seemed to be some sort of argument. But she could not make out the figures. It was frustrating.

It all seemed to be part of the strange behavior of her young husband which had lately made her begin to worry about his sanity. Ever since they had moved into this ancient red brick house with its ivy-clad walls, a change seemed to have come over him. Mercy House, as it was known because it had been built directly adjoining old Mercy Cemetery, had seemed to bring out the worst in him.

When he had courted her the young doctor had seemed as lively and jolly as any of the other young men she'd known. But as soon as they were married he'd become a different person. It was then that he'd shown another side of his personality. He was wildly ambitious to become the most successful doctor in all Edinburgh. He was especially interested in surgery and wanted to become a famous surgeon.

"Can you imagine?" he'd said to her with disgust. "Up until only a little while ago all the surgery was done by barbers!"

"But surely that is changing," she'd said.

"Slowly," her handsome, dark-haired husband had said, a brooding expression on his thin, intelligent face. "Even to this day surgeons are known as mister rather than as doctor. It is a reflection on a noble profession!"

Ann had listened to her husband and felt his tirades were merely part of a young man's enthusiasm for his chosen work. But later she began to wonder. He spent long hours after finishing with his hospital duties and office practice, working in a special room he'd had constructed in the cellar. He called it his surgery and asked that she never enter it.

She had not considered this unreasonable and would have made no objections had he not spent most of his time down there. His surgery had become an obsession with him. At the same time be was becoming strangely nervous. He would remain aloof from her for all but the hours of sleep and then there were disturbances like this one tonight.

Ann could not fathom what it meant. She feared that he was giving so much of himself to whatever he was doing in the cellar surgery that he was gradually changing into an eccentric. Often, when she tried to talk with him and ask for more of his attention, he became angry. It was a difficult situation.

For a time she had worried that even this early in their marriage he had fallen in love with some other young woman. But as she observed Ian more closely she came to a different conclusion. He was caught up in his study of surgery to the point of madness. There seemed to be little else in life which interested him anymore.

The voices outside faded away and were soon lost to her ears altogether. She guessed that the mysterious visitors must have started off again. They probably had finished whatever business they'd had with her husband and had moved on. She crossed to the bed and placed the candle on the bedside table. Then she stood within its limited glow, her eyes fixed on the door as she waited for her husband to return.

Her aunt, Samantha Elliot, who had been both father and mother to her since her parents' death of fever in Italy had left her completely alone in the world at the tender age of five, had not approved of her choice of husband. Dour, spinster Samantha liked to believe herself an astute judge of men, perhaps because she had never married herself.

She had shown a warning look on her plain, long face

which the cruel among her acquaintances called a horse face and with emphasis had told Ann, "I think that young man is too high-strung. Much too nervous. And I hear that he was a student of that mad Dr. Clinton Marsh and has since then continued to be his friend."

Ann had accused her, "You're being unfair. You simply have no wish to see me marry!"

Aunt Samantha had shown annoyance at this by puffing her nostrils and issuing a sort of whinny-like protest which made her seem all the more a horseface. The older woman said, "The Stewarts of Stormhaven may be a fine family and own the largest bank in Edinburgh, but there is a streak of madness in them. It is well known."

"Old wives talk," Ann had replied scornfully. "I do not know a nicer young man than Ian. And I intend to make the year 1801 a memorable one for me by marrying him."

"You'll remember it all right," Aunt Samantha had railed at her. "Remember it and rue it!"

Had her Aunt Samantha been right? Had she married a man tainted with madness whom she did not truly know at all? On nights such as this one she worried that it all might be too sadly so. Each passing twenty-four hours seemed to increase her husband's jittery nerves and irritability. And she was sure these midnight callers were in some way connected with his upset state.

Now she heard his footsteps approaching in the hallway outside the bedroom door. A moment later it opened and Ian came into the room. Even at this late hour and in his bathrobe he was a handsome, commanding figure. His high cheekbones and generally serious mien gave him a look of age beyond his twenty-some years. His curly black hair had been hastily brushed back. He stared at her with an expression of concern.

"What are you doing up?" he asked as he closed the door behind him.

Ann stood there defensively. "It was you and your loud-voiced friends who wakened me! I opened my eyes and found you gone!"

His manner showed impatience. "There was nothing to be worried about. You ought to have gone back to sleep."

"I couldn't!"

"Why not?" he asked, crossing the room slowly to study her.

She found herself losing her nerve under his stern gaze. "I was worried about you," she protested awkwardly. "I feared the intruders might be robbers. Ready to harm you!"

Ian said, "Have you forgotten I'm a doctor?"

"Hardly," she said. "You have not allowed me to forget it."

"When someone in need comes to my door I cannot turn him away!" her young husband said. "That is a rule of my profession."

"Was it someone in need?"

"Yes."

"What sort of need?" she asked.

Her husband's weary, tense face became a little more pale as he said, "That is a question you have no right to ask. You will remember that my relationship with my patients is personal and a matter of trust."

Chagrined, she said, "Is there not trust between a husband and wife also?"

"Trust of a different sort," Ian said. "But since you seem so concerned by our visitors, I will be frank with you. One of them had suffered a wound in a tavern brawl. I repaired the damage and sent them on their way."

"Then why were you arguing with them outside?"

13

He frowned. "So you were eavesdropping?"

"I could not help hearing angry voices. I did not listen to what was being said."

Her husband looked relieved. "I was rebuking them for rousing me from my sleep. For creating the kind of unpleasant situation I am facing now through their drunken squabbling."

Ann listened to his explanation and somehow knew he wasn't telling her the truth. This was merely a glib explanation designed to put her suspicions to rest. She would have been more ready to accept the lie had she not remembered the other nights and those other visitors. There was something dark and sinister going on, of which her husband was a part, and which he dared not divulge to her. So he fed her these lies.

He gazed at her uneasily. "You look as if you didn't believe me."

"What choice have I?" she asked. "I must believe you."

"You must!" he said with a strange intensity. Then he came closer to her and took her in his arms. His eyes gazing into hers with a kind of tragic gentleness, he went on, "You know I love you dearly, Ann! I'm sorry your sleep was disturbed."

"It is of no importance," she said quietly, impressed by his sincerity and wanting to believe him.

"I'm overworked and irritable," he apologized. "Please understand and forgive me!"

"I do," she murmured.

He kissed her tenderly and held her to him for a long moment. Then he said, "And now to bed again. The morning comes early and I have a heavy schedule of hospital rounds."

She nodded with a deep sigh as she allowed him to tuck

her into bed. She watched as he blew out the candle and again worried that he looked so weary and unwell. He took his place in bed beside her in the darkness and lay very still as if something were troubling him and he was trying to straighten it out in his mind.

Ann closed her eyes and tried to sleep. She worried that she might in some way be to blame for the bleak state of their marriage. Certainly she had tried hard enough to be a good wife. But lately Ian had seemed to have no interest in either her or their marriage. At least the interest he showed was purely of a surface nature. Like the moment of tenderness he had shown her just now. In retrospect she could see that it had been a clever performance to placate her.

It was this hiding of something from her which had ruined their relationship. And it had begun when a few months following their marriage they had moved into this ancient red brick house. Ann had been shocked when she'd first seen its great, grim structure. The house was plain to the point of sheer ugliness with only some vines on the walls, gray stone windowsills, a black door and slanted black slate roof to relieve its somber bulk.

"It's so ugly!" she protested when she'd first seen it. "And so large!"

"We need a large house," Ian had smilingly assured her. "I shall have my office at one end of the ground floor. I will need at least three rooms, one a large waiting room. And we'll have three servants to house—Charles, the handyman, Mrs. McQuoid, the cook, and Nancy, who will be the maid."

"Even so," she'd complained, "it is still larger than we need."

"You must think of guests," Ian had pointed out. "We are bound to have some. And I plan to use the cellars for storage and for a special surgery room."

15

She had turned to stare at him. "A surgery room?"

His thin, intense face had been deadly serious. "Yes. You know I intend to become a specialist in surgery. I will need a room for my experiments and dissections."

"Dissections!" she'd shuddered.

"Don't make such a bogey of the word," he'd admonished her. "It's a perfectly respectable practice. The bodies of animals are examined to determine the nature of their structure and pinpoint the ravages of disease. Important!"

She'd told him, "I have no wish to interfere with your work. But mightn't we be able to find some other house which would do as well and be more pleasant?"

"I think not."

She'd pointed to the cemetery gates which were almost next to the house and its small, neglected lawn and said, "I think the proximity to the cemetery is the worst of all. The view from most of the windows will give us nothing more than rows of gravestones!"

Ian shook his head. "There are many houses situated in the various streets bordering on Mercy Cemetery. No one thinks anything of it."

"None of the others are so near it," she protested. "You say the house is itself called Mercy House."

"Yes," her young husband said. "It was built by the same gentleman who planned the cemetery but I can't hold that against it. And there is one strong thing in its favor I haven't discussed with you."

"What?"

"It is very reasonable. I can buy it for less than any of the other houses I have seen."

Ann had stared at him. "Is that so important?"

Ian looked slightly annoyed. "It is. I'm entirely on my own now as a doctor. Because I'm the eldest son of Ian

Stewart everyone automatically thinks I'm rich. I am not! My father is a wealthy banker but that is his money, not mine."

"Some of it will be yours one day," she told him.

"Perhaps," he said stiffly. "Meanwhile I have had my education and now my father expects me to prove my worth."

"I'm sure you will."

"I intend to," Ian said with a slight frown. "Father was upset when I refused to take banking as a career. Now his favorite is my brother, Walter, who is following in his footsteps at the bank. I have chosen to follow the career of my maternal grandfather."

"Your mother told me about him," Ann said. "He was a famous doctor in Glasgow."

Ian nodded. "Yes. He was slain there by highwaymen one winter's night. Mother told me the story first when I was a mere child. I never forgot it nor my grandfather's courage. And with Jock Gregory's encouragement I became a doctor."

"Jock Gregory?" she asked.

"You have not met him," Ian said. "He is presently in America, doing some research at a hospital in the great city of Philadelphia. He is a friend of my mother and father and often visits Stormhaven when he is here in Edinburgh."

"Does he practice medicine here?"

"Only at the hospital," her young husband said. "Mostly he teaches at the college. He is the favorite medical instructor, though not in my opinion the best. The best of all is Dr. Clinton Marsh."

Ann remembered her aunt's description of the university professor and asked, "Do you mean the one they call 'Mad Marsh'?"

Ian frowned at her. "Who told you that was his nickname?"

"Aunt Samantha. She is a great gossip."

"I know that all too well," Ian had said disdainfully. "I have found her never fair to me and she is not being fair to Dr. Marsh. I consider him a genius."

"I'm sure you know him a great deal better than Aunt Samantha and so are better able to judge his qualities," she told her husband.

"He has an unfortunate appearance and he is dedicated to his profession," Ian said. "And these things are unfairly held against him."

The discussion of Dr. Clinton Marsh had ended with this. But she later heard the eminent doctor's name brought up by Ian and his friend, Dr. Harry Turner, when they were together. Dr. Harry Turner had been in medical school with Ian and now practiced in association with his father, the renowned Dr. Edward Turner.

Harry Turner was a bachelor and often dropped by in the evenings to have a glass or two of whiskey and exchange medical gossip with Ian. These were usually the few evenings when Ian tore himself away from his labors in the cellar surgery. Ann prepared special food for their guest and so was often invited to sit and listen to the two young doctors exchange opinions. The gatherings came to mean a great deal to her since they represented almost all their social life other than the occasional visits they made to Stormhaven to see Ian's family.

Dr. Harry Turner was handsome and blond with a quick smile and an excellent bedside manner which was proving an asset to him now that he'd joined his father's practice. But he was openly envious of Ian's skill at surgery.

He'd often say to Ian, "I wish I had the same skill you have in your hands. Then I would be enthusiastic about surgery also."

Ian would reply, "And I think you are by far a better diagnostician than I am."

Humor flecked Harry Turner's blue eyes as he turned to Ann and said, "I'll grant you that. And I diagnose that Ann should have married me instead of you."

His friend's brazen humor seemed to be enjoyed by Ian, who at once turned to her and asked, "Well, what do you say to that diagnosis, Ann?"

Her cheeks burned and she said, "I think the diagnosis has no solid basis. I did not know Harry at the time you courted me. So I have no means of knowing whether I would have preferred him or not. And it doesn't matter now since I am your wife."

"You see!" Harry Turner told Ian, "You are always the winner. The lass loves you even though you scarcely deserve it. And once again I take second place. It was always this way at college!"

And so the banter would go on between them all evening. Ann welcomed the visits of the other young doctor as they meant that Ian would desert his surgery in the cellar, and because the evenings usually left him in a better mood.

She lay fuzzily thinking that Harry Turner had not come to visit them for some time. He probably was busy with his own practice. It was at this moment that sleep finally overtook her.

She awoke the next morning to a gray, April day. Her husband had long gone on his hospital calls and she rose alone and attended to washing and dressing. The maid always left a covered jug of hot water just outside her bedroom door in the morning.

Nancy, the pretty, round-faced maid, also served her at breakfast in the bleak dining room with its gloomy brown wallpaper and ugly still-life paintings in gilt frames for decoration. Ann meant to change the decor of the entire house as soon as she could.

She asked the maid, "Did the doctor leave at his usual time?"

Nancy offered her a pleasant smile. She had full red lips and astonishingly white, even teeth. So many of the working classes had neglected, rotting teeth that one noticed her healthy ones. The girl poured out Ann's tea and said, "Yes, ma'am, he left about seven."

"Did he say if he would return for lunch?"

"No, ma'am," the maid said. "But he is bound to be back for his patients at one o'clock." Ian had afternoon office hours from one to five.

"Yes, I think you'd better plan on his being here for lunch then," Ann said. She was thinking about the intruders who had interrupted their rest and decided that Ian must have had very little sleep. No wonder he was nervous and pale.

She finished breakfast and then went out for a short stroll. Charlie, the elderly handyman, was on his knees, working at the two flower beds in the front lawns. He paused in his labors to tip his cap to her. He had a brown, wrinkled face on which there was almost always a stubble of gray beard. His eyes were sunken and blue but still bright enough. "I dinna ken if there's much I can do with the flowers, ma'am," he said. "They have had so much neglect."

She stood by sympathetically. The desolation of the grounds had been another depressing feature of the property. She told him, "You can only do your best. It will take a few summers to get it all right."

"Might be longer than that," the old man said. And then with a look of interest, he asked, "Did someone make a delivery of something in the middle of the night? I heard sounds and looked out my window to see a wagon outside and two men in conversation with the doctor."

She listened to him fill in some of the details for her and rather apprehensively said, "I don't know of anything being delivered."

Old Charles said, "I thought it might be furniture or something of the sort. I was waiting for the master to call me to see to bringing it in. You mentioned you had ordered some pieces from London."

"They haven't come yet," she told the gardener. "And it is doubtful that they would be delivered in the middle of the night, in any case."

"I hadn't thought of that, ma'am," the old man admitted. "I know that sometimes the ships dock in the wee hours and I thought they might have decided to bring whatever came straight here."

Uneasily, she said, "I don't think it was a delivery at all. The doctor mentioned that someone had been hurt and came to him for help."

"I dinna guessed that," the old man confessed. "I thought the talk was all outside and about some sort of delivery. But then there was nothing to be carried in this morning and the doctor had gone before I had a chance to speak with him."

"He left early," she agreed. "He has a great many patients to see at the hospital just now."

The sound of a wagon approaching made her look up and see an old-fashioned wagon with great, creaking wheels making its way in the driveway. Two men sat on the seat at the front of the gray wagon, the driver with the reins in his hand, and an older, squat man seated next to him. The carriage came to a halt and as she walked over to it the squat man jumped down from his seat to stand on the gravel walk facing her.

"How do you do," he said, removing his three-cornered hat and bowing. He was a strange figure in a shabby purple jacket and dirty yellow vest. His string tie was loosely tied with one end hanging down too far and his peach-colored breeches were stained and faded. But it was his facial appearance which struck her as most remarkable. The only way she could think of it was to tell herself he had the face of a lizard. Thick lips, heavy-lidded eyes, a wide nose with flaring nostrils and a scaly sort of skin gave him the lizard-like appearance.

"Are you looking for Dr. Stewart?" she asked.

The squat man nodded. "Yes. Is he not here?"

"No. He is at the hospital," she said. "May I ask who you are?"

The squat man's heavy-lidded eyes showed a flicker of annoyance at this news. In a rasping voice, he told her, "I was expecting the delivery of something important from him."

"I'm sorry," she said. "There is nothing here for you, I'm certain."

The squat man hesitated. "Could there be something and he not tell you?"

"No. I would know about it. What were you expecting?"

"A box of medical instruments from London," the man said. "They were coming from London by schooner. I did not want them delivered at the college so Ian said they could be sent here."

"I'm sorry," she said, trying not to stare at him. "He is at the hospital and he will be home at the noon hour."

"If you're sure there's nothing I may as well get on my way," the squat man said curtly. "You can let him know I was here. My name is Dr. Clinton Marsh."

Her eyebrows lifted. "From the college! You were his favorite teacher. He often speaks of you."

"Indeed," the old doctor said unsmilingly. "That is most flattering." He offered her his hand and she was shocked to see that it had the same scaly texture of skin and was shaped much like the claw of a lizard. "Good day to you, Mrs. Stewart!"

Reluctantly she took the offered hand and managed a small voiced, "Good-bye!"

The squat man scrambled up onto the wagon seat and said something to the driver. The wagon rumbled off at the same time as a smart black coach came into the driveway. The top-hatted driver leaped down from his perch at the back and opened the door of the carriage to help out a petite, brown-haired girl in green bonnet and dress. The girl came quickly to Ann, her parasol in hand. She had a baby-doll sort of prettiness and was very affected in her ways. Now she rolled her long-lashed eyes and exclaimed, "What an important lady you are today, Ann! So many callers!"

"And all of them unexpected," Ann told her. The girl's name was Martha Todd, the young sister of Samuel Todd, a lawyer who had courted Ann at the same time as Ian and had never forgiven her for choosing the doctor rather than him.

Martha glanced at the rapidly vanishing carriage and said, "What a strange-looking man that was talking to you just now!"

"He's a professor at the college and once he taught Ian," Ann said.

The petite Martha gave a dainty shudder. "He's so ugly!"

"Yes," Ann said, not wanting to discuss her visitor more

23

with the talkative Martha. "Won't you come in and have some tea and cakes?"

"I'd like that," the girl agreed at once. "We were driving by and I saw you in the driveway and asked Thomas to stop. By the way, my brother sends his warm regards to you."

"How kind of him," Ann said and led the other girl into the house.

As they sat in the dark living room the doll-like Martha gazed at the grim furnishings in despair and said, "Doesn't this house depress you. The furniture is awful!"

Politely, Ann said, "These things came with the house. I have furniture on order."

"I should think so," Martha said, daintily sipping her tea. "The Stewarts are so stingy with their money."

"Ian has none of his father's money," Ann was quick to reply. "We are living on his earnings alone."

Martha rolled her lovely gray eyes. "Had you married my brother, Sam, you would have had a fine house and all the nice furniture you could have wished."

"But I didn't marry Sam."

"Worse for you," Martha told her. "He is still in love with you. He hasn't eyes for any other girl."

"I'm sorry. He should soon marry. I'm certain he'd make the right girl a fine husband."

Martha stared at her over her teacup. "You think that, yet you didn't marry him."

Ann smiled in a melancholy way. "I think I explained that to you before and I certainly made it clear to Samuel. I loved Ian and I only liked Sam."

The petite girl sat back with a sigh. "I think it was the name of Stewart which swayed you. The Stewarts of Storm-haven mean so much in Edinburgh. They are at the top of the social and financial world now. But that wasn't always so. There is a dark history to the family."

"I haven't heard of it," Ann said.

"Samuel knows all about it from the senior partner in his law firm," Martha assured her. "There is a record of madness and dissipation in the Stewart family history. Of course Ian won't tell you about it. Nor his parents. But they say his adopted brother, Billy, who was drowned while serving in the navy, was actually the son of some sort of criminal. Sam says the Stewarts weren't too heartbroken to see the end of him."

Annoyed, Ann said, "I'm startled to discover Sam has such an interest in my husband's family history."

Martha smiled cattily. "He only began delving into the subject after you married Ian."

"I'd thank him to refrain from this hobby," she said with some bitterness.

"He thinks there are certain things you should know for your own protection," her former suitor's sister pointed out. "It's possible that Ian could inherit the family madness or your children when you have them."

"That is foolish talk!"

"Maybe so," Martha Todd said airily. "But Sam hears a great deal about what is happening in the city. He says there are strange goings-on in the medical circles. And he wouldn't be surprised if your fine Ian was mixed up in what is taking place."

"What are you talking about?"

"I can't say," Martha told her. "But Sam asked me to tell you to speak to your husband about the resurrectionists."

"Resurrectionists?"

"Yes."

"I never heard such a word before," Ann said. "What does it mean?"

"Why don't you ask Ian?" was Martha's taunting reply. She rose and picked up her parasol. And, as she moved to leave the room, she paused to turn and say, "And Sam also said to ask him about the history of this house."

Ann's impatience with the petite Martha was now strained to the breaking point. She asked angrily, "Is this another of your insinuations?"

"If you want to call it that, do so," the tiny girl said in her overbearing fashion.

"What about this house?"

"I think your husband should tell you," Martha said in taunting fashion. "He is the one who brought you here. I would have expected you to object just because of the cemetery. Imagine waking up to view all those gravestones every day!"

"The house has virtues as well as faults," Ann said coldly. "We have plenty of room for Ian's patients. He has his office here, you know."

Martha smiled cattily. "Perhaps he will not have so many patients if the scandal breaks."

"What scandal?" Ann asked, outraged.

"He can tell you," Martha said, a smug look on her doll's face. "Now I must hurry along. I have to meet my mama at the milliner's!" And she swept out of the room.

Ann preserved an outward calm she did not feel as she saw the catty Martha on her way. Then she went back inside the grim old house and stood thinking of all the taunting remarks the girl had made. What could she mean about scandal? And what did the word resurrectionist signify? And what was there about the history of the house which she did not know?

She walked to the stairway about to go up when another thought struck her. Could that wagon have made some sort of delivery the night before and Ian not have told her about it? If so, whatever had been delivered, and it might have been her furniture, would be in the cellar near the side door where she'd heard Ian talking to the men. Perhaps Ian wanted to keep the furniture as a surprise.

This seemed so reasonable she decided to go down to the cellar and see if there were any new packages there. She went along the shadowed hall and down the steep stairs to the dank cellar. There were several dusty windows to give a small amount of light. She made her way to the cellar door at the side of the ancient house and saw there was nothing there. At least Ian had told her the truth.

On the way back to the stairs she had to pass the door to the room he had dubbed his surgery. It was here he spent hours at a time, working late into the night, dissecting the dogs and cats and other small animals which provided him with the information he sought to perfect his surgical technique. Normally Ian kept the door padlocked when he was not there. But he had somehow forgotten to lock the door on this occasion.

Ann halted before the unlocked door. And though she knew it was forbidden territory to her a sudden curiosity about the room and what her husband did there made her reach out for the door handle and slowly turn it. Her heart pounding with barely suppressed excitement she slowly opened the door.

The shadowy regions of the room were exposed to her. By the murky light of a tiny, single window she saw the big table. Then as her eyes adjusted to the dull light she saw something on the table which made her cry out in horror. The partly dissected remains were not those of a dog or cat but of a human!

Two

Ann drew back in horror at the gruesome sight of the cadaver on the table partially covered by a cloth of some kind, its severed right arm stretched out beside it. She closed the door on the murky room and shut her eyes and bent her head as she stood there still holding the door handle. She was too stunned to move for a moment. She feared she might be physically ill and fought back the nausea which assailed her.

Then she turned and groped her way up the narrow stairs to the hall. She hurried along the dark hall and up the main stairway to their bedroom. There she sat on the side of the bed and stared dully ahead of her as she tried to decide what it all meant. Ian had sworn to her that his experiments in the surgery had been confined to the dissection of animals. Now she knew that he had lied to her. She had just seen the remains of a human body down there!

Her next thought was where had it come from? Doctors were only allowed to dissect the bodies of criminals hung for murder or some similar crime. Where had Ian come upon such a body and why had he concealed the truth about it from her? Perhaps because he was afraid of terrifying her. The knowledge that a corpse was down there in the surgery was not of the most pleasant nature. It must have been somehow preserved and been down there for a long while.

All those late nights when her husband had labored in the cellar surgery room he'd been dissecting the body of some unfortunate. She began to worry more about where the body had come from than about his lying to her.

The comments which the catty Martha had made now came back to nag her. Was it possible that Martha and Samuel Todd knew something which was still a secret to her? Martha had even hinted about some scandal breaking which might involve Ian and hurt his practice. Could the girl have somehow learned that he was dissecting human bodies? There was great opposition to this type of experiment everywhere.

At the moment Ann didn't know whether to condemn or defend her husband. Perhaps what he'd been doing helped to explain the subtle change which had come over him. Some weight of guilt had transformed him from a thoughtful, carefree young husband to a tense, aloof and embittered one. How would she go about finding out the truth? Surely there could be no better action than to face him with what she'd already learned and ask him to fill in the rest.

With this resolved she rose to go down and see her husband at lunch. Not that she felt like eating anything but she wanted a straight talk with him. She went downstairs and met the pretty maid, Nancy, in the front hall. Nancy was holding a tray of food in her hands.

"Where are you taking that?" she asked.

"To the doctor's office, ma'am," the maid said.

"He's taking his lunch in there, then?"

"Yes, ma'am," the girl said and hurried off.

Ann did not know whether she was relieved or annoyed. She had hoped to talk to Ian at once. Now it could be delayed until the dinner hour or later. But there was nothing she could do. With Ian his patients came first.

Already they had begun to arrive. The rich in their carriages and the poor standing in a ragged line along the street and all the way up the front steps. They were a motley crew, some with bandages on heads, arms or bodies with the stain of blood showing through. The wealthy often waited in their carriages while their servants took places in the line. Then when it was about time for them to be ushered in they would exchange places.

Ann knew that Ian would have his lunch tray on his desk and manage a bite now and then between patients or even while he interviewed someone whom he knew. It was a way of saving time. A way she did not approve of but he would not listen to her pleas that he at least take a few minutes to eat briefly with her.

Today she did not care. She couldn't face food anyway so soon after her discovery of what was going on in the cellar. She felt she must get away from the grim old house and the long line of the weak and the wounded. Finding her cloak she threw it hastily over her shoulders and pulled the hood up over her hair. Then she quickly left the house by one of the side doors.

In this way she avoided meeting any of the patients. The driveway was cluttered with carriages and people. So she took a side path which landed her safely away from the house grounds at the gates of Mercy Cemetery. Since she had very little choice, she decided to wander through the cemetery for a little. At least she could enjoy the air and the quiet. The rows of gravestones were divided by narrow pathways along which many tall elms grew and offered shade.

It was a strange, melancholy place and yet at the moment a kind of refuge for her. As she walked down the winding pathway of the cemetery she glanced back over her shoulder and saw the grim red house and the cluster of carriages and people in front of it. What a strange sort of life she had married into. And yet as she had told the catty

Martha only that morning, she was deeply in love with Ian.

That was why the present situation troubled her so. She badly needed her marriage to be a success. She longed for the warmth and love which she had missed as a growing child. Her aunt had been capable but cold in her care of her. So as womanhood approached Ann had dreamed of a marriage filled with love and affection. Ian had at first seemed to offer her that sort of marriage, but now it had all changed.

As a child she had vague memories of a frail mother and a stalwart, red-haired father forever lifting her up in his arms and laughing affectionately at her. Then there had come the dread day when her mother and father had left her with Aunt Samantha. And she never set eyes upon them again.

Years later she learned from her aunt that the reason her parents had departed so swiftly was that the consumption which had been eating away her fragile mother's lungs had suddenly taken a turn for the worse. The family doctor had solemnly pronounced she would not live six months if she remained in Scotland.

So her father had quickly arranged for someone to buy his leather business so he could take his ailing wife to the south of Italy. He decided to leave Ann with Samantha rather than risk her being continually exposed to her desperately ill mother. So she had been left behind in Edinburgh. What ensued was truly a matter of grim irony. Her parents had barely been installed in the villa in the small Italian city they had chosen when the area was stricken by yellow fever. Both her father and her mother fell victims to the plague and so before three months had gone by, they were both dead in that foreign land.

One day Ann hoped to visit Italy and see her parents'

graves. Samantha had even offered to take her as bribe for her not to marry Ian Stewart. But Ann had been too deeply in love to be tempted by the offer. Ian had promised to take her and she had believed him. Now, like everything else, it was left open to doubt.

As her mind rambled over these things she had slowly made her way deeper within the city of the dead known as Mercy Cemetery. She had no idea how old it was or how large an area it took in. But it was a large cemetery for the city and had been started years ago by a man named Jacob Mercy, the same Jacob Mercy who had built the red brick house she and Ian now owned.

With the passing of the years the cemetery had become somewhat less fashionable. But there were still a goodly number of burials. Hardly a day passed that she had not seen at least one solemn procession entering the brick and iron gates. White horses pulling a black hearse, its glassed sides hung with fringed black velvet curtains. Top-hatted drivers and funeral assistants. Carriages creaking slowly behind the hearse, followed by sober mourners on foot. For many chose to walk behind the funeral cortege as a mark of their respect.

The area of the cemetery in which she now found herself was truly isolated, with not even a glimpse of the streets and houses surrounding it. She stood beneath one of the giant elms lining the roadway and gazed about her with a tense feeling. A grim silence cloaked her surroundings. The gray, ghostly shapes of the gravestones loomed around her like a watching, silent throng studying an intruder!

Ann swallowed hard and told herself not to be afraid. She had chosen this place as a refuge and she mustn't spoil its benefits by allowing her fears to take over. She moved along the roadway, a solitary figure in the gray midday, and gave her attention to the occasional more impressive forms of tombstone statuary.

At one point there was a sweet-faced angel poised on a fluted column, the angel's face now pock-marked from long exposure to the weather and one of her wings chipped. Further along there was a child's head on a similar column like some gruesome offering to a wanton Herod. It reminded her of the mutilated body she'd seen in the cellar, and so she turned away from it.

Now on a slight hill to her left she saw a great tomb with the family name of Smith in the granite above its rusted iron doors. In tombs of this sort there were often a half-dozen to a dozen coffins interred. All members of a family resting together in that final sleep. She had been to a funeral where the casket had been placed in a similar tomb and had been grimly fascinated by the practice.

The number of burials possible in these tombs depended on the size of them. Some of them showed only the entrance and front structure above ground, but deep within their dark recesses entire families could be buried. Each casket rested on a dusty shelf and the shelves sometimes rose six caskets high.

All these memories came crowding back to her as she stood staring at the rusty doors of the tomb in front of her. Then, without warning, one of the rust-red doors began to slowly open towards her. She stood there, staring at this door from the grave as it gradually opened, her lips and body frozen with fear!

A head with a wide-brimmed black hat poked out of the tomb and she saw a wrinkled, toothless, grinning face which looked more like a skull than the face of anything living. The brown, wrinkled face had small, sunken eyes which peered at her now.

"Don't be afraid," a hoarse voice said. "I'm not a phantom, though I live among them."

The words served to break through the barrier of panic which had separated her from voice or movement. Suddenly she found herself trembling as she asked the apparition, "Who are you?"

The creature climbed out of the tomb to reveal a long, lanky body wrapped in a tattered cloak of black to match the shabby black hat.

"I am a grave digger by profession," the apparition said in the same hoarse voice. "As the result of reduced circumstances, I have been forced to seek shelter among my former customers. And may I say they are a good deal more friendly than many of those more lively in Canongate."

She drew away from him a little as she gasped, "You live here in the cemetery?"

The face like a rotten, wrinkled plum showed amusement at her horror. "I do. I sleep with the Smiths, though I must admit my slumber does not match theirs in length."

And he flapped his long arms about him and cackled with a maniacal glee.

Ann's pretty face was distorted by fear. "It is wrong of you to live here in a tomb!"

The apparition in black shook his head. "No, ma'am. It would be much more wrong of me to freeze from exposure to the elements. And that is what I would surely do had I not a resting place with the Smiths."

"Is it known you sleep here?"

"Bless you, ma'am, I do it with the permission of the caretaker. It's not easy to find reliable grave diggers who know their business these days. He's glad to have me available under any terms. And my terms include lodging."

She tried to accept it all. "Aren't you afraid here?"

"Now that's a silly question," the man in the tattered black cloak and battered black hat said. "I'm much less liable to harm from this lot around me than I would be from the same group alive in a tavern."

"You terrified me!" she said.

"Not intended," the apparition assured her. "I know who you are, ma'am. You're the doctor's wife. You and your husband have come to live in Mercy House. Name of Stewart."

"You are right," she said. And somehow the fact that he knew her name and all about her made her less afraid of him. He seemed at once less of a specter and more a human being. Though in truth he had come to resemble the dead around him in an uncanny way.

He said, "I have watched you from the inside of the gates."

"Do you ever leave this place?" she asked.

The tall man in black came a few steps nearer to her and she could smell the odor of the grave from him in an eerie sort of way. He smiled, revealing his toothless gums as he informed her, "I only leave when I need a new supply of vittles, or a bottle or two of whiskey. Preserve the body in whiskey, I say, and you'll last 'til Gabriel comes along with his horn."

"So you do go out for food and drink."

"When I have the few pennies required," the thin man said in his hoarse voice. "Grave digging isn't a paying profession anymore. Too many in it. Scoundrels who have no respect for the dead. Villains who live for the bottle alone. Now that could never be said of me."

"How long have you lived this way?"

"I've lost track to be truthful, ma'am," the apparition said. "I lost my woman years back. The bairns have long gone out into the world with no thought of their poor old father. Angus McCrae is quite alone in this world."

Ann studied him with new interest. "You do have a name then, Angus McCrae?"

"That is right, ma'am," the apparition said. He glanced at the Smith tomb and with a gleeful cackle said, "The caretaker says that under the circumstances I ought to change my name to Angus McCrae Smith. But I was never one for three names. Too posh."

She frowned slightly. "Don't you find it scary here?"

"It can be that. When there's a storm and the trees are twisting and moaning in the wind. In a bad rain the water gets down to where I am."

"Do you believe in ghosts, then?"

The ruined, wrinkled plum face became solemn. "Indeed I do!"

"Doesn't that make you afraid to remain here?"

He shook his head. "You let them be and they won't bother you. I never interfere with them."

Ann said, "I can't believe the things you say! You are like one of the dead!"

"I am in most ways," the lanky Angus McCrae said. "I have no ties with the world except with the bottle now and then. And there are worse things in this cemetery to fear than the dead!"

Her eyes widened. "What worse things?"

"Things that a lovely young lady like you ought not to know about," was his unsatisfactory reply.

"I live so near here I should know what goes on. I ought to be aware of any danger for my protection."

The bizarre figure in tattered black waggled a boney finger at her. "Your husband should protect you. Though he can't think much of it, taking you to live in Mercy House."

Ann said, "That is another thing! What is this mystery about Mercy House?"

Angus McCrae looked sly. "Come now, ma'am. It can't be any secret to you!"

"I'm afraid it is," she said.

The weird man chuckled. "Then I must say your husband has played a fine trick on you. I sometimes stop by your back door and your good Mrs. McQuoid gives me any leftovers from the kitchen."

She stared at him. "I have never seen you."

"I have a way of not being seen," the thin man in black said mockingly. "Maybe it comes from my living here."

Ann asked him, "Tell me about Mercy House."

The rim of the thin man's battered hat twisted in the wind and he held his tattered cloak tightly about him. He said, "It is a long story. You had better follow me over where we can be out of this stiff breeze."

Ann followed him without question. It amazed her how quickly she had come to accept this strange Angus McCrae and listen to him. He led her to a hollow and indicated that she seat herself on the top of a small, flat-topped tomb which resembled a granite table. It served them well as a bench and the hollow was sheltered from the wind and not nearly so cold.

She turned to stare up into the wrinkled face and asked again, "What is the truth about the house?"

Angus McCrae compressed his lips, making his toothless gums meet in a weird fashion. Then he said, "You know the house was built by Jacob Mercy who planned this cemetery?"

"Yes."

"Later the house was lived in by the son of Jacob Mercy and his wife, Sophie. It was during this time that a tragedy occurred there."

"What sort of tragedy?"

The thin man smiled bleakly, "It is said that Jacob Mercy found his wife was unfaithful to him. In any event, the two had a quarrel and she went to live with her sister in a house in a fashionable part of the city. Her husband regretted being so quick to quarrel with her and begged her to return to him. But she refused."

"So?"

The thin man in black stared off at a distant gravestone as if he saw something there which was invisible to her. He gazed at this spot for a little and murmured something to himself which she could not make out. Once again she began to be fearful of him, terrified that he might be violently insane rather than merely eccentric.

At last he began to speak again in that hoarse voice. He told her, "The husband felt that his wife must still be seeing the younger man who had stolen her affections. And so he sent a note inviting the young man to Mercy House on some sort of pretense."

Ann said, "Did the young man go?"

"He did," Angus McCrae said. "And he'd hardly been in the house when the outraged husband set upon him and killed him. That afternoon the wife, in the house on the other side of the city, received a hatbox by messenger. The hatbox was from her husband."

"He sent her a gift?"

The plum face crinkled in a weird smile. "Yes, ma'am. He sent her a gift! When she opened the hatbox she found the head of her lover in it! Her husband had decapitated the young man and sent her the bloodied head with its wild, staring eyes as caught in the moment of his death!" The thin man paused.

She was sickened by the story. "Horrible!" she whispered.

Angus McCrae seemed to relish telling the macabre tale. He smacked his lips. "Yes," he said. "She collapsed on the floor by the hatbox. And when her sister found her she had hysterics but managed to call her own husband. And he sent for the police."

"What about the murderer?"

"The police went to Mercy House," the man in black told her. "They discovered the headless body of the young man in the scullery, and in the attic they found the husband hanging from a rafter!"

"A suicide!"

"Yes, ma'am, a suicide; so the law was cheated of the hanging of him."

"What about his wife?"

"She was never right in the head again," Angus McCrae said. "She just sat in silence without seeing anyone or taking notice of anything. It wasn't long before she was dead."

"What a terrible tragedy!" Ann gasped.

"Since then, the ghost has shown itself regularly at Mercy House," the man on the tombstone beside her said.

She asked, "Ghost? What ghost?"

Angus McCrae said, "The ghost of the headless young man. Do you mean to say you haven't seen it yet?"

"No. I didn't know anything about it until just now."

The thin man gave her a wise look. "The house was empty because of its bad reputation. I used to slip in by a cellar door which wasn't fastened and spend the nights there during the winter. It was better than the tomb."

"My husband told me he was able to get the house for a very good price," she recalled.

"It would be bound to go cheap."

"But he didn't tell me why."

"He ought to have done," the apparition in black said. "It wasn't fair of him not to tell you."

She gazed at the tall, thin man in alarm. "Did you ever see the ghost when you were sleeping there in the empty house?"

"I did, ma'am. But, as I told you, I mind my own business and so the ghosts don't harm me!"

"Don't you think it's just a story? A legend?"

"No, ma'am," the spare Angus McCrae said, "I happen to be one of those who seen the ghost!"

"And you think that I will see it?"

"Bound to if you stay there. If I was you I wouldn't stay in that old house. It's a bad luck place. You and the young doctor could find yourselves under its curse!"

Ann gave a tiny shudder. "Ian must have heard the legend. I can't think why he didn't tell me."

"He likely thought you'd be scared out of your wits by the story, ma'am," Angus McCrae said.

"Perhaps so," she said bitterly.

"I wouldn't have mentioned it, but you said you wanted to hear why the old house is said to be haunted."

"Thank you for telling me," she replied.

The thin man got up from the tomb. "Maybe you won't thank me later on. They claim as long as you don't know about the headless phantom you don't ever see it. Now you know about it."

"My own wish," she said, rising. "Now I must go back."

The tall, thin man in the battered black hat and shabby cloak asked her, "Will you tell your cook not to feed me anymore?"

"Of course not," Ann said. "Come by any time you like."

"Thank you, ma'am," the spare Angus McCrae said.

"You are a true lady and I hope the ghost doesn't ever bother you."

"I hope not," she said.

The plum face showed an anxious expression. "And you won't say anything to your husband about my living here?"

"Not if you don't want me to."

"I'd rather you didn't."

"Then I won't," she said.

"Thank you, ma'am," the tall man in black said again.

She started along the path between the gravestones which led to the roadway. After she'd gone a few steps she looked back over her shoulder to ask the thin man another question, but to her amazement he had vanished.

Halting, she turned to try and see some sign of him. He seemed to have disappeared into thin air. She called out to him, "Mr. McCrae, where are you?"

There was no reply as her voice trailed off among the rows of gravestones. The silent, gray stones seemed to be mocking her as she stood there, an intruder among them. In a flurry of fear she wheeled around and ran to the roadway. There she felt a trifle less afraid. But the mysterious disappearance of the weird figure in black had left her in a tense state.

She began walking along the roadway in the direction of the cemetery gates and Mercy House. Had it all been a flight of her imagination? Or had she been talking to a ghost? There was no evidence to show that she had met anyone. He had appeared out of a tomb and then vanished among the gravestones. If she told anyone the story they would scoff at her.

Yet she believed it had all been real. Angus McCrae was truly a drunken, itinerant grave digger who had fallen to such a low state as to actually make his home in one of the

41

tombs in the cemetery. She knew that most grave diggers were drawn from the human scum of the city and had the reputation of being drunken renegades. They did the work because they were fit for nothing else.

The story of the tragedy at Mercy House and the legend of its headless ghost had shocked her. She felt that Ian had tricked her into living in a house under the shadow of a phantom. He at least should have told her. But it seemed he was anxious to buy the house for his own selfish reasons. It gave him plenty of cheap space for his experiments and it was in a central city location for his practice.

She was filled with a mixture of fear and indignation. A few raindrops began to fall as she neared the gates and the ancient red brick house. She saw that the line of patients before the front door was still quite long. There were also some carriages waiting. She again used the path to the side entrance to enter the house.

She made her way directly to the kitchen where she found the ample cook, Mrs. McQuoid, busy rolling out pastry on a board set on the huge kitchen table. The big woman had a jolly face and she greeted her with a smile.

"A busy day for the doctor, ma'am," the cook said. "Nancy has had to watch the door and let in only a few at a time."

"I saw that," she said. Then, giving the cook a questioning look, she asked, "Have you been giving food to a thin old man who lives in the cemetery?"

Mrs. McQuoid halted in her task and her face took on a guilty expression. "I have, ma'am. Why do you ask? I've given him only food which couldn't be used by anyone in the house."

"I wanted to know," she said. "I met him and he told me he came by here occasionally."

"I'll not give him anything more if that's your wish. He is old and a little mad, and I felt sorry for him."

"It's all right," Ann said. "I don't mind his having the food. I just wanted to check and see if his story were true."

The cook looked relieved. "It is true, ma'am."

"Then don't think anything more about it," she said. "Go on as you have been doing." And she left the kitchen to go up to the bedroom.

It was almost six o'clock before she saw her husband again. He came up to join her and tell her, "I've finished with the last of my patients for the day. What a lot! Half of them weren't really sick at all! And a few of them were so close to death that no treatment of mine can save them."

"I saw there was a line at the door."

Ian showed a smile on his handsome, thin face. "Proof that my reputation in the city is growing. By the way, a messenger came from Harry Turner. He's joining us for dinner tonight. It's been a while since we've seen him."

She was standing by the window, gazing out. She turned to ask him, "Did you warn cook?"

"Yes. I let her know as soon as I received the message." He wrinkled his brow. "You are very subdued. Is anything wrong?"

Ann gazed at him in silence for a few seconds. Then she said, "There is."

"What?"

"I found out something today," she said. "I learned the history of this house."

Ian seemed to feel he could pretend there was nothing wrong. He said, "We know the history of the house. It was built by Jacob Mercy and lived in by him and his heirs. Then sold to us."

Her eyes met his with a meaningful look. "You know that is not the whole story."

Her husband looked uneasy. "What do you mean by that?"

"What about the murder?"

"Who has been talking to you?" Ian asked curtly.

"I don't think that is important."

"I do!" her husband said. "Who has been telling you these tales out of school?"

"I'd rather not say!"

"Some of the servants?" Ian asked.

"No."

"Who then?"

"You have had your secret for some time," she said. "Let that be my secret for a while. I want to know why you concealed the dark past of Mercy House from me."

Her husband's face crimsoned. "I didn't think it was anything you should know."

"Why?"

"It has no importance," he said with an impatient wave of his hand. "It was something which happened years ago. A tragedy which occurred to strangers who mean nothing to us. I thought it would only upset you."

Ann said quietly, "I find it more upsetting that you chose to deceive me."

"I didn't deceive you!"

"You just neglected to tell me the truth."

"How much better would you have been for the truth?" her young husband demanded.

"I would likely have refused to come to live in a house reported to be haunted."

"That's ridiculous nonsense!"

"The headless ghost of the man who was decapitated

44

here by a jealous husband . . ." she said. "I know the entire story now."

Ian said, "Whoever told you these things must have done so to upset you. I tried to protect you."

"But you brought me here!"

He moved over to her and earnestly said, "I found this house suited to my needs. And I was startled when I was told how reasonably it might be had. It seemed the ideal answer to our problems."

"Your problems," she said.

Ian spread his hands. "All right, I'm sorry," he said. "But you have seen no ghosts since you came here. So isn't this all a lot of talk about nothing important?"

She said, "I may not have seen ghosts, but I have seen worse."

He frowned. "Worse?"

"Yes," she said. "I have wondered about the nights you have deserted me to spend hours in the cellar, supposedly working at perfecting your surgery. Dissecting cats and dogs and other small animals."

Ian said, "What sort of crime do you think you can make of that? Haven't I a right to dedicate myself to my work?"

Ann said unhappily, "You have every right. But now I discover that you have lied to me in this as well."

"I have not!" he protested.

"I know better," she said. "I was in the cellar this morning. By accident I noticed your surgery door was not locked. And I looked inside!"

Her husband's face paled. Awkwardly, he repeated, "You looked inside?"

"Yes!"

His eyes had taken on a strange light. "I have told you never to go in there," he said in a low, taut voice.

"Now I understand why," she said. "I saw the body on the table. A human body!"

"None of your affair!" he snapped.

"I think it is," Ann told him. "Where did it come from? You know that you could be in serious trouble because of it."

Ian looked shaken. He said, "The surgery is no place for you. But since you have intruded on forbidden ground I'll tell you the truth. The body I'm dissecting came from the university. Because of a special disease involved in the man's death, Dr. Marsh wanted me to do the first experiments."

"Dr. Marsh was here to see you today."

"He was?"

"Yes. He seemed to think you might have something for him. Some sort of package for delivery. He came with a driver and a wagon. Why didn't he tell me what he had really come for?"

Ian sighed. "He wouldn't do that. The body must go back to the college," he said. "I was to have finished with it, but I took more time over the dissection than I originally planned. No doubt he expected the body to be back in its casket of whiskey ready to be returned to the college."

Ann listened to this somewhat faltering explanation, not at all sure that she believed him. Indeed, it was hard for her to accept much of what she'd seen and heard within the past few hours. She was suddenly plunged into a macabre world of partly dissected human bodies, ghostly legends and ancient murder!

She said, "Casket of whiskey? What do you mean?"

"Bodies used for dissection are preserved in tight caskets filled with pure spirits to preserve them," Ian explained. "The one I'm working on now has been thus preserved for many months. It came by ship from London."

"And Dr. Marsh let you have it?"

"So that I might better study a wasting ulcer known to be in this particular body and its effects on the body tissue," Ian explained. "The body on the table below is that of a criminal hung in London months ago for a double murder. At the time of his hanging he was already near death from an interior malignancy. It is the malignancy and its course which interests me."

Ann said, "Wouldn't it have been better for you to have told me the truth?"

"Again I wished to spare you unpleasantness," Ian said. "I swear it is my only crime. I would have finished with the body tonight and sent it along with my findings to Dr. Marsh at the college. Now I will have to leave it for another night since Harry Turner is coming to dine with us and spend the evening."

Ann gave her husband a tender look. "You know I want to help you in all you do."

He took her in his arms. "I know that," he said gently.

"But lately you've alarmed me. These strange midnight visitors. Lying to me about this house. Not telling me the truth about that body in the cellar."

"I meant no harm," her young husband said.

Her eyes looked up into his and she saw nothing but love for her in them. "I want to believe that," she said. "But I'm greatly worried. Today Martha Todd came to see me and made all sorts of insinuations, hinting that you might be in some serious trouble!"

Ian frowned. "You know why. Her brother still is in love with you. He tries to discredit me whenever he can!"

"She knew about the house, though it wasn't she who told me its history. But she taunted me about it!"

"I'll refuse her the house," Ian stormed.

"No, you mustn't," Ann said. "I will not be cut off from those I have known. And there is something else. She told me to ask you what a resurrectionist was."

Ian reacted in a startling fashion. He let go of her arms and stared at her with a shadow of fear on his thin, intelligent face.

Three

"What is a resurrectionist?" Ann repeated.

Her husband's face looked more weary than before. He said, "It's a coined word. A term which has no importance at all!"

Ann said, "Strange, Martha appears to think that it does. Otherwise she wouldn't have mentioned it."

"Martha is a meddlesome troublemaker!"

"Tell me," she insisted.

Ian gave a deep sigh. He said, "A resurrectionist is a term given scoundrels who rob graves and so resurrect the corpses."

"Rob graves?" she asked in a shocked voice.

"There are wild rumors that such things have happened," Ian said with an impatient gesture of dismissal. "It is the sort of gossip a Martha Todd would indulge in."

"Rob graves," Ann repeated. "Why should they want to do that? For the clothes or jewelry of the dead?"

Ian shook his head. "No. These fellows are said to always strip the dead bodies which they've dug up. They are supposed not to take any of the jewelry either. You see, there is no law against the theft of a buried body, but to take the clothes and jewels would be as much an act of theft as if they were taken from a live person."

She was beginning to understand. "So by leaving the clothes and jewelry behind, the criminal hopes to escape being charged with a crime."

He nodded. "Yes."

"And why do they want the bodies?"

There was a tense silence between them as Ian hesitated before replying to her. Then he said, "They sell them."

"Sell them?"

Ian nodded, his handsome face solemn. "The bodies are said to be purchased by medical schools and doctors. I think the whole thing is exaggerated."

It was slowly beginning to dawn on her. Her eyes widened with horror as she asked, "Have you had any traffic with these grave robbers?"

"No!" His protest was vehement. Almost too vehement.

"What about the body downstairs?"

"I told you," her husband said. "Dr. Marsh let me have it. It came from the college."

She listened to his explanation but found it difficult to believe, just as she had been mystified by the unexpected call made by Dr. Clinton Marsh. And yet she didn't want to think that her ambitious husband had gotten himself involved with a group of criminals desecrating graves.

She said, "I do not like your Dr. Marsh. He frightened me! He looks like a lizard."

Her husband frowned. "Too many people are put off by his appearance. He is actually a fine man and a genius of a surgeon."

"I hear they call him 'Mad Marsh'," she said. "Could that be because he is mixed up in this dreadful robbing of graves?"

"He has been criticized by those jealous of him. He was my teacher and he is now my friend," Ian said. "I will not turn my back on him."

"I see," she said quietly, wondering if he would defend her as strongly.

Ian came close to her again and, in a milder tone, said,

"Let us end this unpleasant discussion. If your friend asks you about resurrectionists again tell her you wish to hear no more about them."

"That will not stop her gossiping," Ann pointed out.

"Let her gossip!" Ian said with annoyance. "I doubt if there are many who will pay attention to her. And pray don't mention this matter when Harry Turner arrives. I want to enjoy our evening."

With that he kissed her and left her to change for the evening. As she selected the dress and jewelry she would wear, she reviewed all that her husband had said. And she recalled what the weird old character in the cemetery had told her. Angus McCrae had said that there were worse things to fear than ghosts in the ancient cemetery. She was almost certain he'd been referring to the band of grave robbers.

This brought another troubling thought to mind. Could Ian have deliberately chosen Mercy House not only because it was a cheap buy but because it adjoined the cemetery? What a convenient location if one wanted to deal with grave robbers. And considering her husband's zeal in perfecting his surgical techniques and the difficulty in procuring bodies to dissect, it was all too possible that he'd been tempted into dealing with the evil men who made a business of selling stolen dead bodies. There were grave doubts in her mind as to where the body in the surgery had really come from.

Ann had put on a dress of fine yellow silk and a necklace with a large green stone in it to honor the presence of Dr. Harry Turner. Ian's young friend arrived promptly at seven. He was something of a dandy and on this occasion had on a light purple jacket and fawn breeches. He bowed to Ann and kissed her hand.

Then, regarding her with a smile, he inquired, "Have you

thought about leaving Ian in my favor since we last met?"

She offered him a small smile. "You know I will never do that."

"Just the same, I'll keep trying to make you change your mind and your husband," he promised.

Ian took it with good nature, laughing and placing an arm around his friend. "I vow your bark is much louder than your intent."

"Do not be too sure," Dr. Harry Turner warned him. "You are gradually taking all the patients my father and I have been treating for years. What better revenge than to steal your wife."

Ian ushered him into the living room where they stood before the fireplace. He said, "I would be a great deal more alarmed by your threats if you didn't voice them so loudly and so often."

Harry Turner chuckled and took out a long-stemmed clay pipe. "You do not mind my smoking?"

"Not at all," Ann said, taking a seat by the fireplace where the two men were standing.

Nancy brought them drinks and Harry and Ian exchanged a good deal of banter about the state of medicine and the town. It was a regular part of their meetings that the other young doctor should tease her husband.

Harry Turner winked at Ann and then told her husband, "That's a fine wench you have as a serving maid. Do you attend to the hiring of such females?"

Ian smiled. "No. Ann has that prerogative. Charles came with the house. And it was Ann who hired our cook and Nancy."

The other young doctor offered Ann another smile. "Let me congratulate you on your taste," he told her. "The lass is truly a beauty."

"And a hard worker," Ann said. "She is a great help."

"I should imagine so," the young doctor said. Then he turned to Ian to discuss something else. He said, "I had a patient today just returned from London. He says there is great tension there about what is happening in France. They fear some tyrant may arise to head the country and plunge it into an aggressive war."

"I have heard a few similar rumors," Ian agreed.

Harry Turner took a deep puff of his long clay pipe and exhaled the smoke before replying. Then he said, "King George is having intermittent spells of madness."

"Nothing new," Ian said.

"No. But they seem to be coming more often and to have more severity. Though, according to my informant, the madness has done nothing to dispel the king's popularity. The people appear to prefer him mad to sane!"

Ann felt compelled to join their conversation and say, "The king's worst madness was to lose Virginia and the colonies for us."

"That is long gone by," Ian said. "And there is no hope of our ever reclaiming them."

The dandified Dr. Harry Turner said, "Politics bore me for the most part. And so does much of medicine, though I follow the profession. They are having arguments about vaccinations for the pox in London."

"The benefits have been proven," Ian said.

"But not the methods," his friend replied, pointing the clay pipe at him. "Not everyone is prepared to accept Jenner's theory."

Ian looked shocked. "They would prefer to give direct inoculation of the smallpox vaccine! That is so much more dangerous."

Ann asked the two young men, "What is the Jenner theory?"

Ian showed surprise. "I'm certain I have spoken to you of it. In fact, I have given you an inoculation of his vaccine."

"I remember now," she said. "But I didn't know how it differed from the regular vaccine."

"Very simple," Dr. Harry Turner said, "Jenner studied in London with the great John Hunter. While there, Jenner found that dairymaids who had contracted cowpox from the cows that they milked did not contract smallpox."

Ian nodded. "Cowpox produces sores both on the udder of the cow and on the human skin which resemble the sores of smallpox, but the disease is mild by comparison. And best of all, it isn't contagious."

The good-looking Dr. Harry Turner explained, "Jenner decided to protect against smallpox by giving injections of cowpox. He performed his first vaccination upon a country boy, James Phipps, using matter from the arms of a milkmaid named Sarah Nelmes, who had acquired the cowpox from the animals she had milked. Two months later, he inoculated the boy with the pus from a case of smallpox. The boy did not contract the disease."

Her husband said, "Jenner has published a book on the subject and his method is acclaimed by many. Dr. Marsh approves of it wholly."

"Mad Marsh!" the other young doctor said with a taunting smile.

"We both know he is a genius!" Ian said hotly.

"A mad genius," Harry Turner replied, puffing on his long clay pipe. "A society of anti-vaccinationists has already been formed. Many say smallpox is a visitation from God and originates in man."

Ann was shocked as she declared, "If they can offer an argument like that against vaccination for smallpox, surely they could offer the identical argument against trying to cure other diseases. They could all be termed indictments offered by God."

Ian's thin face showed a frown. "Much of the trouble comes from people confusing vaccination with inoculation. They still believe that vaccine virus is transmitted from person to person as it was in Jenner's early experiment. While, in reality, vaccine virus is obtained from calves and is a vastly purer product than the cleanest milk."

His friend said, "Then I take it you are following Dr. Marsh's lead and using the Jenner method?"

"I am," Ian said.

Dr. Harry Turner offered him a knowing smile as he said, "You'd better be wary of following Marsh in everything. He isn't called mad for nothing. He might get you in a good deal of trouble."

Ann saw the shadow of uneasiness cross her husband's lean face and turned to ask Dr. Harry Turner, "What can you mean by that?"

The young doctor shrugged. "I'm sure Ian understands."

Ian frowned. "I can't say that I do!"

Dr. Harry Turner tapped the ashes from his clay pipe into the fireplace and put the pipe away in an inner pocket before he deigned to reply. Then he told Ian, "There are some ugly rumors going the rounds of the city. Stories about Marsh being the leader of a gang of resurrectionists."

Ann listened with a growing feeling of dismay. Hearing references to the resurrectionists once again was upsetting. She saw that Ian was startled by his friend's words and she waited to see what her husband's answer to this charge might be.

Ian finally said, "There is always that sort of loose talk. The public is suspicious of anyone who is sensible enough to practice dissection on human bodies. They prefer to ignore the good which can come of it."

The atmosphere in the shadowed room had become tense. The wind whistled in the chimney causing the burning logs in the fireplace to temporarily blaze more brightly.

The young doctor gave Ian a warning look. "I wouldn't dismiss the matter lightly if I were you. The rumor is that Marsh has set up a group to obtain corpses for his use and that of other doctors."

"Ridiculous," Ian scoffed, though Ann felt there was not enough strength behind the protest.

"I don't think so," the handsome Harry Turner drawled. "Marsh is obsessed with dissection of humans. And lately there have been instances of new graves being robbed, bodies transported for long distances and suspected murder to provide an easy supply of bodies."

"Suspected murder!" Ann gasped.

The young doctor offered her an apologetic glance. "I'm sorry, Ann. I would rather have spared you hearing this, but Ian seems to think you ought to hear it."

"I do not," Ian said hotly. "If you weren't my oldest friend I'd order you out of the house. What sort of scurrilous accusation are you making against a senior member of our profession?"

"I'm merely repeating what is being said," was Harry Turner's calm reply. "Some highly mysterious killings and disappearances have taken place in the slum areas of Auld Reekie. And the talk is that a lot of these scum have wound up on the dissecting tables of Marsh and his friends!"

Ann gave her husband a frightened glance, but he

frowned again and said to his friend, "You may get yourself in serious trouble if you pursue that line of talk."

Dr. Harry Turner smiled arrogantly and asked, "I simply hope you haven't mixed yourself up in it, because the authorities are ready to bear down on this foul trade."

"Do not worry about me," Ian said rather nervously.

"Don't allow Marsh to lead you astray," his friend warned.

Ian's face was pale and his manner tense. "At least you will admit that human dissection is necessary for the advance of medicine."

Dr. Harry Turner shrugged. "I have no desire to be involved in the issue. My father believes it totally needless. And, should your patients learn that you have dabbled in experiments on humans, you'll find your practice dwindling."

"Why should they complain when it is for their benefit?" Ian asked.

His friend said, "Unhappily, they do not see it that way. They take the religious stand that it amounts to dangerous tampering with the soul."

"Ignorance!" Ian said disdainfully.

"Perhaps so," the other young doctor sighed. "But that is the way things are, and I felt I owed it to you as a friend to let you know what is happening."

"Thank you," Ian said coldly.

"Now I must be on my way," Dr. Harry Turner said, turning to Ann with one of his friendly smiles. "Thank you for your hospitality, Ann."

She rose from her chair to inquire, "May I get you something in the way of food or drink before we send you on your way?"

The young doctor shook his head. "Thank you, no. I

have had enough of everything. It has been a good evening, in spite of Ian's stubborn defense of Marsh."

"You might have expected that," Ian said.

Dr. Harry Turner laughed. "True! You were always one of those who worshipped Mad Marsh! My own favorite is Dr. Jock Gregory. I wonder you don't think more of him. He has long been a friend of your family."

"I admire Dr. Gregory," Ian said. "He is a fine teacher. But Marsh excels him in some things."

"Notably the finding of bodies for dissection," the other young doctor said dryly. "I understand that Dr. Gregory is at this moment on the high seas on his return voyage to Scotland. So we shall soon see him."

Ann escorted their visitor to the reception hall and told him, "Do come back again soon."

"I will," he promised. The maid, Nancy, appeared with his coat and he flashed another of his winning smiles for the pretty girl. Then Ian saw him out to the steps and his waiting carriage in the driveway.

Ann remained in the reception hall, more than a trifle shaken by all that had been said. She could not forget the corpse she had seen on the table in the surgery room in the cellar. She also recalled the mysterious visit of Dr. Clinton Marsh. The weird looking doctor had at once made her uneasy. If even a part of what Dr. Harry Turner had said were true she feared that Ian might have gotten himself into serious trouble by collaborating with the strange old professor in accumulating bodies for dissection.

Nancy broke into her troubled reverie by asking, "Will there be anything else, Mistress Stewart?"

Ann turned to the pretty dark-haired girl and said, "No. That will be all, Nancy. You may go to bed now."

The maid curtsied. "Thank you, mistress." And she at

once turned and vanished in the dark corridor leading to the rear of the house and the servants' quarters.

The front door opened and Ian came back in with a slight shudder. "It's cold out there," he told her. "Spring comes late to Scotland."

"It does," she agreed quietly. "You saw him on his way?"

"Yes," Ian said, placing an arm around her and kissing her on the cheek. "Now it is time we retired for the night. I have a busy day tomorrow."

She said no more as he led the way upstairs with a lighted candle in his hand. But when they reached the privacy of their bedroom she was unable to hold back her worried feelings any longer.

Going to him, she asked, "Was there any truth in what Harry Turner said tonight? I mean about Dr. Marsh and his getting bodies by stealth."

Ian showed disdain. "Harry was always one for gossip. He enjoys sensation."

"You haven't answered my question!"

He frowned. "I thought I had."

"I can't forget the body you have downstairs. The one I saw on your operating table."

"I explained; that came from the college. Marsh loaned it to me."

"You're sure it wasn't stolen from some grave in Mercy Cemetery?" she asked.

The question upset him. This was plain in the look on his lean, intelligent face. "How can you ask me a question like that?"

"I'm worried for you."

"You needn't be."

"But bodies are being stolen," she protested. "And if

gossip is correct murders are being committed to produce bodies for the trade."

"Harry Turner's fantastic stories have no basis of truth in them," Ian said at once. "And you needn't worry about the body in the cellar. I will be returning it to Dr. Marsh at the college within a few days."

"That is good news," she said. "You must be careful. You know that the Turners are jealous of the way you have cut into their practices. And this is true of other doctors in the area. If you are involved in any sort of wrongdoing it could ruin you as a doctor."

Ian took her in his arms. "You must not even think about such a thing," he told her.

That was the end of their discussion. As usual, she found it far from satisfactory, but she knew she'd get no further with him. Long after they went to bed she lay there staring up into the darkness and worrying. At last she slept. And it was small wonder that her sleep was tormented by nightmares.

In her dreams she again found herself in the dark, damp cellar, furtively making her way along in the shadows with only a small candle to provide a faint glow of light in that underground stillness.

She reached the door to the room and with a trembling hand turned the knob. The door opened easily and she again had a view of this private surgical study which was off-limits to her. This time it was not her husband who stood over the corpse on the operating table. It was the evil-looking Dr. Clinton Marsh!

The lizard-like face of the older doctor showed a look of anger at the sight of her. He glared at her with the dissecting scalpel still in his hand.

"What are you doing here?" he rasped.

"Where is my husband?" she replied in return.

A malevolent smile crossed the ugly face of the surgeon. He said, "Your husband is in prison!"

"In prison?"

He nodded. "For stealing bodies such as this one!"

"No!" she cried in protest.

"You have no right to interfere!" Dr. Clinton Marsh said, hatred in his lidded eyes. And he bent over the corpse and uttered some words she could not make out.

Then the horrible thing happened! The partially dismembered corpse slowly raised itself from the table and turned a sallow face with glazed, dead eyes towards her. It was the face of an emaciated old man with wisps of white hair standing wildly on its skull. The corpse uttered a shriek and left the dissecting table, the white cloth still draped over its body, and came stalking her.

It was now her turn to scream and run for safety to the other end of the dark cellar. In her flight she stumbled and fell with her hands sprawled out on the hard, earthen floor. She heard the groaning of the corpse above her and smelled the odor of death from it. Sobbing out her fear, she raised herself a little and scrambled blindly forward in the darkness.

Now the scene quickly changed and she was racing along the pathway of the ancient Mercy Cemetery. The cold wind rustled through her hair causing it to flow behind her in her flight. She dodged this way and that to avoid a collision with the gaunt, gray tombstones which came up to confront her. She was still racing from the specter of the surgical table and certain that the monstrous thing was only a few steps behind her.

Then from out of the shadows came the thin man in black who lived in one of the tombs. The spare figure of

Angus McCrae danced before her. His boney fingers reached out to touch her face and a wicked smile showed on his dried-apple face.

"No!" she screamed in terror. "Let me pass! One of the dead is chasing me!"

The lean Angus McCrae mocked her, saying, "We are all dead here, my pretty one!"

"Please!" she begged, trying to push past him.

He laughed wildly and embraced her. She felt herself drawn into his arms and was sickened by the stench of death which came from him. "Let me go!" she cried. "Let me go!"

She opened her eyes to find Ian, fully-clothed, standing over her and gazing down at her in concern. He said, "You've been having a nightmare!"

Still partially caught up in her wild dream, she looked up at him with puzzled eyes and said, "Yes. I was dreaming of the cemetery!"

Her young husband's face was serious. "It could not have been a pleasant dream. You were twitching like someone in convulsion and several times you cried out!"

"It was a bad dream," she admitted.

"Are you all right now?"

"Yes."

"Then I must be on my way."

She sat up in bed. "Where are you going at this hour?"

Ian scowled slightly. "A night call. Old Squire Murton has had another of his attacks. They sent a servant to fetch me."

"Must you go?"

"I can scarcely refuse. He left the Turners to place himself in my care. He may be having a true heart seizure this time from what the servant says."

"I don't like being left here alone," Ann said plaintively.

"Go back to sleep," Ian told her.

"I'll worry about you!"

"I'll be quite safe. The servant will drive me there and back. I'll not be on the streets alone."

"Take care, then, and hurry back," Ann said.

He bent and kissed her tenderly on the lips. "And you return to sleep. An untroubled sleep this time. You allow that cemetery to bother you too much!"

"I can't help it," she said.

"We'll talk about it tomorrow," her husband said. "I must be on my way now."

She watched him leave the room with a feeling of despair. When he was abroad in the streets of Edinburgh in the midnight darkness she always worried about him. Many times she had heard the story of his grandfather, who had been a doctor in Glasgow. It was while he was on one of those errands of mercy that his grandfather had been cruelly murdered on his own doorstep.

It was soon after that Flora Stewart came to live in Edinburgh and marry the dashing Ian Stewart, the city's most influential banker. It had been a love match and even today, twenty-six years after their marriage, they were attractive, lively people. Ann adored them and especially liked the senior Ian Stewart. She wished that her own Ian had chosen to follow in his father's footsteps rather than decide to be a doctor like his grandfather.

But so he had decided. She had been given to understand that a friend of the family, Dr. Jock Gregory, had been one of those who'd encouraged Ian to become a surgeon. From all that she had heard, this Dr. Jock Gregory was thought to be one of the most talented medical men in all Scotland. He taught at the university and had a private practice as well. Gossip also had it that he had been a suitor of Ian's mother in the old days and was still very fond of her.

Ann believed this was quite possible. She had only met the bald, pleasant man once, but she had liked him. She was glad to know he was returning to Edinburgh and she trusted that he might have some influence on her husband, perhaps get him away from the frightening Dr. Clinton Marsh. Her nightmare had been of this weird old man.

She heard the carriage start up in the driveway outside and knew that Ian was on his way to Squire Murton's house. The stout old squire had been suffering from a series of painful attacks in his chest and Ian had put it down as a form of heart disease. He had confided in her that it was likely one of these attacks might turn out to be a fatal one. That was why he'd offered no argument when the squire's servant had come for him in the middle of the night.

Ann lay back on her pillow and gazed at the empty space in the bed beside her. Had Ian been a banker like his father there would be none of this. Yet she had entered into the marriage willingly, knowing her husband's profession. It was her Aunt Samantha who had shown grave doubts about her husband-to-be.

"Even if the young man is perfect, and I'm sure he is far from that," Aunt Samantha had sputtered, "it is a poor business being married to a doctor!"

"How would you know?" Ann had inquired with a spiteful arrogance of which she had been ashamed later. "You have never been married to anybody!"

"I admit to being that object of derision, a spinster!" Aunt Samantha had snapped back with an angry expression on her plain face. "But I might have married more than once had I not dedicated my life to you!"

She'd run to her aunt and knelt by her chair in an instant mood of penitence. "Forgive me, dear Aunt Samantha! I'm truly sorry! It is just that I love Ian so much!"

Her aunt's plain face had shown sympathy under the fringe of white bonnet as she said, "That is what frightens me! Your love for this young man has blinded you to all the hazards of the marriage."

"Many doctors have happy marriages!" Ann protested.

"Only because their wives are indulgent! Believe me!"

"Then I shall be indulgent!" she said.

Aunt Samantha frowned. "You'll need to be more than that. You will have to be self-sacrificing! Share him with strangers who mean nothing to you but who will make calls on his time and his health!"

"I shall share Ian's dedication to his profession."

"Indeed, that is right, whether you wish it or not," the old woman agreed grimly. "You have young Samuel Todd courting you! A clever, young lawyer who will make his name in the city!"

"I don't love him!"

"He loves you!"

"So does Ian."

"A lawyer makes a perfect husband," Aunt Samantha had declared. "Samuel Todd would never be called from his bed in the middle of the night to attend the sick! Your house would not be filled with processions of the ill and maimed several hours of each day. You would have a privacy as a lawyer's wife you will never find as the wife of a doctor."

"I still want to marry Ian," Ann had said.

Aunt Samantha had sat back in her chair with a sigh. "In that case, let it be on your own head. I only hope that all my sacrifices have not been wasted. That you will have a good life!"

"You know I will," Ann had said, kissing her foster-mother on the cheek.

But now, alone in this dark bedroom, in the middle of the night, she could not help but wonder whether she had been as wise as she'd thought. The warm, considerate Ian had become a husband much less ardent in his attentions to her than he had been during the days of their courtship. Early in their marriage he had shown a cold disinterest in anything which interfered with his profession.

And the lines of sick strangers of whom her aunt had warned did fill the waiting rooms in the house for hours every day. Often she was upset by this intrusion, though she knew it was one of the things a doctor's wife must contend with. Ian had an illustrious family name and so had at once drawn a large number of patients.

The Stewarts of Stormhaven were a well known and respected family in Edinburgh. And young Ian's great talents as a doctor had been evident even before his graduation from the university. His fame had spread and he'd barely put up his sign before he was drawing patients from many of the doctors who had been in practice for years, including Harry Turner and his father.

Ann knew that this had caused some jealousy among the profession. And she feared that the jealous might take advantage of the whisperings about resurrectionists to blacken her husband's name. If Ian had been unfortunate enough to allow Dr. Clinton Marsh to involve him in the illegal accumulating of dead bodies for medical studies there could be serious consequences.

Again, she thought of that body which she'd seen in the cellar surgery. Ian had first lied about it being there and then reluctantly admitted that he had been dissecting a body on loan from the university. Had he told her the truth?

Was it one of the bodies kept in caskets of whiskey in the university for study, or was it some body brought to the house by those ruffians who had paid calls on her husband in the small hours? She couldn't be sure.

Dr. Harry Turner's manner had been teasing when he spoke of the stolen bodies and the murders. But she had sensed that beneath his light manner there had been a chill note of warning. Indeed, he had made this clear before leaving. He had pointedly told Ian that Mad Marsh might well lead him into trouble. And Ian's response had been anger, the same anger which he showed to her whenever she questioned him on a similar touchy subject.

With a sigh she closed her eyes and tried to return to sleep. She tried to rid her thoughts of macabre corpses on operating tables, of the thin, ghost-like grave digger whom she'd met in the cemetery, and of the whole grim business of living in this ugly red house next to Mercy Cemetery.

She slept for a little. But it was a restless sleep and so she wakened at the slightest sound. As it turned out, the sound which wakened her was the twisting of the doorknob at the door leading from the hallway.

Ann at once sat up in bed and called out nervously, "Ian, is that you?"

There was no answer. And for a moment she thought that perhaps it had been part of a dream. But then there was the sound again, but this time as if someone were releasing the doorknob. This was followed by the creaking of a hallway floorboard from the other side of the door.

Now she began to be afraid, afraid as she so often had been in her lonely room in her aunt's house as a little girl! Then she had feared the old woman with a rat on her shoulder, or the ugly man with three heads all covered with warts, or the evil woman with thin, twisting black serpents for hair!

None of these childish fantasies haunted her now, though her fear was as abject as it had been then. Now she saw herself pursued by the unhappy ghosts of those who had once lived in the house. The murderer husband who had hung himself in the attic! Or the lover who had been decapitated in the scullery! Even the ghost of the ugly corpse which she'd seen in Ian's surgery in the cellar!

These were the phantoms which made her stare at the door with bated breath! But after waiting a little with nothing happening she began to doubt her fears. Perhaps her frayed nerves had betrayed her. The sounds which she had heard had been ordinary ones twisted to undue importance by her imagination.

She knew she could not sleep. So she rose and lit a candle. Then, in an effort to prove her courage and reassure herself, she crossed to the door leading to the hallway.

She stood before it for a moment with a shadow of fear on her lovely face. Then she forced herself to open the door quickly and step out into the hall.

A sudden gust of air almost extinguished the small candle flame and sent a chill down her spine. But she forced herself to move slowly along the hall to the landing. And it was there she saw it!

Suddenly, from out of the shadows, a figure took shape—a figure which she knew could only be of a ghostly nature! It was the figure of a headless man with his shirt-waist stained with blood! Ann saw the phantom move across the landing to her and with a piercing scream she dropped the candle!

Four

Ann wheeled around as the phantom advanced on her. A shaft of moonlight showed down the attic stairs. With a sob, she raced to the narrow stairway and made her way up to the attic level. There was a window open at the head of the stairs, and without hesitation she scrambled out of it and found herself on a precariously narrow ledge. Far below was the driveway. The drop down to it meant almost certain death!

But she preferred her new danger to the one to which she had been exposed inside the house. The memory of that headless figure coming after her in the hallway still terrified her. She had only a flimsy nightgown to protect her from the cold, and she began to tremble from a combination of fear and chill. And every moment she expected the headless phantom to show itself in the window.

Minutes passed and nothing happened. The cold was biting into her and her teeth were chattering, but she dared not go back inside. She began moving cautiously along the narrow ledge towards the corner of the house. Each step was a gamble with death. She dare not look down again for fear of becoming dizzy. At last, she reached the corner and grasped a drainpipe anchored there. Holding onto it fiercely, she realized she was at a dead end. She could not go any further.

She doubted that the pipe would sustain her climbing up it to reach the flat, gravel rooftop. She had an idea there was a door somewhere up there leading to steps which went down inside the house. But she dared not risk climbing the shaky pipe. To skirt around it to the other side would also be awkward, if not impossible. And she dared not go back inside.

She remained there, clinging to the drainpipe, tormented by her fears and the chill night. After what seemed a long while she heard the sound of a carriage approaching. It came very close until it was in the driveway. Risking a glance downward, she saw Ian alighting from the carriage with his medical bag in hand. The carriage drove away and he headed for the door.

"Ian!" she called out to him.

He halted at the sound of her voice but did not seem to know where it came from. He stood there gazing around him as he called, "Ann! Where are you?"

"Up here! On the roof!" she cried out, already feeling ashamed.

Her young husband at once looked up and saw her. "What is wrong?" he demanded. "What on earth are you doing out there?"

"I'll tell you later," she said. "Just help me!"

"Don't move!" he commanded her. "I'll be up there in a moment."

"Hurry!" she begged him. "My hands and feet are numb! I can't remain here much longer!"

He had not waited to hear her. He was already in the house and on his way upstairs. These last few minutes of her ordeal were the worst for her. Not only did she have to fight to retain her position on the ledge, but she was terrified that Ian would pay scant attention to her explanations.

She watched the window through which she'd escaped as she expected Ian to join her by this means. But there was no sign of him. Then she heard the sound of a door opened from the rooftop and footsteps approaching her across its gravel and tar surface. A moment later Ian's anxious face showed itself over the edge of the roof.

He said, "I'm sure I can reach you. Take hold of my hands."

"Ian!" she sobbed, and as his hands came within grasping distance she took them.

"All right," he said. "Now I'm going to haul you up. Help as best you can by digging your feet into any crevice between the bricks."

"I will!"

"Now," Ian said, and with a stern effort he literally dragged her up over the edge of the roof beside him.

Gasping, she reached this place of safety and lay still on the gravel, moaning. "I would have fallen in a minute!"

He was gazing at her oddly. "What were you doing out there?"

"The phantom!"

"Phantom?"

She nodded. "I saw it! The ghost of the man who was murdered in this house! The headless phantom!"

"What kind of mad talk is this?" her young husband asked with concern. And he helped her to her feet without waiting for an answer and guided her across the roof to a trapdoor which gave access to narrow stairs inside. He helped her start down the stairs, and when she reached the attic floor he came inside and closed the trapdoor above. Then he came down the stairs to join her.

In their room he gave her a glass of brandy and saw that she was safely tucked in bed again. The brandy warmed her and her teeth ceased their chattering. Then her young husband sat on her bedside and sternly gazed at her.

"What made you do that mad thing?" he asked.

"I told you. I saw a ghost!"

"So you went out on that parapet?"

"It was my only avenue of escape. I saw the open window and I didn't hesitate! The phantom without a head was right behind me!"

Ian showed disdain on his youthful face. "You can't ask me to believe that?"

"I'm telling you what happened, you can believe it or not, as you like," she told him.

"And the ghost didn't follow you outside?"

"No."

"For a very good reason—there wasn't one!" he told her.

"How can you say that?"

He shook his head in despair. "I was prepared for trouble. I noticed the state you were in before I left. But I didn't expect anything like this."

"I'm sorry!"

"You ought to be! You are lucky to be alive!"

"I was too terrified to think after I went out there," she said. "All I could picture was the ghost!"

"Why didn't you shout for help? Charles or one of the other servants would have heard you!"

"I wasn't thinking that clearly," she said.

"You let yourself get into that state," Ian said with some anger. "And, I must confess, Harry's conversation this evening was no help. I vow it will be a long time before I entertain him again!"

"Don't blame Harry!"

"Who, then? You?"

"Blame everything! This house! The old cemetery! Your determination to experiment on bodies in the cellar!"

Ian at once became sternly cold again. He said, "We will

not speak of that. Now you must try and get some rest. I need sleep for the morrow."

So the incident came to a close, Ann finding herself once again humiliated and blamed. She knew that she needed help and that she must find it from someone other than her husband. As she lay there listening to his even breathing as he slept, she began to formulate her plans.

When she awoke the next morning, he had already left for the hospital. She went down and Nancy served her breakfast. She wondered if it were her imagination, but she felt the girl was watching her strangely.

She asked the pretty maid, "Is anything wrong?"

Embarrassed, Nancy replied, "No, ma'am!"

"Did you sleep well last night?" Ann asked.

The girl nodded. "Yes, ma'am. I always sleep sound as a top. That's what my mother says."

"You are fortunate then," Ann said. "I do not sleep well at all."

Nancy suggested, "Perhaps you should ask the master about it since he is a doctor. Or maybe that other fine young gentleman who was here last evening. Isn't he also a doctor?"

Ann eyed the girl with interest. "You mean Dr. Harry Turner?"

"Yes, ma'am," Nancy said, blushing.

"He thinks you are a most attractive young woman," she told the maid. "Did you not hear his comments about you?"

Continuing to blush, Nancy shyly removed a used plate from the table. "It is not for the likes of me to listen to such talk, ma'am."

"You are a pretty girl," she said. "And, regardless of your station in life, entitled to compliments. Just be careful not to let them go to your head. Such educated young men offer that sort of compliment without there being any meaning behind them."

Nancy nodded. "I understand, ma'am."

"I hope you do," Ann said. "When a young man of your own class offers such a compliment it usually means he wishes to marry you. Not so with your fine, educated gentlemen!"

"I know, ma'am," Nancy agreed. "My mother warned me against such things when I went into service."

"That was wise of her," Ann said. "Would you be good enough to tell Charles I'll want the carriage. I mean to go into the city this morning. I have some shopping to do and some calls to make."

"I'll tell him, ma'am," the girl promised and went off to the kitchen.

Ann hurried through her breakfast and then went upstairs to prepare for her excursion into the business district of the ancient city. When she reached the landing where she had seen the headless phantom the previous night she again felt a cold chill coursing through her. The eerie vision which she'd had was still vivid in her mind, and she was desolate that she could not bring her husband to believe what she had seen.

She chose a demure dress of gray and a matching cloak and bonnet. It was not her purpose to attract attention to herself this morning with garish dress. Her errand was an important one, and she wanted to take care of it without being noticed if this was possible.

Charles was standing by the carriage waiting for her when she stepped out of the house. The old man had on his faded livery and top hat. He assisted her into the carriage and then asked her where she wished to go first.

She told him, "I wish to go to the family banking house."

"Very well, ma'am," Charles said respectfully, and he climbed up onto the seat at the rear and started the carriage. The big, brown horse moved along at a brisk trot without any encouragement needed from the old man.

Ann sat back on the horsehair seat which smelled of the stables. As the wheels of the carriage rolled over the cobblestones of the street and the houses with their shutters and the churches with their gray steeples flashed by the small side-windows of the black vehicle, she concentrated on what she was going to say when she arrived at the bank.

She intended to take her problem to the elder Ian Stewart, her husband's father. She had only met the older man a few times. But, in all their meetings, her father-in-law had impressed her. Ian and Flora Stewart had raised five children of their own and an adopted son, Billy, who had been drowned while serving in the navy in 1793. Her husband had not said much about this Billy, but Ann gathered there was a kind of mystery about him, especially after Martha Todd's gossipy reference to his criminal background.

She knew her father-in-law had wanted Ian to be a banker and her husband had refused. So now Walter Stewart was following in his father's footsteps and had already attracted some attention as having the family's gift for sound investments. He had developed a line of trade with the China coast which seemed destined to make all the investors involved wealthy beyond belief. The elder Stewart was rightly proud of this son.

The carriage halted before the columns of marble which flanked the wide entrance to the bank. Charles got down from his perch and helped her out.

Respectfully, the old man asked her, "When do you wish me to pick you up, ma'am?"

"That is hard to say," she told him. "I have to be in the bank for a little. Then I have shopping to do. Suppose you meet me at the drinking fountain for horses on High Street at noon."

"Very well, ma'am," the elderly Charles said. "I shall be there."

This settled, she went into the bank. She approached a clerk at the front counter and was inquiring about seeing Ian Stewart, Sr., when Walter came out a door at the side of the front office and saw her. He at once came over to greet her.

"My dear Ann, this is a pleasant surprise," the tall, dignified young man said. He had the same serious Stewart features as Ian's, but his coloring was lighter. His hair was light brown and his keen eyes were of a hazel shade.

She always felt a trifle uncomfortable in his presence, though he was pleasant enough towards her. She knew there had been youthful jealousy between Walter and Ian when they were young, and that Walter had been delighted when Ian had removed himself from competition with him in the family business. Also, Walter and his wife already had two children, while she and Ian had yet to produce their first grandchild for the family.

She said, "I've come to speak with your father for a moment, if I may."

The tall Walter nodded. "I think that can be arranged. But why do you not come and visit us? Heather Rae is anxious that you see how the children have grown!"

"You know how busy Ian is. We hardly go anywhere."

"That's what comes of his being a doctor," Walter said with an air of regret. "But you mustn't make a victim of yourself. Don't lock yourself up in that grim house he chose for you. Pay us a visit on your own."

"Thank you, I'll do that soon," she promised.

"Don't forget," her brother-in-law insisted. "Heather Rae feels hurt that you come to see her so little."

Ann could not very well tell him that she found Heather Rae a simpering, child-oriented little creature with hardly an original idea in her head. The petite, dark woman talked of nothing but her domestic problems and her children. Ann found her deadly tiresome.

She tried to be diplomatic by saying, "I fear Heather Rae and I have few of the same interests. I often feel that my visits bore her."

"Never," the tall Walter vowed. "As a matter of fact, she is always thrilled when she sees you and invariably talks of your virtues afterwards."

Ann managed a smile. "Then I shall indeed call on her often. I trust your father is not engaged in any serious meeting at the moment?"

"I think you are lucky," Walter said. "He was alone in his office when I last saw him. If you'll wait a moment I'll go in and see if he can't admit you at once."

She thanked him, and he marched off towards a door at the rear of the busy bank. As she waited she observed the male tellers at their counters handling several short lines of customers. Most of the tellers were men of middle age or more as befitted their important duties. Walter was only gone for a few minutes.

He came back to her and said, "Father will be delighted to see you at once." And as he marched along with her to the door of his father's office, he added, "And don't forget about visiting Heather Rae."

"I won't," she promised dutifully.

Ian Stewart, Sr., was standing in the middle of his large, oak-panelled office with his hands stretched out to greet her. He was a handsome man who, apart from his white hair, did not show many signs of age. He had not put on any weight and his face was fairly free of wrinkles. The corners of his eyes crinkled as he gave her a smile of greeting and took her hands in his. He kissed her on the cheek and then led her to a chair before his broad desk.

"Do sit down and make yourself comfortable," the older man, whom her husband resembled so much said. "We do not see you all that often. Can I order you a glass of sherry or perhaps tea?"

"Nothing, thank you," she said, sitting down. And as he sat across from her she lifted her eyes to him in an appealing fashion and said, "Please forgive me for intruding on you at your place of business."

"No apologies needed," her father-in-law said. "I wish you would do it regularly. I see too few pretty young women here."

She smiled. "You are always too kind. I know you are busy and so I will get straight to the point of my visit. I am worried about Ian."

"Worried about Ian?" Her father-in-law looked puzzled. "But I understand he has become one of the busiest doctors in Edinburgh."

"He has. It's not that."

The white-haired man stared at her. "Don't tell me you are having domestic difficulties? I refuse to believe that, after hearing all his declarations of love for you."

Ann blushed. "I can't say that Ian has fallen out of love with me. But I do feel that he no longer cares for me as he once did. And I'm afraid that he is venturing into troubled waters with his profession."

Her father-in-law listened to this with grave attention. "You feel he is neglecting you?"

"Yes."

"That is not strange. In his haste to build a practice, he is no doubt expending all his efforts in that direction. My dear Flora had the same doubts about my love when she first came to Stormhaven, and there were other threats to her there as well. But she was a good wife and saw me through all the worst of it."

"I'm quite willing to do the same if Ian will only confide in me," she said. "He has a coldness towards me when I question him which sometimes frightens me."

The white-haired man gazed at her sympathetically across his desk. "In many ways you are echoing what Flora said to me years ago. She was a doctor's daughter, you know."

"Yes. I have heard about it. And of her great courage when her father was slain by highwaymen."

"A long, tragic story," her father-in-law said. "Now that all the threats have passed and we have a family to comfort us and be proud of it seems that past was only a bad dream. In time you will feel the same way about your situation."

"I hope so."

"I will speak to my son and point out the need of his giving you more of himself," the banker promised.

She said carefully, "There is something beside that. You know that he was a student of Dr. Clinton Marsh."

"I recall that," her father-in-law said. "Ian had a great admiration for him."

"Yes. And I fear that admiration may get him in difficulty."

"Difficulty?"

"Yes."

"In what way?"

Ann hesitated again and then said, "Do you know about the resurrectionists?"

"The grave robbers?" her father-in-law replied, showing at once that he understood the term. "Yes, I have heard about the scoundrels! Outrageous! Even the dead are not safe from theft these days!"

Her eyes met those of the older man. "There is gossip that Dr. Marsh is the head of a ring which provides bodies for medical study. That he is willing to deal with the lowest of rogues who will provide sound bodies for dissection at a price. And that he asks no questions."

"Asks no questions?" the banker echoed.

"As to how they come by the bodies," she said solemnly. "It is rumored that not only do these villains rob graves, they even murder to provide bodies for their grisly commerce."

Her father-in-law looked shocked. "I have not heard that before."

"I fear it is all too true."

"But how is my son mixed up in this?"

"I'm not sure," she faltered. "I think he may have chosen to live in Mercy House next to Mercy Cemetery so that he can act as a convenient go-between for Dr. Marsh and these robbers dealing in stolen bodies. I came upon a body in the cellar which he could not easily account for."

Ian Stewart, Sr., rose from his chair with a shocked look on his handsome face. "I can't think that Ian would be so reckless as to endanger his good name and that of the family by engaging in such a foul business."

"I'm afraid that Dr. Marsh has somehow persuaded him that it is all in the best interests of medicine. Ian firmly believes that surgeons should be allowed bodies for the purposes of anatomy studies."

"They are," her father-in-law said. "The law gives them the use of scoundrels executed for murder."

"Ian contends that this is not enough. Many more bodies are needed."

"And you think that he and this Marsh may be taking matters in their own hands?"

"Yes."

"I'm glad you've come to me with this," the banker said at once. He was pacing up and down. "Fortunately my good friend, Dr. Jock Gregory, is arriving tomorrow or the next day. He is one of Edinburgh's finest medical men, as you must have heard."

"I know of his reputation," she agreed.

"He also has a great deal of influence with Ian," her father-in-law said. "I'm sure I can get him to talk to my son, and if there is any involvement have it ended."

Relieved, she said, "I think it might be most helpful."

Her father-in-law halted by his desk and his face lighted up. "We shall have a party for Jock's return. It is far too long since we've had a good party at Stormhaven. I'll speak to Flora tonight. We'll arrange it at once and send out invitations. And I shall explain the situation to Dr. Gregory and have him talk to Ian. My son must be warned."

"Thank you," she said. "I'll go now."

Her father-in-law placed an arm around her. "I'm glad you had the good sense to come to me directly. This is not anything which you should bear alone. If Ian were caught in a foul trade like this it would not only bring ruin to him but directly hurt the family. In banking, we must be above suspicion."

She gave him a worried look. "Please don't tell Walter or the others."

"Don't worry about that," the banker said. "Trust my discretion. Only Dr. Jock Gregory will hear of this."

He saw her to the street and she went on her way feeling

a great deal better. She felt sure that Dr. Gregory would be able to dissuade Ian from his dealing in stolen bodies with the evil Dr. Marsh. The meeting between Ian and the returning doctor would come within the framework of a party, so it would not seem that it had been arranged. Best of all, it would take place within a few days.

Ann had her favorite shops. Now she moved from one to another. There was a small shop not far from the fountain where she was to meet the old carriage man which dealt in buttons, lace, ribbons and other items necessary to millinery and dress-making. Whenever she found items which interested her she took them to her seamstress and had them made up.

On this particular morning she tarried over a choice of silks. She finally decided on several yards of a fine lavender shade. Then came the problem of finding buttons and lace to match. When she finished with this it was time to meet her carriage.

She hurried out of the tiny shop onto the brick sidewalk. And as she did so she almost collided with a well-dressed young man in brown jacket and breeches. It was none other than the lawyer, Samuel Todd, who had once hoped that she would become his wife. The young man at once doffed his hat and greeted her cordially.

"You are the one person I didn't expect to meet," Samuel Todd said. "You have become such a recluse of late." He was on the stout side with a broad face and smug expression. He had sandy hair and almost invisible eyebrows which gave his face a rather odd expression.

"Martha comes to visit me," she said.

"So she tells me," the young lawyer said, studying her with his sharp blue eyes. "But you never return her visits. Is it because you fear I might be at home?"

Embarrassed, she protested, "You know that is not so."

His eyes showed a mischievous light. "Why not? You left me for a lesser man. It wouldn't be surprising if you felt some shame."

"You are jesting," she said.

"Not entirely," he replied. "I fear you may have managed to get yourself in a pretty predicament. Do you know the authorities are looking into this business of stolen bodies?"

Faintly, she said, "I have not paid much attention to it."

"You would do well to. And so would your husband. There's trouble brewing. I promise you."

At this moment a number of carriages and wagons came rumbling by. Between the clamor of the wagon wheels and the rude shouting of the drivers, it was impossible to conduct a conversation on the sidewalk. Samuel Todd registered an expression of annoyance on his freckled face and with an impatient gesture took her by the arm and almost literally dragged her up a narrow alley away from the street and the clamor.

"We can talk better here," he told her as he released her arm.

She felt annoyed at being treated in this almost childlike fashion and adjusted her sleeve. "You almost tore my dress!" she accused him as she straightened out her clothing.

A certain smile played on his face, and she realized for the first time that one of the things she disliked about him was his almost bovine look. He said in a low voice, "If I were to tear your dress my choice would be to begin at the neckline."

Her temper flared and she said, "How dare you talk to me like that! I'm a married woman!"

He chuckled mirthlessly. "The courts may settle that. It could be they'll string your precious Ian and his criminal friends up! Robbing graves and committing murders are not looked upon as social pastimes by the average judge and jury!"

Ann now became uneasily aware that they were at the very end of an alley with stone walls all around them. Stone walls in which there were no windows. And the stout young lawyer blocked the only path to freedom. The distance between them and the street seemed to grow in a frightening way. With all the bedlam of sound out there, it would do her little good to cry for help. For the moment she was at the mercy of the bovine Samuel Todd, and he was all too obviously enjoying this knowledge.

She said sharply, "I must go. My carriage is waiting for me!"

"No hurry," he said, edging a little closer to her. "You could do worse than cultivate my friendship again. You may have sore need of a good lawyer."

"If a good lawyer is my need I surely will not find it in you," she shot back in anger.

The sandy-haired man reached out for her, and she dodged back to escape his grasp. But he had her at a complete disadvantage. There was no place to retreat. She found herself backed against the stone wall as he struggled to take her in his arms. Then he was holding her close to him, his body rigid against hers, and his lips enveloping hers in a lascivious, repulsive kiss! She fought fiercely, scratching at his face so that he finally let her go.

"I like your temper," he said, taking a handkerchief from his coat pocket and applying it to his bleeding cheek. "It only goads me on! Remember that!" And with this final jeering comment he turned and headed for the street.

She stood there, dishevelled and sobbing. The parcels she'd been carrying were scattered on the cobblestones. It took her minutes to restore her clothing to a proper state and compose her tear-ravaged face.

Then she carefully picked up the packages she'd dropped and made her way back down the alley to the street. She was sickened by the memory of the hateful encounter. She knew she had only to tell her husband of it and he would make Samuel Todd pay dearly. But at the same time she realized she dare not involve Ian in any argument with the lawyer at the moment. It might only serve to enrage Todd and have him work to bring the whole matter of the resurrectionists out into the open sooner.

Because of the plight in which Ian had placed himself, she would have to remain silent about the attack on her by the young lawyer. Samuel Todd had obviously thought this all out. He had never behaved so outrageously towards her before, and he had only done so now because he felt he was safe. She couldn't imagine what she had ever found in him to attract her, and she knew she had made a wise decision in turning him down in preference for Ian.

But Ian was in serious trouble. She had no doubt of this now. She could only pray that his father would somehow get him out of the predicament in which the malevolent Dr. Clinton Marsh had involved him.

These thoughts were uppermost in her mind as she made her way along the sidewalk towards the drinking fountain for horses. Charles was there with the carriage as he had promised. She gave him the parcels and allowed him to help her up into the carriage. She sat back with closed eyes as the journey home began. Her only hope was that she could live with all this dreadful knowledge until things had improved. Dr. Jock Gregory was due back home and he could be the answer to all this evil.

When she reached Mercy House she was astonished to find Ian home ahead of her. Her young husband met her in the reception hall.

"I wondered where you were," he said.

Nervously, she replied, "I had some shopping to do."

His weary face revealed a thin smile. "Indeed! I have never known you to set out on a shopping expedition so early in the day."

"Mrs. Hocking, my seamstress, is coming," she told him. "I needed some materials for her. I decided the sooner I did the errand the better." She worried that he might have learned of her visit to the bank and her talk with his father. It was hard to tell with him.

But he at least made no mention of it. Instead, he said, "I managed to get home early and I looked forward to our having the midday meal together before I began my office hours."

"That was thoughtful of you," she said.

He smiled again. "I try to remember my husbandly duties now and then. I'll be waiting for you in the dining room."

"I won't keep you long," she promised and hurried upstairs to put away her parcels.

As she quickly tidied herself to join him at the dinner table, she wondered about his sudden change of manner. He was at once more thoughtful of her. Could his father have somehow managed to get in touch with him and offered him a lecture? She decided this was not likely. Yet something had worked to make a change in him. Perhaps she should accept it with gratitude rather than question how it came about.

With this in mind she went down and joined him at the

table. The attractive Nancy served the meal, and they had barely started on the main course of fine roast beef when Ian began to reveal what had brought about the sudden change in his manner towards her.

Sighing, he studied her across the table and said, "What happened last night worries me."

"I am not exactly happy about it either," she reminded him.

He said, "You could easily have fallen from that narrow ledge and killed yourself."

"I know."

His eyes met hers directly. "You are not happy in this house."

"I haven't been from the first," she said. "And now that the ghost has revealed itself to me I'm less happy."

Ian frowned. "I don't believe in the ghost. It is a product of your upset mind."

"No." She replied quietly but stubbornly.

He made a deprecating gesture. "Why should I argue about it? I know we'll never agree. If there was a headless ghost stalking these corridors I'd have seen it long ago. And I haven't."

"What are you trying to tell me?"

He hesitated, then he said, "I think you need a rest. I believe you should return to live with your Aunt Samantha for a few weeks. In your absence I will try and find us another more suitable house."

In a flash it all became clear to her. Her husband was really in this resurrectionist thing deeply. So deeply that he feared she was finding out too much about it. His solution was to coax her to leave the grim old house so he could continue the grisly trade in bodies without interference from her.

She eyed him with concern. "You want to be rid of me!"

"Certainly not! I'm thinking only of your good!"

"I somehow doubt that," she told him. "I think you are in trouble and you don't want me to find out about it. Let me assure you, I will not leave this house without you."

Ian looked stunned. After a moment he said, "You're behaving in a childishly stupid manner!"

"I'm sorry," she said. "I intend to remain here. And I beg you to give up whatever dark doings you and that Dr. Marsh are engaged in!"

Ian touched his napkin to his lips and jumped up from the table. "I have nothing more to say to you. Whatever happens to you is on your own head!"

"The same might well be said of you," she told him.

His lean face went pale, and he turned and strode from the room. She knew he would be going directly to his office as the line of patients usually formed earlier than this. It was unlikely she'd have the opportunity of talking with him for the balance of the day. This was of small account since he would not listen to her anyway. She had to depend on his father and Dr. Jock Gregory to reason with him and somehow try to save him.

Leaving the dining room, she went as far as the hall. She saw that Ian was already receiving patients. And as she stood there watching the line across the hallway, it suddenly struck her that this would be an ideal time to make a more complete examination of the cellars and find out if there was more going on down there than she knew. She found a candle and lit it, and then she made her way to the door leading to the cellar and descended the narrow stairway to the eerie, damp darkness!

Five

This was an excursion she only dared to make while Ian was occupied and during the hours of daylight. She would not have the courage to descend into this dark place during the night when the phantoms were abroad. She could only hope that she would be safe in daylight, in spite of the pitch blackness of the cellars, and be able to properly explore the place.

The small candle flame gave only a limited glow of light around her and cast everything in a weird pattern. The most ordinary objects such as packing cases and kegs took on a different aspect. The pillars which held up the old house and the arches between them gave the dark cellar the air of a deserted cathedral.

Moving along cautiously, she was aware of the quick-ened pounding of her heart and conscious of her breathing. There was no sound from above that reached these deep, dark regions. She could also imagine that no sound from where she walked could be heard above. She was as isolated as if she were on some strange planet.

She came to the door of the surgery and hesitated. Dare she look inside it again? Bracing herself she turned the door knob and slowly opened the door. Then she held the candle a little higher to see within. There on the table under a white covering was the distinct outline of a human body. Ian was still dissecting a human cadaver, whether it was the one she'd seen before or not. She closed the door quickly!

Now she moved on to explore an area of the cellar she

had not reached before. A cobweb from above fell and besmirched her pretty face. She quickly brushed it off with a feeling of revulsion and pushed on towards the opposite side of the cellar. Within a moment her venture into the dark regions offered shocking new evidence of her husband's guilt.

Straight ahead of her, neatly arranged against the cellar wall, were a number of rough, wooden caskets. When the first fright of seeing them wore off she began to count them. There were six in all and on top of one of them was what appeared to be a body sewed in a canvas covering. This would make a total of seven cadavers stowed there in the cellar!

How many of them were stolen bodies, freshly robbed from their nearby graves in Mercy Cemetery? How many of them had been murdered to supply bodies to the grisly trade? The legitimate need for dead bodies for medical study had been perverted into this cruel, criminal activity! And her husband was a part of it!

She stood there staring at the caskets and the canvas sack and feeling ill. Then from directly behind her there came the sound of a dry cough! It shot through her like a sharp knife! With a feeling of terror such as she had never known before she turned quickly in the direction from which the cough had come to see Dr. Clinton Marsh standing there with a lantern in his hand.

She gasped, "What are you doing here?"

In a harsh voice, he said, "I might ask you the same thing. Or do you make a practice of roaming about in the cellar?"

Ann feared she might faint. She struggled to maintain a defiant front as she declared, "This is my house. I have every right to be down here!"

The doctor smiled but his lidded eyes seemed to narrow with hatred as he informed her, "It is also your husband's house, and I am here with his permission."

She said, "Because of those caskets?"

Dr. Clinton Marsh showed no emotion. He told her, "The cases to which you refer are property of the university. And I shortly propose to remove them from here."

"I doubt they have ever seen the university," she replied angrily. "I say they are stolen bodies! That you are a grave robber or worse!"

The lizard face took on a leering smile. Dr. Marsh said, "Your husband warned me you were emotionally unstable. I see how right he is."

"You have contrived to make him a fellow criminal," she told the doctor. "I will not forgive you for that."

"You are filled with wrong ideas, young woman," Dr. Marsh said. "I advise you not to interfere with things of which you have no understanding."

"The authorities are ready to close down on you," she warned the ugly Dr. Marsh. "It's time you put a stop to all this!"

"I don't know what you're talking about," was his reply.

She saw that she could not reason with him, and she found herself wanting to escape the macabre atmosphere of the cellar with its stock of caskets. So she turned and ran from him as she headed for the stairway. She did not halt until she reached the upper hallway. Then she could not bear to remain in the grim old house. The line of patients on the steps told her that Ian was still busy. She went out by the side door and avoided any contact with them.

It was a sunny afternoon and she hurried towards the cemetery gates. It was strange to find herself using Mercy Cemetery as a sanctuary. But that was how she felt about it at the moment. She hurried along the narrow roadway and then took one of the pathways leading off the road. She was soon deep in the country of the dead.

She was strolling between the headstones in a stunned state when she was alerted to the sounds of someone shoveling a little distance away. Like a person in a trance, she followed the sounds of the shoveling until she came to a half-dug grave with the weird, spare Angus McCrae standing in it.

He paused in his labors to squint up at her. A grin crossed his dried-apple face and he said, "It is you again, Mistress Stewart!"

"You remember me!"

"Am I liable to forget such beauty," the old grave digger said. "And does your cook not supply me with luscious scraps from your table!"

"Are you preparing a grave?" she asked.

"That I am," he said with some pride. "I'm not one of those who dig bodies up. I can swear to that! Would you believe that a grave I dug three days ago was vandalized last night and the casket taken from it. They used to take only the bodies, but now they're so brazen they take everything including the casket."

"That makes the crime more grievous in the eyes of the law," she suggested.

The thin man in black nodded. "It's a hanging matter! No less!"

"Do you think the authorities are going to act?"

"You can be sure they are," Angus McCrae told her with grim relish. "Before long some necks are going to be stretched. And some of the grave robbers will find themselves in their own graves!" He gave a rasping laugh.

Again she felt sick with worry. She said, "I must not keep you from your work."

"The party coming to sleep in this hole isn't impatient," the weird scarecrow of a man chuckled. "They aren't coming with him until tomorrow. And if the vultures are around there's no telling how long he'll lie here in peace."

"Have you ever seen these grave robbers?" she asked.

He looked sly. "You'd be fair shocked if you knew just half of what I see in this place."

"I'm sure I would."

"Dark shadows moving in the night," he told her. "Then I hear the digging. And in the morning what do I find but an empty grave!"

"Aren't you afraid?"

"I keep to myself," Angus McCrae told her. "I don't mix where I'm not wanted. I like people a lot more when they've a tombstone to weight them down! Back to work!" And he began vigorously shoveling once again and singing some weird sort of folk song.

By the time she reached the red brick house again, the line of patients had vanished. She went inside and met the maid, Nancy, in the hallway.

"Where is the doctor?" she asked.

"He left a while ago," the maid replied. "With the gentleman with the ugly face."

"Dr. Marsh?"

"I expect that is his name," the girl answered. "He waited to see the doctor after he'd finished with his patients. Then they left in the doctor's carriage."

"I see," she said. And she went on upstairs.

Ian did not appear again until the dinner hour. Then he arrived and joined her at the dinner table. He was quiet and polite to her. She expected him to make some reference to her being in the cellar and seeing the sinister old doctor there, but he made no mention of it.

She played along with him in this. And when he excused himself to go down to work in his surgical room she made no comment, though the knowledge that there were a half-dozen or more stolen cadavers in the cellar had thoroughly frightened her.

Perhaps by tomorrow there would be word from his father. They would be invited to the party at Stormhaven and Dr. Jock Gregory would attempt to reason with her errant husband. She only worried that even a day's delay might be too late. The authorities could raid the house and charge Ian with possession of stolen bodies at any moment.

She was in bed when Ian came up to join her. He bent and kissed her forehead tenderly. Ann pretended to be asleep and kept up the pretense as he prepared for bed and then got in beside her. It was ironical that her pretense ended in her truly falling into a deep sleep.

Somewhere in her sleep the nightmares began once again. She was fleeing down a long corridor with the headless ghost following close on her heels. She screamed and awoke bathed with perspiration to discover that she was alone in the bed. Ian had vanished somewhere.

Fear crept across her face as she sat up in bed. And then from the driveway outside she heard the sound of loud, rough voices. Someone uttered a dreadful curse and this was followed by coarse laughter. Then the voices became hushed as if someone had warned them!

She rose from the bed and went to the window. She clearly saw lanterns waving in the darkness. And there was the heavy sound of something being loaded on the wagon. She did not need to penetrate the darkness to guess that the caskets she'd seen in the cellar were being removed. Dr. Marsh was moving them on somewhere.

Her first feeling was one of relief. At least they would no

longer be on the premises as evidence against her husband. But this momentary easing of her tensions was followed by the sickening realization that it would happen all over again. More graves would be raided and other caskets would arrive. This would go on until the wicked practice was ended.

And that could mean her husband standing in the gallows! There were more mutterings from below and then the wagon rumbled off and the lanterns vanished. She hurried back to bed to again appear to be asleep when her husband returned. He came back shortly after with a dressing robe thrown over his nightgown. She again simulated sleep and he returned to bed without bothering her.

The following morning she received a message from her mother-in-law. One of the servants from Stormhaven brought the letter. It was an invitation to a party for Dr. Jock Gregory on the following evening. Flora Stewart made it explicit that she expected Ian to attend and she also requested that Ann visit her on receipt of the invitation to help with the plans for the affair.

Ann was happy to have an excuse to get away from the old brick house. Also, she always enjoyed the time she spent with her mother-in-law. Flora was a lively, pleasant, youthful person who took an active interest in all the family problems. Ann shrewdly guessed that Ian's father had undoubtedly confided to his wife the plight their son was in. He could do this safely since Flora might well be a help in the unhappy situation.

Charles drove Ann to the imposing old castle in which the Stewarts lived. Stormhaven was always like some fabled mansion in a storybook to her. The Chippendale furniture and the exquisite Chinese sideboards were only a part of the treasures of the great house. The paintings on the walls along with the fine Persian rugs on the hardwood floors and the exquisite services of china and silver served to make it one of the finest homes in all Edinburgh. The Stewarts did not make a vulgar display of their wealth, but everything was of fine quality.

Flora received Ann in the modest parlor which she reserved for her own use. It was in the north wing of the old mansion and decorated in soft gray. The fine Chippendale furniture and the impressive family portraits on the gray and silver of the walls were in keeping with the rest of the great house. But this room had another quality of simple graciousness which some of the rest of the mansion lacked. Ann felt the room reflected the nature of the mistress of the house.

Flora rose from her writing desk to greet Ann and kiss her gently on the cheek. The mistress of Stormhaven had a young face framed by pure white hair. It was claimed that in her youth she had been an outstanding beauty and her looks were still well preserved.

"How good of you to come so promptly," Ian's mother said as she and Ann seated themselves on the lovely chaise longue.

"I appreciate your having the party," Ann said.

Flora smiled knowingly. "What better occasion for it? Dr. Jock Gregory arrived in Edinburgh this morning. Tomorrow night we shall celebrate his return."

"It will be good to have him back," Ann said.

"He is our dearest friend," Flora assured her. A sad, reflective look crossed the older woman's face. "And we have lost so many of our friends."

"I'm sure you must have."

"Jock is the oldest one left and truly dear to us. He takes an interest in all the family. Especially Ian. Your husband is like a son to him. It was his example which made Ian decide to be a doctor."

"So I have been told," she said. She was now more certain than ever that her father-in-law had confided in his wife about the problem she and Ian were facing.

Flora gave her a discerning look. "You're very pale, child. Have you been getting proper rest?"

"My nerves have been bad lately. I find Mercy House a depressing place in which to live."

"I don't blame you! I was surprised when Ian chose the house, and I still think it a mistake. We must talk to him about it."

She sighed. "He claims it is a good location for his practice."

"Nonsense!" Ian's mother said. "His patients will follow him anywhere. He has built himself an excellent reputation."

"I think that," she said.

Her mother-in-law rose and stood a few steps away from her. "All marriages bring problems," she said. "Especially new marriages." She turned to look directly at Ann. "I can tell you it was not easy for me when I first came here."

"Really?"

"I felt the house hostile toward me and full of mystery. There were so many things I did not know and understand about the Stewarts. My husband wasn't too helpful at first so I had to depend on myself a great deal."

"Yet it has worked out well."

Flora smiled. "Better than I dreamed. Ian and I have been blessed with five good children of our own and then there was Billy." She glanced at the portrait of an attractive-looking woman on the wall. "That was Billy's mother! She was my husband's sister. After her death we adopted Billy who was her love child."

"He is dead now, isn't he?" Ann said.

The older woman nodded. "Yes. Poor lad! He was like one of my own! It is sad that he had so short a life!"

Ann said, "I've heard only a little about him. Who was his father?"

Flora Stewart sighed. "I think that is better left unspoken. His background was cloaked in mystery. It was one of the problems I faced when I came here. So you see even the most forbidding shadows can be dispelled."

"I want to believe that," Ann said sincerely.

"You must," was Flora's reply. "And even though Ian may seem unattentive to you at times you must never doubt his love. I know my son and I know it is his nature to be true to those he loves."

"I have always tried to tell myself that," she said, "even now when I find myself sorely tried."

Flora nodded. She moved across the room and looked out the window at the small pond which had been constructed on the grounds. "About tomorrow night. We are having food and dancing in the great hall. About the middle of the evening we have arranged a display of fireworks out by the pond."

"Fireworks! How exciting!"

Her mother-in-law smiled. "Everyone seems to enjoy them. We have a man to work them who is excellent at it. Of course it depends on the weather. Should it rain there will be no fireworks."

"It will be a gala occasion," Ann said.

"I'd like to make it one," Flora agreed. "And I shall want you to take a turn at presiding over the teacups along with Heather Rae and Mary."

It was the first time she'd mentioned Mary who was her older daughter. Perhaps this was because Mary and her husband travelled a good deal and spent only a portion of their time in Edinburgh. Though a young woman, Mary had married the elderly Lord Inglis, a widower, when he was near his sixtieth year. Yet it seemed a happy May and December marriage though the couple had no children.

"How is Lady Inglis?" Ann asked.

Flora turned to her with a smile. "Lady Inglis! I find it hard to think of Mary as that! And yet it is her name now. I still see her as a child and as a quiet, solitary girl growing up. Yet now she has blossomed both physically and in personality. I have been told she was the most popular young hostess in London last season."

"Lord Inglis is very understanding of her."

"He dotes on her," Flora agreed. "He is both father and husband to her. I confess I was upset about the match at first, but now it seems to have worked out well. It shows how little we know."

Ann smiled. "I'm certain they are happy, but I doubt they will ever have children. Walter and Heather Rae are the only ones who have made you grandparents."

Her mother-in-law said, "But you and Ian are bound to have a family."

"I hope so," she said. "If nothing happens to us." She was again thinking of her young husband being threatened by the gallows.

"You mustn't talk like that," her mother-in-law said at once. "Nothing is going to happen. You two will live long and happy lives. I'm positive of it!"

Ann was grateful for the courage which her mother-in-law offered. She said, "You are right! I must be more optimistic."

"Sophie is languishing with love for her music instructor," Flora went on briskly. "And I don't know how I'll deal with that. He is Italian and barely speaks our tongue and he can do nothing beyond play the violin."

"I understand he is an excellent violinist."

"But hardly a suitable husband for Sophie. She is still only eighteen. I plan to send her to London to be with Mary. It will get her away from this fellow and she will see a more lively social life there than we have here in Edinburgh."

Ann said, "It might be that she would meet someone more fitted to court her in London."

"Perhaps," her mother-in-law agreed. "At least someone to take her mind off this music teacher. Sophie is a pretty girl and I'd like her to marry well. Someone whom we could take into the business. Walter cannot carry the burden of the bank alone, and one day my husband will be too old for it."

"What about Roger?" she asked.

"That boy!" Flora replied with a sparkle of delight in her eyes. "Have you seen him lately? He is as large as his father and he is only sixteen! He wants nothing to do with the bank! He loves the outdoors and he claims he wants to be a builder!"

"Perhaps he'd be very good at it."

"I'm sure he will be," Flora said. "And he has a mind of his own. I warn you that having children can be a torment as well as a blessing!" The older woman laughed.

Ann joined in her laughter. "I have no doubt of that. Life is a series of challenges to all of us."

Flora sat down at her desk again. "And now I must acquaint you with the details of the party and give you a list of our guests."

They spent the rest of the morning on the party plans, and it was a lesson for Ann. One which she could apply when she had parties of her own. Her mother-in-law worked out every detail in advance so that there would be no problems on the night of the event. Or at least she reduced the risk of any problems to a minimum. In the excitement of all this Ann forgot for a little the black shadow still threatening her marriage. The cellars of Mercy House with the caskets and dead bodies were forgotten for a while. Yet the terror of it all lurked in the back of her mind, waiting only for a suitable moment to return.

She left Stormhaven in the mid-afternoon, and when she arrived at Mercy House there were still a dozen patients on the front steps along with those who were already in the waiting room. She once again used the side entrance to avoid the crowd and went up to her room.

Just being with her mother-in-law had made her feel more assurance. Flora was a wonderful woman with a strong will. And she felt sure that Dr. Jock Gregory would have influence with Ian. If he could only talk him out of collaborating with the mad Dr. Clinton Marsh there might be no scandal. The risk was that Ian would again act as go-between for more stolen bodies.

She informed Ian about the party at dinner that night, and he was far from enthusiastic in receiving the news. He complained, "That is very short notice! I'm in the middle of some important work!"

She glanced across the table at him. "In your surgery?"

"Yes," her young husband said with a frown. "And don't make it sound like something criminal. My experiments are training me to be a better surgeon."

"I did not intend to sound disapproving," Ann said. "But I do think you might tear yourself away from the cellar for at least one night. It is an occasion to honor Dr. Gregory and I'm sure he'll have a great deal of news for you about his work in the medical centers of America."

Ian gave a great sigh. "I suppose I will have to attend. My mother sets great store on her friendship with Jock Gregory. He courted her in the old days. They lived in the same lodging house when he was a student and she had just arrived in Edinburgh."

Ann was pleased. She said, "I'm sure you'll not regret attending. You are fond of Dr. Gregory, aren't you?"

"Of course. He was my idol when I was a boy. I'm sure that is why I chose to be a doctor rather than enter banking."

"Your mother has a large guest list and is making great plans for the event," she told her young husband. "If the weather is suitable there will even be a firework display by the pond."

"I find that tedious," Ian said. "I'm only interested in seeing Jock again and talking with him."

She said nothing more, not wanting to risk turning him against going to the party. As soon as dinner was over, he left her to return to his surgery in the cellar. It was as if he grudged every moment he was away from it. The evening passed quickly with Ann preparing her dress for the party. The night which followed was without event.

The day of the party was pleasantly warm and sunny. Ann was pleased as she knew her mother-in-law planned to make use of the vast grounds of Stormhaven for entertaining. She remained at home during the day to rest and prepare for the party. In mid-afternoon she had a visitor, the petite Martha Todd.

The lawyer's sister was in a state of excitement as she confided to Ann, "Samuel is taking me to Stormhaven tonight. We have both been invited."

"How nice," Ann said politely, though the possibility of meeting the bovine young lawyer again did not thrill her.

His behavior of the other day had turned her against him.

"You and Ian will be there, of course," Martha said.

"Yes. We will be there," she said quietly.

"I wondered," the rattle-brained Martha admitted. "I mean everyone knows that Ian is in trouble with those awful grave robbers and may bring disgrace on the family. I thought maybe his father would prefer not to have him seen at the party."

Ann got to her feet and, standing before the girl, said sharply, "I don't think you should indulge in such loose talk! What proof have you that Ian is in any way involved with the criminals robbing graves?"

Martha looked uneasy. Her vapid face under her wide bonnet showed mild dismay. "I only repeated what others have told me."

"By others," Ann said tautly, "I imagine you mean your brother, Samuel."

Martha's cheeks crimsoned. "Samuel is well informed!"

"Perhaps not so well as he pretends to you," Ann said in a cutting tone. "And I will thank you to make no more harmful comments about my husband."

Martha quickly rose. "I was only trying to warn you!" she protested.

"I do not need your warning and I do not wish your company," she replied in an outburst of annoyance. "Please do me the kindness to leave!"

"Very well!" the other woman said indignantly. "But I warn you, such behavior will not help Ian's case should he come to court!" And she marched out of the room.

Ann feared that she had made an enemy, but she felt that the time had come when she must speak in Ian's defense. It was only making things more difficult to agree with such gossips as Martha Todd. She had no doubt that

Martha went about picking up all the information that she could and then adding more from her own imagination to it.

She made no mention of the scene to Ian. That evening he took her to Stormhaven to the party for Dr. Jock Gregory. The driveway was lined with carriages by the time they arrived. It was a fairly long wait before a lackey came to take their carriage and help her and Ian down. They joined the procession of Edinburgh's best society streaming in through the main entrance door. The silks and satins exhibited in the clothing of the men and women were bright in color and the latest in stylish tailoring. Torches burned on either side of the main entrance to light the gala scene.

There to greet everyone was the senior Ian Stewart, flanked by his lovely wife, Flora, radiant in a lovely blue dress. Beside her was Dr. Jock Gregory. He was not a large man, but he had a kind of vitality about him which one could notice at a glance. Ann knew that the good doctor was completely bald, but he now wore a brown wig which made him appear a good deal younger.

The doctor's face lit up when Ian came to him in the reception line. They chatted for a moment and she heard Dr. Gregory making a point of the fact he wished to speak with him later. She shook hands with the doctor and they moved on to the end of the reception line with Mary and her husband, Lord Inglis. Mary was radiant in a silk dress of many shades, and her elderly husband was pleasant and courteous despite being hard of hearing.

When they finished with the line they went to get some punch and listen to the Scottish Highlanders playing their pipe music. When the Highlanders moved out an orchestra took its place at the end of the grand ballroom and began to play a lilting waltz. As Ian was fond of dancing he at once led her out onto the floor.

She smiled at him as they joined the swirling couples in the softly-lighted big room. During the dance she saw many people she knew. Dr. Harry Turner was there dancing with a pretty redhead; she also saw Samuel Todd there, plodding through the dance with his sister. She felt they deserved each other. Neither Samuel nor Martha noticed them, for which she was grateful.

Perhaps an hour later the party was at its best when Dr. Jock Gregory threaded his way through the clusters of people in the big room to reach them. She saw Ian go stiff and rather edgy at the sight of him.

Jock Gregory smiled and said, "I feel ill at ease to be the guest of honor here tonight. It is too much!"

Ann said, "No! Everyone is delighted to have you back in Edinburgh."

"Thank you, lovely lady," the doctor said. And he gave Ian a glance with his eyes twinkling and inquired, "And are you also as pleased to have me back, young Dr. Ian?"

Ian said, "I wish there was not so much fol-de-rol and that we might have a chance to talk some about your findings in the New World."

"We can find time for that," the older doctor said, taking him by the arm. "Suppose we seek out your father's study. It is bound to be empty and I have much to discuss with you."

"All right," Ian said nervously. He glanced at her, "But what of my wife?"

"I shall manage," she exclaimed, pushing him towards Dr. Gregory. He glanced over his shoulder at her as he said, "We won't be long!" And then he and the older doctor were lost in the crowd.

"Good evening, Mrs. Stewart," a voice with a familiar ring rasped in her ear. And she turned quickly to see the ugly Dr. Clinton Marsh standing at her side. He wore a jacket of crimson silk, a fawn vest and breeches in a lighter shade of fawn. There was a sort of gloating smile on his ugly, lizard-like face.

Ann could not hide the look of surprise on her face. It had not struck her that Ian's parents would include the much-discussed doctor in their guest list. But then, she realized, it was perhaps clever of them to do so. He was an outstanding member of the university staff and a colleague of Dr. Jock Gregory's. There would have been bound to be gossip if he had not been there.

She said, in a faint voice, "Good evening."

The heavy-lidded eyes studied her with grim humor as the old doctor said, "Don't you recognize me, Mrs. Stewart?" It was said with proper sarcasm, since probably even he knew that whoever met him was not liable to forget his ugliness.

"Yes," she said, slowly recovering from her surprise. "You are Dr. Marsh. We met at Mercy House."

"We did," the ugly Dr. Clinton Marsh said. "An extremely interesting old house, don't you agree?"

"I find it grim and unpleasant."

"I'm surprised."

"At what?"

"That your husband should keep you there if you feel so strongly against it," Dr. Marsh said, the half-closed eyes fixed on her.

Ann said, "My husband did not ask my approval of Mercy House, and he turns a deaf ear to my complaints at living in a haunted house."

This seemed to please the evil-looking old doctor more. He said, "So you are aware of its peculiar history?"

"I know murder and suicide took place there," she said.

"Perhaps you have even seen the ghost as well?"

"I have," she said, hating the odious man who had gotten her husband in such trouble. "And I have seen worse than that. I have seen caskets in the cellar! Caskets with stolen bodies!"

"Have you?" Dr. Clinton Marsh inquired with a scathing sarcasm. "And how were you able to identify them as stolen bodies?"

"You know well enough!" she said angrily.

"I'm afraid I must confess a complete innocence on the subject," the lizard-like doctor said. "When your husband returns from talking with Dr. Gregory, I must question him about this!"

"As if you needed to!" she gasped.

Before the conversation could continue further Ian's brother, Walter, came to her. He bowed to Dr. Marsh, who nodded and withdrew, and then asked her, "May I have this dance, Ann?"

She was hardly aware of the music, so great was her upset. But she said, "Yes. I should like that." And a moment later Walter guided her out onto the floor and she was moving swiftly through a folk dance with him as her partner. It went on for what seemed a great while and when they finished she was breathless.

Walter led her from the floor, saying, "I felt I had to rescue you from that monstrous Marsh—or Mad Marsh as he is called! I can't guess why mother invited him!"

She managed a wan smile. "He is a friend and member of the staff with Dr. Gregory. She could not very well leave him out."

"That must be it," Walter said with a frown on his pleasant face. "Marsh and Dr. Gregory are both on the medical staff of the college, though I do not think they are friends."

"Thank you for the dance," she told him.

"Where is Ian?"

"With Dr. Gregory."

"No doubt they have much to talk about," Walter said.

"I'm sure they have," she agreed, knowing that to a point the party had been arranged simply so her husband and Dr. Gregory should meet and the older doctor give her impetuous young husband advice.

The crowd seemed to be moving from the ballroom outside and Walter told her, "The fireworks display is about to begin! Please excuse me. I must find Heather Rae. I promised I'd stay by her during the display. She becomes very nervous and has been known to come down with the vapors!"

"Please do go to her," she begged the nervous young man. Without any need of second asking, he hurried off to find his wife.

Bleakly amused by this, she moved along with the crowd to the outside. She supposed that Ian and Dr. Gregory were still having that earnest conversation which she hoped would put her husband on a safe path again. Meanwhile she would watch the fireworks alone.

A lone piper had been stationed on one of the balconies of the great mansion, and now he began to pace back and forth and play. The people crowded across the lawns to the pond, the paths lit up by flares. Great torches burned at intervals in the gardens. The first of the rockets was set off close by the pond. It shot high in the air and filled the sky with a spectacular stream of colorful light! There were shouts of approval and applause.

Ann drifted off by herself and moved nearer the pond. She could clearly make out the dark figure of the man in charge of the fireworks. He had a lighted taper in his hand

and moved quickly from one spot to another. As he touched off the various pieces, great luminous flows of stars in assorted colors streaked through the dark above them!

The explosions of rockets came loudly before the show of myriad lights! More applause from the enraptured crowd as the bagpiper played on in the background. Entranced by it all, she moved closer to the pond and a distance apart from all the others. She found herself standing between two tall green hedges which cut her off from the main body of the onlookers.

Another rocket exploded, filling the night with its brightness! As it was at its height, she was suddenly aware of a phantom figure which had appeared directly between her and the pond! The figure of the headless ghost!

Six

Ann was shocked by the sight of the hideous phantom and uttered a scream! It was unfortunate that at the identical moment of her scream there were also loud explosions of the fireworks. No one heard her cry! And the headless phantom roughly seized her and dragged her down to the edge of the pond. She fought back and screamed several times as the phantom attempted to fling her into the black, chill water!

Her horror of the headless figure was matched by her terrified attempts to free herself from its grasp. She felt a stinging pain as her left arm was twisted upward behind her, and she found herself falling head first into the pond. The cold water served the purpose of reviving her from her near-fainting condition. She heard frantic shouts from the grassy bank and was vaguely aware of someone plunging into the pond to rescue her.

It was Walter Stewart who took her up in his arms and carried her out of the pond. She was moaning as he put her down on the bank. The fireworks were still going on, and only those in the near area were attracted to her plight.

Kneeling by her, her brother-in-law asked, "What happened to you?"

Thoroughly soaked in the chill water and with her arms still aching from her struggles she told him falteringly, "The ghost! I was thrown in the water!"

"Ghost!" Walter said incredulously. Then he added, "I'd better get you inside." And, once again, he picked her up as he might have a child and strode towards the lighted mansion with her.

By chance Ian and Dr. Jock Gregory were coming out of the door of the mansion nearest the pond as Walter carried her in. Ann was aware of their startled expressions as they saw her.

Ian spoke first, demanding, "What does this mean?"

"Ann met with some sort of accident," his brother told him. "I dragged her out of the pond!"

"Take her into the room off the reception hall," Ian said at once.

Walter took her into the small room and sat her on the chaise longue there. It was the coatroom used by guests during the cold winter months. It had the advantage of being close at hand and empty.

Now Ian gave his attention to her. "Tell me what this is all about?" he said.

Feeling somewhat better, she partly sat up and said, "I was watching the fireworks. I'd wandered off by myself when all at once a figure appeared. It was the same ghost I saw at Mercy House! The headless ghost!"

Ian frowned. "Headless ghost!"

"Yes," she went on, even though she noticed the disapproval in his tone. "The monstrous thing came towards me. I struggled to escape it but without any success. I cried for help, but no one seemed to hear me over the sound of the fireworks and the shouts of the crowd. Then he flung me into the pond. After a while Walter came to my rescue."

Ian glanced up at Walter and asked, "What did you see?"

His brother looked embarrassed. "I thought I heard a scream. Next, I saw Ann struggling in the pond."

Still kneeling by the chaise longue, Ian demanded, "You saw no headless phantom?"

Walter's pale face was unhappy. "No," he said.

Dr. Jock Gregory spoke up briskly. "I don't think any of that is important. But I do think this young woman should be taken upstairs to dry off and change her clothing. She obviously has a chill."

Ian got to his feet. "I realize that. But I would like to know what took place."

The older doctor gave him a meaningful look. "I understand your concern. But first things first. We must get her warm and dry. And I'm sure your parents would not like to have their party spoiled. So we must hurry to see about this discreetly, before the crowd returns inside to the dance."

"Very well," Ian said grumpily. And he told Ann, "I'll take you upstairs to my mother's room."

"I can walk by myself," she told him, recovered enough to be independent and to be aware that he was more angry with her than sympathetic.

Walter suggested, "You take Ann upstairs and I'll call mother and have her help her." And he hurried out.

Dr. Jock Gregory's kindly face showed concern for her as she got to her feet. "You're sure you're not hurt in any way?"

"Thank you, no," she said. "It's just the shock and the cold water!"

"Come along," Ian said impatiently. "We'd best be on our way. The fireworks must be coming to an end."

The hallway was still deserted when Ian guided her out. He placed an arm around her waist as he helped her mount the broad stairway leading to the upper area of the old mansion. It was his only indication of tenderness for her.

She said, "I know you are blaming me for what happened! But it was no fault of mine! I was attacked!"

He glanced at her grimly. "Attacked by a headless ghost?"

"It is true."

"I do not believe in ghosts. And the headless ghost is a legend of Mercy House, not Stormhaven. I can not imagine it appearing here."

"I know what I saw!" she protested.

Her husband said, "For some time now you have been allowing your nerves to mercilessly hound you. Tonight is a result. I have treated enough female victims of hysteria to be familiar with the pattern. You saw a ghost because you wanted to see one!"

"And did I throw myself in the pond as well?"

"That happened as a result of your upset state of mind," her husband said. "Let us talk no more about it!"

He escorted her into Flora Stewart's bedroom, and within a few minutes his mother and her personal maid arrived to look after her. Ian left the room and went back downstairs.

Flora Stewart saw that after Ann was dried and seated in a warm bathrobe, she had a hot drink of rum. The older woman studied her anxiously. "Do you feel well enough to return home, or should you remain here for the night?"

"I'd prefer to go home," Ann said, "if you can find me some dry clothes."

"You are about the same size as Sophie," her mother-in-law said, naming her youngest daughter. "I'll get you an outfit from among her things."

"Please go back to your guests," Ann implored her. "I'm in no hurry."

"I'll get the clothes and then Mary can help you dress," Flora Stewart said. "I'll see that Ian has the carriage ready to take you home."

"I'm so sorry!" Ann lamented.

"Nonsense!" Flora said. "The real worry is that you might have drowned. The pond is deep!"

"Ian doesn't believe my story," she worried.

Her mother-in-law patted her on the shoulder to comfort her. "I'm certain he will when he thinks it over. It is plain enough to me. Some ruffian attacked you in the darkness and threw you in the water!"

Having delivered herself of this opinion, her mother-in-law left with the maid to get some of Sophie's clothes. Meanwhile Ann sat alone, finishing the rest of the hot rum. None of them believed her story of a ghost. But at least her mother-in-law didn't think she'd been hysterical. She would have to take whatever small satisfaction she could from that.

The maid returned with the clothes, and she dressed and went downstairs. The party was now going on at full swing in the ballroom again. She heard the lively music of the dancing and felt sad at having to leave. But Ian was waiting for her at the bottom of the stairway, his young face showing a troubled shadow.

Taking her by the arm, he led her to the front door as he told her, "Charles is waiting with the carriage by the gate."

They did not reach the doorway before they were halted by a call from behind. It was Ian's mother who called to them. They turned to see Flora and the elder Ian approaching them. Both Ian's mother and father showed concern on their pleasant faces.

Ian's father placed an arm around Ann and told her, "I'm most distressed by what happened! I've quietly had the servants search the grounds for some hint of the lunatic who pounced on you."

"It doesn't matter," she protested weakly.

"But it does," Flora said at once. And she told her son, "Be kind to this poor girl! She's been through an ordeal!"

"I will," Ian said with a hint of impatience.

His mother kissed Ann and said, "Do let me know how you are in the morning. I will expect a message from you."

"You have been so kind," Ann thanked her in a voice taut with emotion.

Ian's father also gave her a kiss on the cheek. "We regret this happened," he said. "And I swear I will get to the bottom of it!"

"Do not distress yourself," Ann said. "Your guests must be your first concern."

"You are a guest," the handsome Ian Stewart, Sr., pointed out.

They saw her and Ian out the door and to the carriage. Ann waved to them as the carriage drove off in the darkness. She turned to gaze at the blurred outline of her young husband seated ramrod stiff in the shadowed interior of the carriage. She ventured, "Your parents are most kind."

As the carriage rolled on, Ian replied coldly, "By that I assume you are inferring that I am not."

"I didn't say that!"

"You meant it!"

"Let us not talk about it!" she said despairingly. "You refuse to believe me! I'm sorry I spoiled your evening."

Speaking almost to himself, Ian said, "I was glad to get away from it all!"

"Glad to get away?" she echoed in surprise.

"Yes," he said sternly. "I have no doubt that you are aware I spent the better part of an hour receiving a lecture from Jock Gregory!"

"I know Dr. Gregory took you away to talk with you. That is how I happened to be alone for the fireworks."

"Better if he'd spared his time," Ian went on in an angry voice. "I have no doubt it was arranged. That either my father or my brother put Jock up to it. They've heard these monstrous stories about grave robbing and that Dr. Marsh and some others have been suspected of establishing a ring for the purpose."

She knew this to be true but only dared to venture, "Is that what he talked to you about?"

"He talked around it first," Ian said. "Then he came straight out and warned me that my career would be ruined if I were mixed up with Marsh in the grave robbing in any way."

"Dr. Marsh was at the party."

Ian's reply was bitter. "My parents are clever enough to have seen to that. But they don't really respect Marsh. They think him mad like everyone else."

"He is very strange."

"He is a genius."

"Genius can border on madness."

"That is what Jock Gregory said," Ian commented in the same bitter tone. "Jock talked to me in the same way he did when I was a youth. I'm no longer a student paying homage to his every word. I'm a doctor, licensed in my own right. I have the right to choose what I will or will not do!"

"I'm sure anything Dr. Gregory said was meant to be helpful," Ann said.

Ian turned to her almost fiercely. "Everyone wants to be helpful, and yet you all want to interfere. Why can't you let me make my own decisions?"

"Is that what you told Dr. Gregory?" she asked.

"Just about that," he said. "I respect Jock for being a fine teacher and a good doctor. But he is backward when it comes to his views on the dissection of human bodies! God in Heaven, does he think we can find the answers to cure suffering humans by cutting up frogs and rats?"

"I'm sure he agrees with you about the need for human dissection," she said. "I think he only wanted to warn you that robbing graves to provide bodies for the purpose is no sensible solution."

"Do you think me a grave robber?"

"No," she said. "But I do worry about you . . . about those men who have come in the night . . . the caskets in the cellar . . ."

"All that is no concern of yours," Ian snapped.

"But I am your wife!" she protested. "I do worry about you."

"There is no need," was his reply.

For the rest of their journey home he sat aloof from her and silent. Only after they had prepared for bed did he seem to have a change of heart and show a different and more kindly approach towards her. When she was in bed he came to her and bent down to tenderly kiss her lips.

She stared up at him. "You are so strange! I don't understand you at all!"

His eyes were sad as he gazed down at her. "Perhaps you had better not try."

"You make me believe that! But I do want to help you! So do your parents! We are all anxious about you!"

His lean face went cold again. In a stern voice, he said, "I ask you to rely on me to judge what is best for us." And with that he extinguished the remaining candle and took his place beside her in bed.

Soon he was asleep. She listened to his even breathing and stared up into the shadows. Tonight she had gone through a dreadful ordeal. Ian insisted that he loved her and yet he made no attempt to believe her story. Instead he preferred to think that because of overwrought nerves she had become hysterical during the time she stood alone at the pond watching the fireworks. But she knew better! She would not soon forget what she had seen and the brutal treatment she'd received. The image of the headless phantom was etched on her mind!

It rained the following morning. Ann awoke in a depressed mood, and when she went down to have breakfast she found Mrs. McQuoid, the cook, also in an unhappy mood.

The usually jolly Mrs. McQuoid came in to serve her breakfast instead of the pretty Nancy. Before Ann had a chance to ask where the maid was, Mrs. McQuoid explained, "I don't know what to think, ma'am. Nancy is missing."

"Missing?"

"Yes. She went out somewhere last night and, as far as I can tell, she didn't ever come back."

"Does Dr. Stewart know about this?"

"No, ma'am. I didn't tell him when he came down. I thought Nancy might have overslept. But when I went out and checked her room, I found her bed hadn't been used at all."

Ann stared at the stout woman. "What do you make of it?"

"I don't like it, ma'am. Nancy has never done anything like this before. She's a saucy little creature and vain about her looks, but she's always been dependable."

"Where did she go last night?"

The housekeeper looked embarrassed. "I couldn't say for certain, ma'am, but I think she went out to meet a young man. You know how it is with these girls."

"Has she been meeting any particular young man regularly?"

"I think so. Though I don't know his name. I have an idea they may have been meeting in the cemetery."

Ann's eyebrows raised. "In the cemetery?"

"Yes, ma'am. There are many who use it as a lover's lane."

"It's not a place I would seek out," Ann said.

"There are many who aren't so fussy," the older woman said. "I'm fair upset about the girl. And so is old Charles."

"I'm worried as well," she said. "Nancy has come to be like one of the family."

"That is true, ma'am," Mrs. McQuoid said with a sigh and went on serving breakfast.

Ann lingered over her tea, worrying about what could have happened to the pretty maid. She felt responsible for the girl since she was in their employ. Perhaps Nancy had suddenly taken a notion to run off and get married. But it seemed unlikely that she wouldn't leave some word. After debating about this, she rose from the table and was about to leave the room when Mrs. McQuoid came in again.

In a low, conspiratorial tone, the cook leaned forward to her and said, "He's here again!"

"Who?" Ann asked, surprised by the woman's manner.

"Him!" Mrs. McQuoid said. "From the graveyard! The grave digger!"

"Oh! Angus McCrae!"

"That's him, ma'am. And he has a strange story to tell. I think you should hear it."

"Really?"

"Yes. It has something to do with Nancy," the cook said.

Ann was at once concerned. "Very well. I'll go out and talk to him," she agreed.

When they entered the kitchen with its big stove and steaming kettles they discovered the odd, thin grave digger seated contentedly at one end of the big kitchen table, munching mutton and bread. He got to his feet and touched a hand to his temple respectfully on seeing Ann.

"A good day to you, ma'am," the scarecrow figure in black said. "Though to be truthful, it is anything but that."

"Good day," Ann said. "I understand you had something to tell about Nancy."

"The maid, ma'am?"

"Yes," Ann said.

Angus McCrae ran the back of his hand across his lips and his rotten-apple face took on a knowing look. "I've seen her in the cemetery quite a few nights."

"Has she been alone?" Ann questioned him.

"She usually comes alone, but she meets a man. I've seen them together."

"Would you recognize him?"

"I wouldn't say so, ma'am. I've never been that close to him. But she's walked by me many's the time."

"Did you see her last night?"

"I did."

"And did she meet anyone?"

"That, I can't say," Angus McCrae declared. "I mean by that I didn't see them together later. But I watched where she went."

"Where did she go?"

"Over to the new section of the cemetery. I expected to see her later, but I didn't."

Ann said, "So she just vanished somewhere in the cemetery?"

"That's right, ma'am," the old grave digger said.

Ann sighed. "And that's all you can tell us?"

Mrs. McQuoid spoke up and advised the grave digger, "Don't hold back! Tell her the rest."

Angus McCrae's ruined face showed uneasiness. He paused a minute before going on. Then, he said, "It might not be important . . ."

"What?" Ann interrupted.

The thin man blinked at her. "Well, just where I saw her standing last, there was something happened . . ."

"What happened?" Ann cut in sharply, a little annoyed at the way he was drawing it out.

"Just where she was standing a grave was robbed. When I went over there this morning, I found the grave dug up and the coffin gone!"

Ann gasped. "So the grave robbers have been at work again?"

"Yes, ma'am. And it struck me funny that she should have been standing there in that spot."

Ann asked him, "Do you think Nancy might have had anything to do with the body being stolen?"

"I don't know, ma'am," the thin grave digger said. "I wondered if maybe she'd been standing guard while the young man and his friends dug up the grave and robbed it."

"She's been going to the cemetery regularly," the cook said.

Ann was puzzled by this new turn of events. She asked the grave digger, "Then you think Nancy might be one of the gang robbing the graves?"

"It occurred to me," Angus McCrae admitted. "Of course, I might be wrong."

Ann asked, "Is that everything?"

"Yes," the thin man said. "That's everything. And thank you for the vittles, ma'am."

"You're most welcome," she said. And turning to the cook she added, "See that Angus gets whatever he wants. And don't ever turn him away."

Mrs. McQuoid nodded seriously. "If that's your wish, ma'am."

"It is," she said. And she gave her attention to Angus McCrae once more, telling him, "Just one thing more. If you get any information about Nancy at all, no matter how trivial, will you please let me know?"

The thin man nodded. "Depend on it, ma'am. I hope you find her. She's a pretty one!"

Ann nodded without speaking and then, after a further word to Mrs. McQuoid, she went on out to the main area of the house. The news that Nancy was missing had been disquieting enough, but now to complicate matters Angus McCrae had come along with this story of her being near the grave which had been robbed. It might be only coincidence and mean nothing; on the other hand, it might be something related to the series of grave robberies.

She went into the magnificent living room and stood gazing out at the falling rain. Never had she felt so frustrated and so uncertain about what she ought to do. She was thinking about this when she saw a rig come into the driveway. An instant later, a male figure quickly dodged out of the rig and hurried towards the front door. The driver and the rig went about waiting in the rain for the passenger.

The doorbell rang and Mrs. McQuoid came hurrying out to answer it, another of Nancy's jobs which had now fallen to her. Ann waited to see who it might be. When the door was open she saw that it was Dr. Jock Gregory. The doctor saw her, bowed to Mrs. McQuoid, and entered. He came directly across to greet Ann.

"My dear girl," he said, "I have made a special visit to see your state of health. I remained overnight at Stormhaven, and Flora begged me to check on you."

She managed a weary smile. "That is good of you and

kind of her. As a matter of fact, I'm feeling very well despite my unpleasant experience."

"I'm glad to hear that," the doctor said.

Mrs. McQuoid came and helped him remove his dripping wet coat and he thanked her. Then he turned to Ann and, with a suggestion that he had more to discuss with her than her health, he said, "You won't mind if I remain for a little?"

"I'd be delighted," she said. "What about your carriage?"

"The driver has a rubber coat against the storm," Dr. Gregory said. "He won't mind waiting."

"Please come in and sit down," she said, inviting him into the parlor.

He followed her, saying, "This is an extraordinary old house. I well remember the scandal connected with it."

She glanced at him. "You mean the murder and suicide?"

Dr. Jock Gregory nodded. "Yes. Sad business! I saw the woman afterwards. She was lost to the world. The shock of it sent her into a withdrawn state. A kind of madness that is fairly common."

"I learned the story shortly after I came here," she said.

"Did Ian tell you?"

"No."

The doctor showed surprise. "He kept it from you?"

"Yes," she said grimly. "I learned it from a grave digger in Mercy Cemetery."

Dr. Jock Gregory rubbed his chin. "Rather an odd source," he said.

"My life has been filled with odd experiences since Ian brought me here to live."

The man in the brown wig eyed her sharply. "The last one being at the party, when the headless phantom followed you there."

She gave him a troubled look. "Do you think I was hysterical or perhaps just plain mad? Do you think it was all a fantasy on my part?"

"No."

"Ian does."

"I'm sure the episode upset and puzzled him," the doctor said. "Perhaps he prefers to hide his frustration behind the mask of a skeptic."

"And you?"

"I think you were attacked by what you believe to be a ghost but what was probably something quite different. I would vote that your attacker was some enemy in disguise."

"You think that?"

"Yes. Someone trying to frighten you badly for a reason. Perhaps to get you out of this house."

Ann smiled bitterly. "Anyone who would try to get me out of this house would be a friend, not an enemy."

Dr. Jock Gregory explained, "The motive might be that of an enemy, although you might consider the end result beneficial. But surely your experience last night could have ended in your death."

She shuddered. "I don't like to think that."

"Ian's parents are very upset. They seem to feel it may have been some mad prowler, some lunatic who intruded on the grounds."

"It was no ordinary man. I could see no head! I was attacked by a figure without a head!" she protested.

The doctor frowned. "That is why I stay with my theory you were the victim of an enemy . . . an enemy of yours or possibly of your husband's. Can you think of any such person who was at the party?"

She considered and then after a brief moment, said,

"Yes, I can think of one person."

"Who?"

"A lawyer who used to court me. His name is Samuel Todd. He was there with his sister. I saw them dancing together."

"Did you see him after the incident?"

"No. But I saw very few people. Ian took me home as soon as I changed into warm clothing."

Dr. Jock Gregory said, "So there is at least one suspect. Do you think Samuel Todd capable of such a masquerade?"

"He's capable of making the attack on me. But I would hardly suspect him of being able to so disguise himself," she said.

The doctor's pleasant face showed serious thought as he warned her, "You never can tell. People are capable of much more than we give them credit for, both good and bad."

"I suppose he could somehow disguise himself," she said.

"Can you remember? Did this phantom without a head have any likeness to this lawyer fellow?"

"I can't say. It all happened so quickly. I really can't honestly say!"

"That's a sensible answer," Dr. Jock Gregory said. "In my opinion, a quiet investigation of where Samuel Todd was during the fireworks might be of value."

"It could be," she agreed. "He has been one of those casting slurs against Ian, suggesting that he and Dr. Marsh are involved in robbing graves. He has never forgiven Ian for taking me from him."

"Then it all fits in," the doctor said. "As you must know, I talked with Ian about this business of the stolen bodies last night."

"I hoped that you'd warn him against Dr. Marsh."

"I did that also," Jock Gregory said. "But I fear much of what I said was resented by Ian."

"I know. He told me as much on our way home."

"He has a hero-worship for Marsh," the doctor confessed. "And I must be truthful and say he is not all wrong in that. Marsh is a surgeon of outstanding ability and a great teacher in the steps of Hunter. But he is obsessed with human dissection. He sees it as a great factor in improving his profession."

"But the means for securing bodies is the hinge of it all," she said. "I can't deny he is right in wanting to use human bodies for his experiments. But surely he should be satisfied with the bodies of criminals which are rightly his by law."

"There aren't enough of them for all the medical schools," Dr. Jock Gregory told her.

"So now bodies of decent people are being stolen. And worse, good people are being murdered for their bodies. That is the current rumor in Edinburgh."

"I hope it is only a rumor," Dr. Jock Gregory said in a worried tone. "Any scandal touching the profession is a setback for all of us."

She gave the elderly doctor a very direct look. "I happen to know another grave was robbed last night."

His eyes opened wide. "How do you know?"

"It happened in Mercy Cemetery, next to us. One of the grave-diggers comes here for snacks. He told my cook the story and she had him tell it to me."

"You are directly next to the cemetery, of course."

She nodded. "Yes. I wonder if Ian chose the place because it was convenient for the dealings he had with Dr. Marsh. I can tell you there have been strange visitors here in the middle of the night."

126

The doctor showed alarm. "Have you actually seen any traffic in bodies going on?"

"I have seen six caskets stored in the cellar and a dead body in a canvas as well. These all disappeared overnight."

"It sounds bad," Dr. Jock Gregory said.

"That is why I sought help from Ian's parents and they turned to you."

"And thus far I have failed to be of any help."

"I hope," she said, her eyes meeting his, "that it is not too late."

"Please, explain," he begged her.

"Something else has happened since I saw you at the party last night," she said.

"Oh?"

"Yes. The maid employed here—a healthy, pretty girl whom everyone liked—has vanished."

"Vanished?"

"She has been meeting some man in the cemetery. She went out for one of these regular meetings last night and didn't come back."

"That is worrisome," the old doctor said. "This girl has been completely reliable up until now?"

"Yes."

"Then she wouldn't likely run off without telling you," he ventured.

"I'm sure she wouldn't."

The doctor gave her a troubled look. "Do you think it could be possibly mixed up in this other business in any way?"

"The thought terrifies me," she said. "And I do believe there may be a link."

"Of what sort?"

"The grave digger who told me about the open grave

said that he last saw Nancy standing near the grave which was robbed."

"Very strange!" Dr. Jock Gregory agreed.

"I'd say so," she told him with meaning. "He claims she was standing there as if she might be a lookout for whoever was going about the grave robbing."

Seven

More than two weeks had passed since Nancy disappeared. It had been a time of torment for Ann. She was sure that in some way the girl's vanishing was associated with the grave robbers whose exploits had scandalized the city. When Ian had heard about Nancy's disappearance he had at first pushed the news aside as not being important.

"It is clear enough," he'd told Ann. "The girl has gone off with some man. She was always too pretty for her own good."

"She was not brainless," Ann had replied sharply. "I do not see her doing such a thing."

"She has people in the Highlands, hasn't she? Perhaps she has gone back there," Ian suggested.

"A few months ago she told me that her mother was the only one left and she'd gone to another town to live with a widowed sister. I don't think she had any home to go to."

Ian had then showed impatience. "I was the girl's employer, not her guardian. I'm extremely busy and can't be accountable for what my servants do."

"I think that we are," she said gravely. "I am extremely worried about this, especially as she was last seen in the cemetery."

"Why make so much of that?" her husband asked. "It is a likely place for lovers to rendezvous."

"I do not see it so," she said. "Though I know Nancy had been meeting someone there. According to my informant, she was last seen standing near a grave which was afterwards robbed."

Ian's blue eyes flashed angrily. "So we come back to that again!"

"I do not mean to harp on it," she told him. "But the facts can't be denied."

"Facts which you've had from some mad scarecrow who drinks himself into stupidity and sleeps in a cemetery tomb. He does not strike me as being too reliable!"

Her cheeks crimsoned. "Just the same, he does work in the cemetery as a grave digger and so he knows what goes on there."

"I shouldn't be surprised if he were mixed up in the robbing of graves himself," Ian said.

"Never! He condemns it!"

"A truly virtuous character!" Ian said with sarcasm. "I do not want to hear any more about grave robbing. I've had my fill of it!" And he stalked out of the room.

Ann had let him go. She did not dare press him too far. He was unaware that she was the one who'd arranged with his parents for Dr. Jock Gregory to lecture him on his reckless association with the doctor called Mad Marsh. And he was also unaware that Dr. Gregory had come to see how she was the day after the party. It was better that he did not find this out. If he guessed they were conspiring against him he would simply be less reasonable than ever.

Dr. Gregory suspected that the appearance of the headless phantom at the party and the attack on her had been the work of an enemy. He was trying to find out if Samuel Todd might be the villain. So far he had not had much luck. And she had not seen the phantom since that night. But she lived in fear of it returning. Mercy House had become a somber prison from which she only wished to escape. But Ian didn't see it that way.

The old house served him perfectly as an office. And despite the dark rumors linked to his name, his practice was continuing to grow. His sessions in his surgery room in the evenings also went on. She had not ventured into the cellar recently and did not dare to guess what gruesome horrors it might contain.

The sad business of Nancy being missing was enough for her to cope with. She did not like to bother Ian's father and mother with more of their problems, and so she avoided going to Stormhaven. It was natural in her upset state of mind that she should think of her own Aunt Samantha and turn to her.

Aunt Samantha lived in a cozy stone house tucked between two shops on a busy street of Edinburgh. In the days when Ann had been growing up, the old woman had presided over a house in the suburbs of the city. But with Ann's marriage the house became too large. Samantha had owned this tiny house in the city which she'd rented. Now she had taken possession of it herself and lived there with an elderly woman who served as a maid and companion.

On the bright summer-like afternoon on which Ann elected to visit her Aunt Samantha, the downtown street was excessively busy and noisy. When she alighted from her carriage she asked Charles to return for her within an hour. And she was forced to shout this at the top of her lungs to make herself heard over the bedlam of voices and carriage sounds which filled the air.

There had been a heavy rain the previous night, leaving soft sections in the street. A carriage belonging to the gentry by its decoration had sunk a wheel in the mud and a half-dozen straining and shouting males were trying to lift it out of the muddy rut and send it on its way. At the same time the drivers of other carriages were screaming for the bogged-down vehicle to clear the way as a general traffic jam was in progress.

Vendors of fish and purveyors of sweetmeats called out their wares as they wheeled their carts along. A chimney sweep blocked her way as he passed with a long ladder under his arm and two soot-besmirched lads following him with brass plates on their caps telling the name and address of the sweep. The cobblestoned sidewalk was crowded with shoppers, young and old, gawking in the multi-paned display windows.

She wended her way through this chaotic confusion and reached the stone step of her aunt's house and lifted the heavy brass knocker on the door under the plate bearing her aunt's name. She waited, parasol in hand, warm in her blue taffeta dress and wide-brimmed blue bonnet, until finally the door opened.

The buxom, red-faced woman who opened the door at once broke into a smile and exclaimed, "It's Miss Ann come calling!"

"Good afternoon, Helen," she said. "Is my aunt at home?"

"She is!" the old woman said, standing back for Ann to enter. "And glad she will be to see you. She has not been well of late."

Ann was at once concerned. "Aunt Samantha ill?"

"The surgeon has bled her twice. He fears she may be on the verge of a stroke. But I think he is only drumming up business. I swear there is nothing more wrong with her than an indisposition of the liver!"

"I do hope she is getting proper medical attention!" Ann worried.

"Well, you know what these doctors are like!" the old woman said grimly. And then remembering, she apologized,

"No harm meant, Miss Ann! I clear forgot you are married to one."

"That is all right," she smiled. "Take me to my aunt."

Aunt Samantha received her in a small back parlor which was as cool and quiet as the street outside was hot and noisy. The bedlam of the street did not penetrate the stout stone walls of the well built old house.

The old woman was seated in a high-backed chair and looked as regal and as horse-faced as Ann remembered her. She did not look ill, hardly any change noticeable in her.

Ann bent and kissed her and said, "Dear Aunt Samantha!"

The old lady looked pleased but afraid of showing it. With a peevish gesture she directed her to sit in a chair by her. "I must say you were long enough in coming!"

"I have been so busy establishing my new home," Ann said.

"That is a mere excuse and you know it," her aunt snapped. "You have neglected me because you know I do not approve of your husband or his family."

Ann said, "That's so silly, Aunt Samantha. Ian is the son of an old and respected family. Stormhaven is one of the finest mansions in Edinburgh."

"Fine plumes do not make a pheasant!" the old woman in the chair said tartly. The face under the white cap with its black velvet ribbon showed scorn. "There is madness in the Stewart strain, and the family records attest to it!"

"That is beside the point," Ann said. "I am here to see you. How have you been?"

"None the better for getting older," Aunt Samantha said in her bitter fashion. "I've had my doctor here, but he's done me little good."

"Why don't you have Ian see you?" Ann suggested. "He is an excellent doctor."

Aunt Samantha gave her a withering look. "I have heard he is more than that. There are stories going about the city that he is one of the doctors behind these grave robberies!"

She gasped. "You have heard that?"

"Is there any truth in it?"

"Ian is a fine, intelligent man."

"That is no answer to my question," her aunt said.

Ann was at a loss. She said, "It is because my husband is so popular that they are spreading these rumors. Some in his own profession wish to hurt him."

"I wonder about that," the old woman said dryly. "From what I hear, the waiting rooms of Dr. Turner and his son, Harry, are perpetually crowded."

"Harry is a friend of Ian's," she said. "He comes to our house often."

"His name has not been mixed up in any of these ugly rumors," the old woman pointed out.

"That is because his father's eminence rules any such talk out. Ian is new to medical circles and has gone too far in too short a time. That is why he has been made the target of such gossip."

"What about this professor at the university? Don't they call him Mad Marsh? I understand he and your Ian are as thick as two toads!"

Ann winced under the accusation. She thought the reference to toads especially apt because of Dr. Marsh's unfortunate looks. She said, "He does think Dr. Marsh a genius. And I believe he is. Unhappily he is deeply involved in the dissection of human remains."

"And doesn't care where the bodies come from!" Aunt

Samantha said angrily. "Decent folk no longer can be sure of resting easy in their graves!"

"I wish Ian would dissolve his relationship with Dr. Marsh but he won't," Ann said.

Aunt Samantha gave her a sharp look. "I know you! I can tell when you're troubled. You have come here today because you are in a panic. Now why not be sensible and come straight out with it? I am your flesh and blood and whether I approve of your choice of husband or not I shall do all I can to help you."

Her aunt's frankness broke down her facade. Slowly and unhappily she recited the whole story for the old woman's benefit, including the attacks on her by the headless phantom. She ended by saying desolately, "I cannot get Ian to listen to me! He simply won't pay any attention!"

Aunt Samantha stared at her with bleak amazement. "My dear child, why didn't you come to me sooner?"

Ann bit her lip. "I didn't want to! I knew you would only remind me that you'd warned me."

"Fie on that!" the old woman exclaimed. "I don't wish to gloat over this misfortune you've come upon. I wish to help you."

Ann said imploringly, "And I do need your help, Aunt Samantha."

The old woman tapped her fingers on the arms of her chair. She said, "You still believe in your husband?"

"I must."

"But do you think him capable of being a member of this grave robbing group?"

"It would depend on circumstances. He might be in it if Dr. Marsh has persuaded him it is for the benefit of medical science."

"Ah!" the old woman declared with satisfaction. "Then you think he may be guilty?"

"I don't know," she said miserably.

"If he isn't then he is the victim of some evil person who wishes you both harm. Someone who has been starting these rumors. It could be the same man whom you suspect of playing ghost and attacking you at the party."

"Samuel Todd?"

"That is the lawyer fellow's name, isn't it?"

"Yes."

"It might very well be him," the old woman said. "I recall how bitter he was when you returned his ring. I never did like his appearance. As I remember, he has no eyebrows."

"No."

"Odd! It gives him a strange appearance! Nasty person! And you claim Dr. Gregory has tried to find out whether Todd could have played phantom that night?"

"Without any luck. He has not been able to get definite information as to Samuel Todd's whereabouts at the time of the accident from anyone."

Aunt Samantha thought about this for a minute. Then she said, "I think it is something you should do yourself."

"What?"

"Investigate this fellow."

Startled, she said, "But that is out of the question. I don't want to see him again. The last time we met, as I've told you, he brutally took me in his arms."

"And you quarreled with the sister?"

"Yes. I ordered Martha from our house."

"That was unwise," the old woman said.

"You think so?"

"I do!"

"Why?"

Aunt Samantha said, "Until you quarreled with her, you had a direct link to Samuel Todd without having to see him. With the quarrel you cut this source of information off."

Ann said, "I suppose you are right. But she made me so angry. She is such a vacant-minded little creature!"

"All the more reason for seeking her out," the old woman assured her. "She was with Samuel that night. You claim you saw them dancing together. She should know best where he was during the party and whether he could have played the phantom."

"I suppose so. But she is angry with me."

"Go to her. Apologize."

Her eyebrows raised. "But Martha was in the wrong!"

"No matter. You can't afford not to cultivate her if you are to get the information you need about her brother."

Ann was forced to see the wisdom of this. She said, "I cannot but agree. I will take my pride in my hands and go to her."

"It would be wise," her aunt said.

"But then there is Nancy," she worried. "The mystery of what happened to her still hangs over us."

"You fear the maid was also somehow mixed up in the grave robbing?"

"I no longer know what to think," she confessed. "But I am very worried about her."

"One thing at a time," the old woman advised her. "Take care of patching up your quarrels with Martha Todd first and work gradually from that."

"I will," she promised, rising.

"And don't make a stranger of me," Aunt Samantha told her. "I am your only living relative, and what happens to you is of concern to me."

"You have been too kind!"

"I could be kinder," the old woman said in her usual acid fashion. "Just be sure and keep me advised what happens."

"I shall," Ann promised and kissed the old woman goodbye.

The buxom Helen accompanied her to the front door again, anxiously asking, "Would you say she has failed any?"

"I don't think so," Ann replied. "She seemed to be in very good spirits. I wouldn't worry about her."

"Thank you, Miss Ann," the housekeeper said. "I wanted to have your opinion."

"I have rarely seen her more alert," Ann said.

Ann left the small stone house determined to carry out Samantha's suggestions. The turmoil on the street still continued, a cart driver in loud argument with a vendor of periwinkles, while a fat woman with a tray of ribbons and a selection of buttons was one of the many accosting Ann as she sought out her carriage.

Charles was waiting down the street and she gave him Martha Todd's address and swiftly got inside. As the carriage started to move slowly a boy pressed his face against the side window and stayed there for a little. Then they were free of the worst of the uproar and on their way to a quiet side street where the Todds lived. Ann was following her aunt's advice and losing no time in seeking out Martha.

She sat back and closed her eyes, thinking about all her wise old foster-mother had said. Aunt Samantha still seemed to think that Ian could be guilty of criminal acts and she, herself, was no longer able to argue the old woman wasn't right. Perhaps the streak of insanity in the family had descended to him and accounted for his wild recklessness.

The carriage halted and Charles, in his faded livery, came to help her down. He asked, "Shall I wait, ma'am?"

"Yes," she said. "I may not be long. And this street is quiet."

"Yes, ma'am," the old man said.

She hesitated to ask him, "Have you any new thoughts concerning Nancy's disappearance?"

The old man shook his head. "No. Except that I don't think it was anything which she planned. She talked to me that night as if she expected to be around the following day."

"Thank you, Charles," she said. And she made her way up the flagstone walk to the cottage in which the Todds lived.

The door was answered by a down-trodden maid who informed her that Miss Martha was having tea in the garden. Ann inquired whether the sister of the lawyer was entertaining and the maid informed her that her mistress was quite alone. So Ann had the girl show her out to the garden behind the cottage.

Martha was seated in a small, latticed summer house. Seeing Ann approach, the girl came to the door of the summer house and peered out as if she could not believe what she saw.

Martha's petite figure was primly drawn up as she waited for Ann to join her at the entrance of the summer house. The girl said, "Well, I must say, I didn't expect to have you for a visitor!"

Ann went directly to the purpose of her being there. She said, "I have come to humbly ask your forgiveness."

Martha's rather pretty, if stupid, face showed real surprise. "Are you apologizing?"

"Yes," Ann said, determined to do it properly. "I was

wrong and I wish to admit it and ask your pardon."

Martha turned pink and looked pleased. "Well, I must say, that is generous of you."

"Not at all. I was in the wrong."

Martha was not to be outdone. "I did tantalize you!"

Ann waved this aside. "That is of no importance. Can you accept me as a friend again?"

"Of course I can, dear Ann!" the petite girl exclaimed and embraced her warmly. "And now, do come in and have tea with me. I was sitting here so lonesome."

"Thank you," Ann said, secretly amused that she should have won her point so easily. And when she was seated in the small summer house across from Martha, she asked, "Did you enjoy the party at Stormhaven?"

"The Stewarts' affair? I thought it was delightful," Martha said, all smiles. "Of course, I went with my brother and Samuel is at his worst with me. And I had to avoid you and that made it a trifle awkward. But it was a good party for all that!"

"I'm glad," Ann said, sipping her tea. "What about Samuel?"

Martha's face shadowed. "I suppose he had a good time. He complained continually about having to dance with me. And he kept wandering off!"

"Did he?"

Martha said, "You must know what he is like since you were engaged to him. Not that he would show anything but his best side to you. But with his sister he behaves differently. He left me alone all during the fireworks and I was terrified."

"He wandered off during the fireworks?" Ann echoed her, wanting to be sure on this point since it was so important to her.

"Yes. Even before they started. I thought I might faint. Then I met another young man who was most kind to me."

Ann gave her a knowing look. "You made it sound as if a romance might have budded that night."

Delighted, Martha said, "I think it may have. I have been secretly seeing him since."

"Secretly?"

"Yes. He wants our courting to be our own affair until we are able to reveal our engagement."

"Then you can't tell me his name?"

"Not anything about him. But you will know soon enough. I'm certain he wishes to marry me. The engagement will soon be announced."

"I wish you luck," Ann said. "I hope he is a suitable young man. But I can't imagine my husband's parents having anyone at the party who wouldn't be socially desirable."

"Exactly," the petite girl said. "I know you will approve of him. And I'm so glad we are friends once again. I've had no one my own age to talk with."

"We aren't all that long a distance apart," Ann said.

"Not really," Martha agreed. "You are at one end of Mercy Cemetery and this street is on the other end of it. And have you heard about the recent grave robbings?"

"Yes."

"It gets worse," the other girl said. "The city is alive with rumors. And Samuel says that the high sheriff knows certain ruffians dealing in bodies and expects to raid their place of residence soon."

Ann stood up. "I must be getting home. Doesn't living so near the cemetery make you nervous?"

"I'm not afraid of it at all," Martha exclaimed. "We have lived here so long I have become used to it. But I don't like the things that have been happening there."

"Nor do I," Ann said, starting out of the summer house.

"How is your husband?" Martha wanted to know.

"As usual," she said.

"Shall I tell Samuel that we are friends again? He blamed me for starting our quarrel."

Ann gave her a small smile. "Do as you like. And he was wrong to blame you. It was my fault entirely."

"I'll tell him you were here and that you said that," Martha said happily. "And you will keep mum on the subject of my romance."

"Depend on it," Ann said.

So the visit ended. As she rode back to Mercy House in the jolting carriage, Ann went over it all in her mind. She had established friendship with the petite Martha again and almost at once had learned that Samuel Todd could have been the villain who'd attacked her in the guise of the phantom. He had wandered away from his sister at that particular time. Yet the mere fact he'd wandered away didn't prove him guilty, it merely darkened the suspicions she had about him.

When she reached the forbidding Mercy House the early afternoon sun had faded and the day had become cloudy and bleak. She left the carriage and entered the grim red brick house with its tangled ivy on the walls and its gloomy view of the cemetery.

Mrs. McQuoid was there to greet her with, "The master has gone out."

This surprised Ann. Ian usually was kept busy with calls until near time for the evening meal, and he almost never left the house between his calls and dinner time.

She said, "Was there some sort of emergency?"

"There must have been," the housekeeper said. "All I

know is that he dismissed the few patients he had not seen and went off with the gentleman who had arrived insisting on talking with him at once."

"Do you know who the gentleman was?"

"No, ma'am," Mrs. McQuoid said. "He was a stern sort and seemed in a state. Nothing would do but he talk with the master between patients. So I announced him."

"He must have been the relative of some patient taken with an emergency," she surmised. "Probably the doctor will return soon."

"I hope so," the cook lamented. "I have a fine dinner of veal cutlets, green goose, carrots and damson pie."

"I'm sure he'll be back," she assured the worried woman. But, at the same time, she found herself concerned. What could the urgent call have been about? Why hadn't Ian left some sort of message as to where he had gone and when he would return. She hoped it had nothing to do with Dr. Marsh and his questionable affairs.

She went up and freshened herself for dinner. When she came back downstairs she hoped that her husband would have returned, but he was nowhere in sight. Either the patient he'd been called out to visit was seriously ill and required his constant attention, or something was wrong.

She carefully concealed her fears from Mrs. McQuoid who was complaining that her dinner would be ruined. And in the end she sat down to dinner alone, complimenting the upset cook on the excellent fare. Yet she was so upset herself she had to force herself to eat the excellent food.

When dinner ended she went to the window and stared out at the driveway. What had happened to Ian? Her eyes wandered to the cemetery in the distance. Her thoughts turned to the grave robbers. She hoped this was not the beginning of something new in that line!

And then a carriage showed itself on the street and came into the driveway. Her heart leaped with relief but was almost immediately cast down again when she saw that it was not Ian who got out of the carriage. It was a finely-dressed Dr. Harry Turner. It had been some time since the young doctor had called on them, and she was troubled that he should arrive when Ian was absent.

The doorbell rang and Mrs. McQuoid showed the good-looking and brash young doctor in. With a merry smile he came to her and kissed her on the cheek. "You look lovelier each time we meet, Ann. Where is your second-rate spouse?"

"Ian is out somewhere," she said faintly.

"Out?" the young doctor echoed. "Thunderation! He invited me over for the evening and I turned my back on a patient to be here on time!"

"I don't know what can have happened," she confessed. "He didn't finish his office calls. Someone came for him and he left quickly."

Dr. Harry Turner looked wise. "I can imagine. Some old patient of his has the gout, or fits or perhaps a stroke and he is fettered at their side."

"You know the problems of doctoring well," she said.

"He'll be back," the jolly young man predicted. "And in the meantime, I shall make ardent love to you!"

She blushed. "Do come into the parlor," she said. "It is coolish tonight and Mrs. McQuoid has started a fire in the fireplace."

Following her into the parlor, Dr. Harry Turner asked, "And where is the girl, Nancy? The pretty maid who showed me in last time."

She gave him an anxious look. "Haven't you heard? She is missing."

"Missing?"

"For some weeks now," Ann said. "It is dreadful. We have no idea what happened to her."

"Did she leave without notice?"

"Without even taking her few belongings," Ann said. "We fear that some harm may have befallen her."

"That is bad news," the young doctor said. "But she had a pretty face and figure. I'll venture some lad has made off with her."

"She was meeting someone."

"Oh?" He produced his long-stemmed pipe. "Do you mind if I smoke?"

"No."

"Does anyone know the chap she was meeting?"

"She somehow kept his name a secret. She went out each night for a rendezvous with him in the cemetery."

"In the cemetery?" the young doctor said in wonder. "Well, I suppose it had the virtue of being quiet."

"A grave digger whom I have met saw her. And he saw someone with her. But he wasn't close enough to them to identify the man."

Harry Turner had lit his pipe and now he puffed on it contentedly. "I wouldn't worry too much then. Sounds like the two ran off. We've lost a good many female servants in the same fashion."

"I try to tell myself that it is all right," she said.

The young doctor smiled at her. "You were a treat to the eye at the dance your in-laws gave."

"Thank you."

"But you left early. I inquired for you and you had gone."

She didn't want to reveal all that had happened, so she said, "I wasn't feeling well. Ian took me home."

"You looked ravishing," he said. "Had you been in my

company you would not have tired of the party so easily. I know Ian. He can be tiresome."

"You think so?"

"I know it," the young doctor continued. "At school he was disgustingly assiduous in his studies and far too clever. Made the ordinary clods like myself look as if we weren't trying. And, I assure you, we were. But such virtuous men can be dreadfully dull!"

Ann felt she must defend her husband, so she said, "I have never found him dull."

"Ah!" the young doctor said, "but that is because you have no means of comparison."

"That is not true," she objected. "I was courted by a line of young men! Samuel Todd among them!"

Dr. Harry Turner grimaced and groaned. "Samuel Todd is a toad!" he declared with disgust. "Anyone would seem a fine gentleman compared to that lawyer!"

"Really?"

"It is true!" the young man said, coming uncomfortably close to her and his eyes looking deep into hers. "Now if you lived with me you would see life differently. I would make it sparkle for you. Try to be worthy of your beauty!"

"You are too skilled a lover for my poor self," she said, with a mock show of humbleness. "Pray do not try to woo me. I might succumb to your blandishments and it is my wish to be true to my husband, however dull he may be."

The young doctor regarded her sadly. "Now that is truly tragic. I hope that one day you may change your mind. Should you consider leaving Ian, there is another doctor waiting to be your most obedient servant."

"Thank you," she said with cool politeness. "I value your friendship, though I must spurn your love."

Harry Turner warned her, "Do not count too much on your Ian. He may break your heart one day."

"Then I must risk that."

"You do not know the shadow you are living in," he said.

She gave him a frightened glance. "What do you mean by that?"

The young doctor shrugged. "Where is your precious Ian at this moment?"

"I don't know."

"That is part of what I mean."

"You are being unfair. He meant to be here. Otherwise he would not have invited you."

Harry Turner smiled grimly. "I suspect that something else came up which seemed more important to him."

"Such as?"

"Perhaps Dr. Marsh called him."

Her heart skipped a beat. She said, "I'm almost certain he has avoided seeing Dr. Marsh lately."

"Mad Marsh!"

"Whatever you wish to call him."

The young doctor took a few steps away and then turned to her again. "When I tell you that I am in love with you I am most serious. So I would not willingly worry you if I could avoid it. Yet I feel there are things about Ian which you must know."

"Tell me."

"For one thing, he has always been much under the influence of our ugly friend, Dr. Marsh. This began when Marsh was his instructor at university."

"I know that."

Harry Turner said, "What you may not know is that Marsh is fanatical in his pursuit of surgery. He has always

147

ranted at not having enough bodies for dissection."

"I'm familiar with that as well," she said.

"And as his disciple, Ian has agreed with him."

"I'm sure they are both right. More human bodies are needed for dissection."

The young doctor nodded. "If they are come by in the right way. Lately, I have been told, Marsh has had more bodies than he can use."

"Who told you that?"

"Never mind," the young doctor said shortly. "Suffice that I know this. I have heard that he has passed bodies on to others. That almost anyone in Edinburgh can have all the bodies they want if they are willing to pay for them!"

"I'm sure they are vicious rumors," she protested. "And even if they are not, how can you connect Ian with them?"

He said, "I don't think I need answer that for you. You know that Ian picked this house. And you know that there have been a series of grave robberies in Mercy Cemetery next door to you!"

"I won't—" she began angrily, but she didn't finish. The doorbell rang and interrupted their conversation.

She heard voices as Mrs. McQuoid opened the door and she immediately recognized the low, urgent tone of Dr. Jock Gregory. At once it hit her that something was wrong with Ian and the old doctor friend of the family had come to inform her about it. She rushed to the doorway leading to the hall and Dr. Gregory, his hat in hand, met her there.

"Dr. Gregory!" she exclaimed. "What brings you here?"

"Grim news," the doctor said. And he glanced at Dr. Harry Turner as he asked, "Shall I continue in the presence of Dr. Turner?"

Harry Turner came to join them and said, "Anything

you have to say is also important to me. I consider myself Ian's best friend."

The older doctor's face was solemn. "He will need friends. The body of your maid, Nancy, has been found, Ann. Found in a casket of whiskey. Ian is being questioned about her murder."

Eight

The older doctor's words had a shattering effect upon Ann. She might well have collapsed at that very moment had not young Dr. Harry Turner moved forward solicitously to place a supporting arm around her. There was no question that she needed this kindly gesture. She was trembling and she'd gone completely pale.

It was Harry Turner who spoke first, addressing himself to the older doctor, "Just how serious do you think all this is for Ian?"

"I do not like the appearance of it," Dr. Jock Gregory said.

"Tell me all," Ann said faintly.

Harry Turner told her, "You had best sit down." And he guided her to a nearby divan where she sat. He took a place alongside her.

Dr. Jock Gregory moved across the room to stand before them. His lined face was gloomy as he said, "You want the whole story as I know it?"

"Please," she begged him still feeling that she might black out at any moment.

The older doctor frowned. "I suppose you might say it began with the disappearance of your maid, Nancy."

"How?" Harry Turner wanted to know. "I mean, how does what happened to Nancy link with Ian?"

Dr. Jock Gregory said, "I think I can satisfy you on that point. The high sheriff has been closely watching a group of ruffians in the slums of the city."

Harry Turner nodded. "I have heard of that."

Dr. Jock Gregory's pleasant face was gaunt. He said, "This afternoon a party raided a dwelling in the heart of the slums. The place was rented by a Joe Scott and his wife, Sadie."

"Go on," Ann implored, though she dreaded what he might have to tell her.

The older doctor twisted his three-cornered hat nervously in his hands. "The authorities were looking for two men, this Joe Scott and a henchman by the name of Hard Hannigan. These two are known grave robbers and have been under surveillance for a good while. But someone must have warned them and they slipped away just before the raid on the dwelling."

"Where does Ian fit into this?" his friend Harry Turner asked.

"Patience, please!" the older doctor said. "I shall get to that part in a moment. Though the roughnecks mentioned earlier had fled, the raiding party took into custody Sadie Scott, the wife of Joe Scott."

"So they did catch one of them?" Harry Turner said.

"Perhaps the most innocent of the lot, though she has had criminal charges of another nature brought against her!" Dr. Jock Gregory said.

Harry Turner said, "Will you please go on, sir?" This time he was the epitome of patience in his appeal.

"Just so!" the older doctor said. "The raiding party made a thorough search of the dwelling, despite a continued struggle put up by the woman Scott. And as they expected, they came upon several caskets filled with whiskey to preserve the bodies in them. One of these bodies was that of a nude Nancy."

"How awful!" Ann gasped.

"No one can but agree with you, dear lady," Dr. Jock Gregory said. "They then began to question the harridan of a woman, Sadie Scott. For a while she was sullen and would say nothing. Then she began to talk grudgingly. She informed them that the girl, Nancy, had been lured to their house and given drink until she passed out."

Ann asked, "Did they say who brought her there? She had been meeting someone in the cemetery?"

"To the best of my knowledge, she didn't divulge that," the older doctor said. "But she did say that as soon as Nancy was unconscious from drink the man called Hard Hannigan placed a bed cushion over her face and suffocated her with it!"

"Murder!" Dr. Harry Turner said.

"Without a doubt," his older colleague agreed. "The woman then described how a stolen casket from which the body had been removed and sold was prepared to house the body of the unhappy Nancy. It was carefully sealed so it would not leak and then the girl's body placed in it. After this the casket was filled with whiskey sufficient to cover the girl's body and preserve it. Then the lid was placed on the casket and it was set apart for delivery."

"To whom?" Ann asked tensely.

Dr. Jock Gregory showed concern. "That is the bad part. Mrs. Scott swears that a young doctor who had frequently bought stolen bodies from her husband and the other character before, came that night and bargained with them for the delivery of the body of Nancy. It was finally settled that the doctor should give the two the cost of the whiskey plus ten pounds profit!"

"What rogues!" Dr. Harry Turner cried.

"They can't believe such a story!" Ann protested, her fear for her husband overcoming everything else. "Ian would not want Nancy's body for dissection. She was like one of the family."

Dr. Gregory nodded. "I understand that. They sent someone here to fetch Ian and he went to the court with them."

"True," she said. "But he would only wish to clear his name."

The older doctor said, "I'm sure he went there for that and to try and help deal with the criminals involved. When he found himself charged as an accomplice in the crime, he sent for his father at the bank."

"The wise course," Harry Turner agreed from the place where he sat beside her.

"In turn, his father sent for me to accompany him," Dr. Jock Gregory said. "In view of the seriousness of the situation, I did not hesitate to act."

"Was he able to get the woman to change her story?" Ann asked.

"To a degree," the older doctor said.

Ann pointed out, "She would have to have proof to make her evil story plausible. What proof did she have?"

"Only her word," Dr. Jock Gregory said.

"Her word against Ian's!" Dr. Harry Turner said with disgust. "I shouldn't think there would be any difficulty making a choice."

Dr. Gregory sighed. "You may not think so, but while I was at the court it seemed a matter of touch and go. The woman insisted it was Ian who had been a go-between a number of times. And since everyone recognized that only doctors or the university would be in the market for these stolen and murdered bodies, her story took on an air of truth."

Harry Turner pointed out, "While doctors would be the

buyers of the bodies, I can't imagine any of them being so reckless as to show themselves to the grave robbers. They would surely send a servant. And it would be the servant whom this woman had seen."

"Exactly what I stated in defense of Ian," the older doctor said. "And I may say it was the first argument to carry any weight. I then asked the woman if she could describe this supposed young doctor."

"And?" Ann broke in tensely.

"Sadie Scott could neither describe the doctor nor tell anything about the sound of his voice. We had Ian speak along with several others from the adjoining room and she could not identify Ian's voice. Then, when he was brought into the room to confront her, the woman was not able to recognize him."

Ann said, "Then that must have vindicated Ian?"

"I'm almost positive there will be no charges placed against him at this point," the older doctor agreed. "I did not leave the courthouse until I was reasonably certain of that. But Ian is still there, and the questioning of the woman goes on."

Harry Turner jumped to his feet. "A dastardly affair! I knew Ian would come to some such harm if he persisted in associating himself with Dr. Marsh."

"Dr. Clinton Marsh has also been called to the court for questioning," Jock Gregory said. "His name was also mentioned by the Scott woman."

"No doubt it was some young lackey of his posing as a doctor who worked out the perfidious deal," Harry Turner said. "Marsh is the evil star influencing everyone else and urging them to crime."

"I only partly agree," Dr. Jock Gregory said calmly. "I know Marsh is advanced in his opinions about human dissection. But I have never thought of him as evil by nature."

"He is so ugly!" Ann said with a shudder.

The older doctor nodded. "That goes against him. But I must express my doubts that he is guilty of all the crimes with which rumor links him."

"I am a member of the medical profession, sir, and so is my father," Harry Turner said angrily. "And we are ashamed that we practice in this city. Edinburgh has gained a wicked reputation throughout the country as being the center of organized body stealing. And I say the one responsible for this is Dr. Clinton Marsh!"

"You are entitled to your views," the older doctor said.

"I'm concerned only about Ian at the moment," was Ann's contribution to the conversation.

"And quite right," Harry Turner said. "Since it is evident that Ian will not be here to share a pleasant evening, I think I shall be on my way. It is possible I may be of some help to him elsewhere."

Dr. Jock Gregory said, "You might stop by the courthouse. Every voice in his favor will be helpful. And I will remain here with Ann until we hear some word. So she will not be alone."

Ann got to her feet. "Please do go see Ian, Harry," she begged the young doctor. "You can be of real help to him at this dreadful moment."

"Count on me, Ann," Harry said, bowing to her. "And remember all that I said."

She saw him on his way and then she and Jock Gregory stood facing each other in the grim parlor of Mercy House. She said, "This house has been bad luck for us. I felt it from the moment I saw it!"

"It is not all that pleasant," the elderly doctor agreed.

Ann eyed him anxiously. "What do you really think?"

"I think it will be all right," he replied slowly.

"I'm not saying that Ian hasn't ventured close to the center of this evil, since I think he has."

"I know."

"But not Nancy!" she declared in a tense voice. "He would not see her murdered and haggle to buy her body."

"I agree."

"Yet he may have been one of them, without knowing Nancy was a victim. Marsh might have kept it from him!"

"If Marsh is to blame."

She gave the elderly doctor a frightened look. "You are a friend of all the family so I can speak plainly. There were bodies in this house. In the cellar! My husband claimed they were here waiting to be transferred to the university. Marsh came here and behaved in an odd manner. And I saw a partly-dissected body on the operating table in the cellar which Ian insisted was on loan from the university."

"It well could have been. And those other bodies might have been quite legitimate shipments of criminals' bodies destined for the university."

"Then why the secrecy?" she demanded. "Why the deliveries at such after-midnight hours? And why were they sent here first rather than the university?"

He spread his hands in a gesture of despair. "I can't say! These are the things which are bound to be worrisome. I can only suggest the secrecy was to avoid observation of the bodies being handled. Rumors and suspicions have been at a peak in Edinburgh these last few months. Few people any longer worry about the state of the government or the threat from France! All the talk in this city has been about grave robbers!"

"It is true," she agreed.

"The danger is that Marsh is a fanatic and most fanatics

156

finally go too far. If he has led Ian along in this madness it may have tragic consequences."

She sat down, lost in thought. "Someone lured that girl to the murder den. But who?"

"That did not come out."

She looked up into the older man's face. "But it is the most important point! The link! Nancy was so entranced by some evil gentleman that she must have allowed him to take her to her death. If we knew who that man was we might have all the answers. One thing I do know is that she was meeting him in the nearby cemetery."

"Perhaps the Scott woman can be made to reveal his name."

"If she knows it and she may not," was her worry. "But at least some attempt should be made to find out. Nancy went to meet him almost nightly."

Dr. Jock Gregory said, "I would hope that Ian might make some mention of this."

"He will still be at the courthouse," she said.

"I assume so. His father and a lawyer are with him."

"Will they keep him there?"

"I can't quite believe that," the old doctor said. "Though they might if the Scott woman persists in her story that he bought Nancy's body."

A frightening thought crossed her mind. She gave the old doctor a troubled look. "Do you think the authorities may come here and search this house?"

"It's a possibility. But there can be nothing here to find now. You said the bodies had been transferred."

Fear was in her face and in her voice as she quavered, "That doesn't mean there could not be other bodies. Ones that were sent here afterwards without my knowing."

Dr. Jock Gregory wrinkled his brow and he showed that he understood the dangerous possibility. He said, "Perhaps we ought to make a search of the cellars ourselves?"

She nodded. "Yes. I think so."

They had a worried Mrs. McQuoid fetch candles and Ann took the opportunity of asking the upset cook, "Have you been in the doctor's surgery lately?"

"No, ma'am! I never venture in there!" the cook exclaimed. And then she asked, "Is it true that they have found poor Nancy?"

"They have found her dead body," she told the older woman. "I'm sorry." And as Mrs. McQuoid vanished in tears, Ann solemnly handed one of the candles to the doctor and then lit her own and his.

She stood with him in the shadowed hallway, their faces grim and pale in the glow of the candles. Her old friend said, "You'd better lead the way since you are more familiar with the cellar than I."

Ann opened the door and they cautiously descended the narrow stairs into the dank depths. She waited for the doctor to catch up with her and indicated to him the area where the caskets had previously been stored.

"The caskets were at that end of the cellar," she said.

"Let us look there," he said.

They crossed the hard, uneven earthen floor of the cellar but found nothing. Yet the eerie atmosphere of the place chilled her to the bone. She knew it had been a place of horror and could be again.

Candle held high, she whispered, "No sign of anything."

"So it would seem."

"I hate the cellar more than anything else," she said. "You know this house has seen murder and suicide."

The old doctor's face was grim in the glow of the candle

which he carried. "That is the past. It need have nothing to do with you and Ian."

"But it has!" she insisted. "The curse is on anyone who lives here! That is the legend, and I believe in it!"

As if to underline her statement there was a squeak and a scurry. Ann screamed and leapt back as a rat raced across the top of her foot and was lost in the darkness.

Dr. Gregory took her by the arm. "Let us get out of here. This is doing you no good."

"No," she protested. "One thing more, first."

"What?"

"The room where Ian does his surgery . . ." she said. "We must look in there."

"I suppose so," he said reluctantly.

"It is across this way," she said.

They made their way to the door of the surgery, and once again she felt that same familiar hesitation about opening the door. On earlier occasions she had been shocked by what she had seen inside. There was no reason to suppose this visit might be any different. Because of the presence of the doctor at her side, she fought back her lingering fears and forced herself to throw the door open.

She ventured into the dark room and the first thing they saw was a skull grinning at them from its place on the operating table. The grisly, gray-white skull with its black, hollow eye-sockets had almost an appearance of living malevolence, as if it were scoffing at them.

Her friend must have felt her tremble and read her thoughts. He said, "Skulls are weird! They sometimes give you the feeling they are mocking you!"

In awe she glanced at him. "That is exactly how I felt. How did you know?"

He said, "I drew on my memories as a medical student.

I'm not bothered by the sight of a skull anymore."

"What would Ian be doing with it?"

"Most doctors have one for reference. He may have been checking it to decide where a patient had a head injury."

"At least there's no body with it," she murmured.

"No," he said, glancing around. "It is a well-kept room. Neat. You say Ian spends a good deal of time down here?"

"Yes."

"It would be helpful."

She held her candle high again so that its small flame gave light to a large area. "I see no sign of any casket here."

"So your worries were for nothing," the doctor said.

"Yes," she sighed with relief.

"Then let us go back upstairs," he said. "I fear this gloomy atmosphere down here is bad for you."

"Very well," she agreed.

He stood by the open doorway and said, "I'll allow you to show me the way again."

But she was diverted by something else. "One moment," she said. There was a closet. Ian used it for odds and ends, including keeping the dirty sheets from his operating table in there. She now opened the door. There was a smock hanging from a nail at the rear. On the floor there were several sheets thrown in a heap. And something else! A cotton bag tied at the top.

"Are you ready?" the doctor asked.

"Wait, I'll be there," she promised. At the same time she bent down and undid the cord tying the cotton bag. Then she opened the bag and saw that it contained a woman's discarded clothing! Girl's clothes to be exact! The very clothes which Nancy had been wearing that fatal night when she'd vanished! Ann had seen them often enough to recognize them as Nancy's best.

"Anything wrong?" the doctor called from the door.

"No," she replied, trying to eliminate the shock and horror from her voice. For now she was alone in this! She dare not tell even the friendly doctor of her discovery. It was too damaging!

"I'm waiting."

"Yes," she said, closing the top of the bag quickly and in a numbed state of terror bringing it along in her free hand.

The doctor saw it. "You found something?"

She grimaced. "A poor find! Dirty clothes!" The answer was true yet did not tell all the truth. How had Nancy's clothes reached Ian's room if he hadn't been mixed up in her death?

"We must get upstairs," Dr. Gregory said, staring at her. "You look as if you could collapse at any moment."

"I'll be all right," she insisted. She knew that she must be.

"It really was a mistake coming down here," he said as they crossed the cellar in the direction of the stairs.

"I wouldn't say that," Ann replied tautly, clutching the bag with the murdered girl's clothing in her hand.

"I came to Edinburgh as a youth to study medicine, so I'm not sure I was here when the murder was committed in this house," he said. "But I heard about it. Everyone who has ever lived in the city has heard the story."

"I'm sure they must have," she agreed, her thoughts many miles distant as they started up the stairs.

They reached the ground level of the old house and she quickly opened the door of a hall closet and put the bag with Nancy's clothing in it. But merely disposing of the grim clue didn't ease her shock.

They reached the parlor again and she was about to offer the doctor a cup of tea when there were sounds of the front door opening and voices. A moment later Ian, accompanied by his father, appeared in the doorway of the parlor.

"Ann, my darling!" Ian exclaimed, looking wan and miserable. He came and embraced her at once.

She looked up at him and said, "I was afraid they might keep you."

Ian's father spoke up. "There were no solid grounds for detention. The Scott woman is a known liar and she changed her story four or five times until everyone was disgusted."

Dr. Jock Gregory gave Ian a friendly glance. "You have no idea how glad I am to see you. I didn't know what would happen. It looked bad."

Ian nodded. "I know. I can't imagine what those villains have against me to make up such a story."

Ian's father's distinguished face was grim. "I think the Scott woman seized on your name since she knew you were a doctor and Nancy was in your employ. It was the first thing she thought of without considering the dire consequences to you."

"A woman like that isn't apt to think of anyone," Ian said bitterly. "What truly disgusts me is that it has come to this! That innocents like poor Nancy should be murdered to provide bodies for sale. And that my profession should be involved!"

"Much involved," his father said bleakly. "I did not much like the account Dr. Marsh gave of himself in the questioning. He strikes me as a most unreliable person."

"You are wrong in that!" Ian defended him.

"I trust that I am," the elder Stewart said. "And even though we managed to get you free tonight, do not think you are finished with the matter."

Ian looked shattered. "You think?"

"I think our name will suffer through this," his father said with brutal frankness. "The Stewarts have been looked up to in Edinburgh. I fear you have brought us to the shadow of scandal."

"It may not be all that bad," Dr. Jock Gregory suggested.

Ian's father gave his old friend a troubled glance. "You were not there until the end. You do not know the mood then. I am certain there will be serious scandal and that Ian's practice may be ruined. If that woman goes back to her original story he might even see the inside of a jail. And the Lord forbid, the gallows!"

"No!" Ann protested, her eyes filling with tears.

"I'm sorry, my dear girl," Ian's father said, going to her and taking her hands in his. "I went rather far in my predictions. You mustn't think of what I've said. Though I do feel you should know this is not a mere game. Ian's reputation and perhaps his life is at stake."

Ian exclaimed, "It would seem that my fate is in the hands of those foul rogues. If only they can find Hannigan and Scott. They might sing a different song from the wife!"

"That would be helpful," his father agreed. "In the meantime, there is nothing to be done until morning. You will come to my office. My lawyer will be there waiting."

Ian showed bewilderment. "I can't! I have my hospital rounds."

His father was stern and unbending. "Someone else will have to do them."

Ian gazed at him in uneasy confusion. "You mean that, sir?"

"I do," his father said. "The family name is at stake. You must have a common wish with me to spare your mother and your brothers and sisters the worst of this scandal."

Ian said bitterly, "Sir, there have been scandals at Stormhaven before if I have heard rightly. The murder of a brother by a sister, and the begetting of an illegitimate Stewart by a highwayman!"

"None of that concerns you, young man," his father shot back. "This has all to do with you. And I warn you that sullenness and resistance are not appropriate at this moment!"

Ann placed a restraining hand on her young husband's arm and said, "Your father is right."

"Of course he is!" Dr. Jock Gregory spoke up. And he told Ian, "I will look after your rounds at the hospital for you. And I will take care of your calls and the patients who come here in the afternoon."

Ian stared at him as if he could not believe what was happening. He said, "I thank you, sir. But will it not seem that I am truly guilty if I do not appear for my regular duties?"

"I don't see why it should," the older doctor said. "It is bound to be known you have been accused in this affair and will need time to consult a lawyer."

Ian's father said, "He is right. You will do well to listen to him, son."

"Very well, then," Ian said quietly, as if he were completely broken.

Ann found it almost unbearable. She kept thinking of her find in the closet and what the others would say if they knew.

Ian's father turned to Dr. Jock Gregory and said, "I have my carriage outside. I can drop you off on my way to Stormhaven."

"Thank you, that would be excellent," the old doctor said. And he went to Ann and told her, "You must bear

164

up, my dear, for your husband's sake."

"I know," she murmured.

He patted her on the arm. "I have no doubts about your courage." Then he turned to Ian. "I shall be at the hospital early to cover for you, Ian. And I'll come here in the afternoon. Leave a list of any calls you wish made."

"Thank you, doctor," Ian said humbly.

Ian's father kissed Ann when she saw the two older men to the door. He gave her a warm hug and said, "Don't let this shatter you. I'm sure with good legal advice we can extricate Ian from this grim business."

She stood with Ian in the doorway until the two men were in the carriage and had vanished in the foggy night. Then they closed the door and Ian placed an arm around her and sighed.

"I'm confused," he said. "In a daze!"

"How could you help not be?"

"I had no idea what they wanted with me," he continued as they stood in the nearly dark hall. "But they would not take a refusal. When I arrived at the scene they showed me Nancy. It was horrible!"

"Don't go over it!"

"I can't help it," Ian said unhappily. "And Father seems to think it will get worse."

"He's probably right."

"This mad, gin-sodden woman insists on accusing me!" Ian said unhappily.

"So I've heard."

"I can't think why!"

"You are a doctor and Nancy did work here."

"But I wouldn't do a thing like that! Not for a hundred bodies!" her husband declared.

She watched him and listened to his despairing words

and wondered if this were an acting performance. Was he playing this scene purely for her benefit, or did he truly feel shattered by the woman's accusations and innocent of all wrongdoing? She would be ready to believe him were it not for that silent witness against him—the bundle of Nancy's clothes in the closet!

She said, "You have been dissecting human bodies."

"That is my right."

"And you have helped Dr. Marsh in securing bodies for the university."

"That is also my right," he declared.

"Your rights do end at some given point, though. You must admit that."

He stared at her with puzzled eyes. "What are you trying to say?"

"That you have been playing with fire and that you shouldn't be so shocked if your fingers get burned!"

Ian's eyebrows raised. "I must say, that's a fine, sympathetic attitude for a wife to take!"

"I have no choice," she said. "I would to Heaven that I knew you to be innocent of any misdeeds in the past or present! The terrible thing is that I cannot be!"

Ian grasped her roughly by the arms. "Are you accusing me like that gin-soaked slut?"

Tears sprang into her eyes, not entirely from the hurt of his fierce grip on her arms, but from her inner desolation as well. She said, "Abuse will not change my mind!"

Looking startled, he let her go. "Why are you turning against me?" he wanted to know.

"Why have you consorted with Marsh and behaved like a madman?"

"That is my affair!"

"And so now you find yourself charged with a murder

and suddenly it becomes the affair of us all!" she berated him.

"You're echoing my father's words!"

"They are true!"

"All of you are turning on me!"

"Because you won't listen!" she declared. "You have never given heed to any of my warnings!"

"If I need a sermon I can go to the kirk!" he sneered.

"You might do well to do just that!" was her reply. "Why have you not been frank with me?"

"I have been. In all that is important."

"And what between a man and wife is not important?" she wanted to know.

"Nothing of consequence."

"So you say!" She went to the closet and opened the door. Then she brought out the cotton bag with Nancy's clothes and dropped it in front of him. "What about that?"

Seemingly bewildered, he stared down at the bag and asked, "What is it?"

Her eyes met his. "Nancy's clothes!"

"Nancy's clothes?"

"The ones she wore on that last night of her life!"

His mouth gaped. If he were acting he was doing a fine job of it. "How did they get here?"

"I found them."

"Where?"

"In your surgery. Hidden in the closet under some dirty sheets!"

Anger flared in his eyes. "You have instructions not to enter the surgery!"

"And there seems to be good reason for that!" she said with scathing sarcasm. "What do you have to say?"

Ian stared down at the bag of clothing. "If they are her

clothes I don't know how they got here. I have never seen them before!"

"They were in your closet!"

"I can't help that!"

"You won't make an attempt to explain?"

"I can't," he said. And then his face took on a wary expression as he asked in quite another tone of voice, "Have you told anyone else about these?"

"No. But I will have to. You realize that!"

"Why?"

"I will protect you against any crime short of murder," she said. "But I can't live with this and not share what I know with someone else. I kept it from Dr. Gregory tonight, but tomorrow I shall tell your father."

Ian took another step towards her. "No! You mustn't!"

"I'm sorry!"

There was a desperation in him now, something which she felt she had never seen in him before. He said, "I'm in enough trouble in that direction. You know what strong feelings he has about family. If you tell him all will be lost!"

"You can give me no reason for the clothes being here? I cannot protect a murderer!" She was surprised at the calmness with which she uttered these words.

"Then you think I may be Nancy's murderer?" he asked in a strained voice.

"Until you prove to me otherwise," she said. "It is up to you!"

His answer was to stare at her in utter dismay for a moment. Then he turned and rushed to the door and threw it open as he ran out into the foggy night. She hurried across to the door, but by the time she looked out he was only a thin, distant figure in the fog and darkness heading in the direction of the ancient cemetery. She could not help ask

168

herself whether or not he was returning to the scene of the crime.

Despair trickled through her as she shut the door on the cool, foggy night. Then it surged through her in a torrent. She had handled the situation badly; she was blaming herself for that almost at once. And yet, what else could she have done? Ian had made no effort to explain or defend himself. He seemed to think she should be eternally trusting in spite of his suspicious actions and all the evidence which was piling up against him.

She slid the bolt in the front door and extinguished the single candle which offered light in the lower hall. Then she wearily began to make her way upstairs. She and Mrs. McQuoid were alone in the grim old house on this night of shock and terror. In her utter despair she had not even bothered to move the cotton bag with Nancy's clothes in it from the place on the rug where she had shown it to her husband.

She was at the first landing when she realized this. And she knew she could not leave the damaging evidence there for Mrs. McQuoid to find. She could not let anyone know about the clothes until she discussed them with Ian's father. So now she turned and began descending the stairs again. When she reached the dark lower hall she groped about for the bag and could not find it.

Her heart began to beat wildly, and she found the candle in its holder and struck a match to it with trembling fingers. She tried to remember. Had Ian seized the bag and taken it with him when he fled? She had been very tense at that moment and so she could not be sure. But it seemed to her that he hadn't! That he had simply turned and fled! Candle in hand, she searched the hall. It was no use!

The all-important bag of clothes had vanished! Vanished as if whisked away by a ghostly hand!

Ann felt ill and unable to cope with a series of frightening events which were taking place far too rapidly. She stood there in the midnight stillness of the dark hall, bathed in the faint glow of the candle's flame! What did it mean?

Had Mrs. McQuoid risen from her sound sleep to take the bag? Not likely! Had a ghostly hand removed the bag? She did not want to believe in ghosts, especially not at this terrifying moment! Had Ian taken the clothes with him to destroy the evidence against him? It was the most likely explanation and the one she finally accepted—made herself accept!

She started up the stairs again. The house was deathly quiet. But just as she neared the landing the chimes in the big clock below solemnly struck the midnight hour! As the last of the chimes struck she had the eerie feeling that something frightening was about to happen! She had paused for the chimes and now she made herself move on towards the landing! Then she saw it!

Nine

A terrible scream crossed her quivering lips as she gazed up at the thing in horror! On the landing above her the decapitated head of a man seemed to be floating in the air! She was instantly conscious of every grisly detail of it—the opened, staring eyes, the black hair wildly askew, the lips drawn back from huge, yellow teeth as if in a final snarl at life! It was the most fearful and ugly thing she had ever seen in her life, this sallow face!

And then she saw that the head wasn't really floating on its own, but it was held by boney hands. Issuing from the shadows was the figure of the headless man proffering her this horrific head as if serving something on a platter! She screamed over and over again, frozen there on the top step, her hand clinging to the railing!

Suddenly the head was thrown at her and with a final scream as she saw the gruesome object rolling through the air at her, she lost her grip on the railing and tumbled backward. Down the long flight of stairs she fell, finally resting in a crumpled heap at the bottom. But she was no longer aware of what was happening, since she had mercifully blacked out.

The next thing of which she was conscious were the wails of Mrs. McQuoid over her. The cook was in what might be called a dreadful state.

"Ma'am, speak to me! Please say something, ma'am! Could it be she's dead!" the woman was frantically wailing both to Ann and to herself.

Ann stirred and opened her eyes. Then fear transformed her pretty face. "The head!" she cried.

"You're not dead then!" Mrs. McQuoid said with delight.

Ann had raised herself up on an elbow. She looked around her in terror, her eyes darting from the carpet to the floor beyond. "The head! I don't see the head!"

Mrs. McQuoid was so happy that she had found her alive that she seemed not to be listening to anything. The cook said, "It is a blessing you fell onto the carpeted area. You might otherwise have been killed! Indeed, you would have been!"

She gave the old woman a frightened look. "Did you see the ghost? And the head? He was carrying his head!"

Mrs. McQuoid showed distress. "The ghost, ma'am?"

With weary impatience, she said, "Don't tell me you saw none of it?"

"I don't know what you mean, ma'am," the old woman said. "I heard your screams as you fell! When I came out you were here on the floor! I was sure you'd fallen to your death!"

"And that was all you saw?"

"That was all."

Ann sighed and gazed up at the dark landing above. She knew it would be useless to pursue the reason for her terror. Once again she alone had experienced an encounter with the phantom who plagued the old house. And no one else would listen to her or believe her account of it.

Mrs. McQuoid asked, "Where is the doctor? I expected he would have heard you and be down by now."

She struggled to her feet. "The doctor is not here. He had to leave."

The old cook hovered near her. "Are you all right, ma'am?"

"Yes, I'm all right now," she said in a dull, toneless manner which really indicated nothing.

"Is there anything you would like?" Mrs. McQuoid asked, a ludicrous figure in her long flannel nightgown and with her thin, white hair falling on her shoulders.

"No," she said. "I'm sorry I gave you such a scare. Now we must get some sleep. Go on to bed."

The old woman lingered to ask worriedly, "Is it going to be settled soon? Is the master safely out of it?"

"I hope so," she said, gazing down the hallway where she'd last seen the bag of Nancy's clothing. There was no sign of it anywhere. "I hope so," she repeated.

She went upstairs and bolted the door of the bedroom. She was almost certain Ian would not return in the night. If he did he would simply have to knock on the door and wake her. Not that having the door bolted gave her any great sense of security; the thing which threatened her was not stopped by walls, locks, or doors.

And yet, as she slowly prepared for bed, she began to wonder. Was the phantom she'd just seen more real than she'd guessed? The grisly business of the head made her more suspicious than she might otherwise have been. Possibly the phantom might have overplayed his hand. Who would have access to the head of a dead man more readily than a grave robber? Could it be that one of the grave robbers had returned to the house to get the bag of clothing and, at the same time, terrify her to the breaking point by playing the headless phantom?

This seemed something for solid consideration and she thought about it long after she had gotten into bed. No matter where her thoughts began, she wound up suspecting one person more than any other—her disgruntled former suitor, Samuel Todd. Yet she knew he could not have managed all this wickedness alone. He surely had helpers.

Her sleep that night was filled with nightmares as might have been expected. Headless bodies throwing their decapitated heads at her through the air abounded in her terrifying dreams. She twisted and turned in the bed and sometimes cried out in her sleep. When morning came, she felt as if she'd had no real rest at all.

She'd barely finished her breakfast when a carriage rolled up at the front door of Mercy House. In it were Ian's father and mother. The two came in to her in a greatly upset state. Ian's father had the carriage wait and faced Ann with a question she could not answer.

"Where is my son? He was to meet me at Stormhaven and he did not appear," her father-in-law demanded.

"He's gone off somewhere!" she said unhappily.

Flora, her kindly mother-in-law, at once placed an arm around her and said, "Gone off? Where?"

"I don't know," was her abject reply. "We had a quarrel soon after his father left last night. He ran out into the darkness. The last I saw of him, he was going in the direction of the town."

The aristocratic face of the elder Ian Stewart showed dismay. "This is a pretty pass! His running off in that manner is practically a confession of guilt!"

Flora spoke sharply to her husband, "I will not believe that! Not ever!"

Ian's father looked frustrated. He gave his attention to Ann as he asked, "May I inquire what you quarreled about?"

She hesitated and then decided it was time to tell him. He had a right to know, since he was so deeply involved. She said, "I made a discovery. I asked him to explain it."

Ian's father frowned. "What sort of discovery?"

"A shocking one! I found Nancy's clothing in a closet off his surgery room in the cellar."

There was a hushed moment following this dramatic announcement. Ian's mother stepped back from her in shock and turned to her husband with imploring eyes, as if begging him to say something which would make it all right, something to remove this nightmare moment they were all facing. But the handsome older man merely stood there in grim silence.

At last in a strained voice, he said, "You found the clothes the murdered girl had been wearing?"

"Yes."

"In my son's surgery room?"

"Yes."

Ian's father gazed at her with tortured eyes. "Where are they now? I'd like to see them."

"I'm sorry," she said. "I don't have them."

"What?" he asked, blankly.

"I simply do not have them!"

Ian's mother gazed at her in distress. "What did you do with them?"

"Nothing! They vanished!"

"Vanished?" Ian's father echoed incredulously.

"I only realized they were gone after Ian left," she told them. "I went upstairs after leaving them where they were in the middle of the hall. Then I went back to get them. They were no longer there. Either Ian had taken them or someone else came and got them."

"I find that difficult to believe," Ian's father said.

"I'm sorry. I've told you all I know," she replied. She could have told them about the phantom and the floating head, but they would have been only more skeptical. Better to keep her silence.

Flora Stewart turned to her husband. "What now?"

"I don't know," he said unhappily. "I'll go on to my office and try and think this all out. Unless you have some easy explanation, Ann?"

She said, "There are no easy explanations. I'm beginning to wonder if whoever is trying to make Ian the scapegoat for the grave robberies and murders didn't come here last night and get those clothes. After first planting them here to incriminate Ian."

"Ian didn't say anything?" his father commented bitterly.

"No. But this could have been from shock."

"I'm sure that has to be it," Flora said. "I do not think my son capable of these criminal offenses."

Ian Stewart, Sr., hesitated, then told Ann, "I will have to get on to the bank. But I will consult with my lawyers and see what they can come up with. I'd like to try and save Ian in spite of himself. More particularly, I want to spare the family name from other needless scandal."

Flora remained after her husband had left for the bank in his fine carriage. Ann had Mrs. McQuoid bring tea and cakes to them in the grim parlor of the old house. Even on this sunny day the room remained dark and cold. Flora and Ann sat before the tea tray and Ann poured.

The older woman accepted her tea in the fine China cup and said, "I have the feeling you didn't tell my husband everything about last night."

Ann gave the handsome older woman a surprised glance. "How were you able to guess that?"

Flora shrugged. "I can't exactly say. But I'm sure I'm right. Please confide in me."

Ann surprisingly found herself filling in all the rest of the macabre story for her mother-in-law. She finished by saying, "I didn't tell Ian's father because I was afraid he'd think me a mad female."

"Probably you were well advised," Ian's mother said. "I can now understand why you hate this house. When all this is at an end, Ian must get you out of it."

"If things ever do come to an end," she said.

"They must. And Ian will be proven innocent. I know all appearances are against this. But I know my son also, and I will go on believing in him."

Ann said bleakly, "I suppose beneath all my doubts and suspicions I still want to think him innocent."

"His father will do everything he can to help him. And I say a thorough investigation should be made into the movements of this lawyer, Samuel Todd."

"Samuel Todd's guilt is my only hope," Ann agreed.

"But how to prove it?" Ian's mother said.

"I know."

"There has to be a way."

"I will think about it. And when Dr. Gregory comes this afternoon I will ask his advice. I depend on him greatly."

Flora nodded. "He is a good man. No one knows that better than I. I almost married him once."

"He has remained a bachelor."

"Yes," Flora sighed. "I wish that he had found himself a suitable wife. But he preferred to transfer his affections to my family."

"He appears happy enough. And he is dedicated to his work. That alone gives him major fulfillment."

"True," the attractive older woman said. "You can count on his advice being sound. What really worries me the most is Ian's disappearing in this manner. His father is correct in saying it does make him look guilty."

"I know."

"Walter will be in a rage. My second oldest son is a very proper person, and any hint of scandal immediately strikes him as a threat to our family name and to the bank!"

"There is bound to be a scandal. Ian has been publicly questioned about this murder and the grave robberies."

"I hope my husband can deal with Walter," Flora worried. "He is the only one liable to make a fuss. Though my daughter Mary is married to Lord Inglis they are not liable to be disturbed by this. They are in London at the moment. Sophie is too much in love with her Italian to be worried and Roger couldn't care less. He is occupied with his horses and the outdoors. And he is still only sixteen."

"Walter and Heather Rae will make much of this," Ann sighed. "I'm sorry. We have no wish to bring them shame."

"They should recognize that," her mother-in-law said, rising. "And if they don't then let them stew! It won't do them any harm!"

Flora left soon after this, assuring Ann that she would do everything she could to see Ian safely through the crisis. Left alone again, Ann found her confidence in her husband's innocence wavering. She wanted him to be freed of blame, but she was increasingly concerned that she might be looking for a miracle.

At length she could not stand the house any longer. Ian had not returned, and Mrs. McQuoid was asking questions about lunch and dinner.

"Dr. Gregory will be here for lunch," she told the worried housekeeper. "I don't know about dinner." And with that she strode out of the house.

It was easier for her to go for a stroll in Mercy Cemetery than anywhere else. If she wandered along the downtown streets she might meet people who would ask her questions she couldn't answer. In the cemetery she would at least find peace and solitude. She made her way along the roadway and then went further along the side paths to reach the thick forest of tombstones. She stood in the shade of a giant elm, tombstones arrayed about her. Some were of recent vintage and straight to the sky; others were more weathered, and slanting; some had the lettering on them obliterated by the passage of time and were badly bent or broken.

As she was standing there she became aware she was no longer alone. She turned quickly and saw the scarecrow figure of the black-clad Angus McCrae standing behind her. In his wide-brimmed black hat and black cape he looked as shabby and bizarre as ever.

"You arrived so silently!" she said in mild protest.

"Popped out of my tomb," the thin scarecrow of a grave digger said in his cracked voice. He followed this with a cackle of laughter.

"Have you seen my husband?"

"The doctor?"

"Yes."

"He may have been," the thin specter of a man said, cracking his boney knuckles as he spoke. "Another grave was emptied last night!"

"Oh, no!" she protested.

"A fresh one! Dug it myself! Now there's an empty hole, casket and body gone!"

"It has to stop!"

"So the high sheriff says," the tall Angus McCrae said with a grin on his rotten apple face. "But they don't do much."

"They will," she insisted. "You're sure you didn't see my husband here?"

"I never leave the tomb after it gets dark," the man in black said. "Then it is the ghosts walk. You can't tell the living from the dead! This place is busier than you'd imagine! They stumble around and groan! I've heard them!"

His words sent a coldness through her—the coldness of a sharp knife. He was talking about the ghosts. And certainly she had seen at least one of them.

She suddenly felt weary and ill. It struck her that this spare old man with his wizened face and his haven in a tomb was utterly mad! She was wasting time talking to him. He was one of the macabre manifestations with which she'd had to deal since coming to live in the accursed Mercy House!

She said, "I must be on my way."

"I will watch for Dr. Stewart," the man in black promised.

"Thank you," she said, feeling it wasn't important.

Slyly, he said, "The Stewarts of Stormhaven are important people!"

Ann looked at him in surprise, wondering if there wasn't some hidden venom behind his words. She asked him, "What do you know of the Stewarts?"

"Only that they are the gentry. Bankers, doctors and the like! All Edinburgh knows them!"

"You sound as if you don't like them!"

"Nay!" the man lifted a thin hand in protest. "I have a love for all the living and the dead as well. It's just in the small hours that I shy away from the dead. Then they are restless! It is then they do harm!"

His mind was surely wandering again. She gave him a final glance and then began walking back to the roadway. Within a few minutes she was close to the cemetery gates which opened onto the grounds of Mercy House.

During the walk back she'd thought about Angus Mc-Crae. His sudden show of hidden malice had upset her. She began to worry that she might have underestimated his powers for evil. Could he be an ancient enemy of the Stewarts, posing as the headless ghost? And might he not be the organizer of the grave robberies since the cemetery was his domain? His plan might be to deliberately involve Ian as the guilty one to settle an old grudge. He seemed a very odd person to be a grave digger. Had he been something else before he'd fallen to drink and this low estate? Perhaps a businessman ruined by the dealings of the Stewart bank.

She was so much in a turmoil with these thoughts that she did not at first see Dr. Jock Gregory waiting on the front steps for her. When she saw him she waved and he waved in return.

Ann hurried up the steps to join him. "I was lost in my thoughts," she apologized.

The doctor took it good-naturedly. "You have a right to be, with all your troubles. I understand that Ian has disappeared. No sign of him yet?"

"No."

"That is too bad."

"If I only knew where he's gone. He didn't show up at Stormhaven either."

Dr. Jock Gregory frowned. "The worst thing he could do is vanish at this time. The city is filled with talk of the raid, the finding of Nancy's body and of Ian being questioned."

"You did his hospital rounds? What were the reactions of his patients and colleagues?"

"Pure shock!" Dr. Gregory said. "Ian is very popular. He is a good doctor and has a multitude of friends."

"He may need them now," she said bleakly. "Mrs. McQuoid has lunch ready for us. You must eat. The office patients will soon be arriving. If any come."

The doctor said, "I think more than usual will turn up.

Curiosity will bring them today if nothing else. Of course, if the rumors and gossip continue his practice is likely to fall off!"

"And when they find you here in his place, what then?"

He sighed. "It won't make a good impression."

At lunch she brought up her newly-born suspicions of the old grave digger. She said, "First, I was inclined to think Samuel Todd at the bottom of all this. But now I begin to wonder if the real villain might be that weird Angus McCrae."

"The problem is you haven't solid evidence against either of them," Dr. Jock Gregory warned her.

"I know. And then there is Dr. Marsh. That evil, ugly man fits in somewhere."

"Very possibly," the older doctor agreed. "I am at a loss now myself."

She lifted her eyes from her plate to meet his. "Do you know what?"

"Please tell me."

"It is very clear what I should do next. I ought to speak with that woman—that Sadie Scott who has accused Ian of so much."

Dr. Gregory's pleasant face mirrored his concern at her announcement. "I won't encourage you in that, my dear. She is a hardened, drunken type of whom you know nothing. You have never had contact with such a woman. I warn you, she will not be easy to deal with. And I don't see what you hope to gain."

"Information," she replied. "This Sadie Scott, if she chooses to talk, can tell me who the one was who hired Hannigan and her husband. If I know that, I know all."

"She already says it was Ian who hired them."

"But then she changed her story."

"And so she will continue to," Dr. Jock Gregory advised her. "She is a devious creature! Up to every trick!"

"She is in jail and she faces sentencing for her crimes. Surely she wishes to help herself. She could do so by telling the truth and sending us to the heart of this fester!"

The old doctor touched his napkin to his lips. "I wish I could encourage you, but I cannot. Such women have a weird loyalty to the men they consort with. My feeling is you will learn nothing from Sadie Scott."

"And I feel strongly I should at least see her."

He shrugged. "If that is your desire."

"Do you think it might be allowed?"

"Ian's father has the influence to arrange it," Dr. Jock Gregory said. "If you went to the jail armed with a letter from him it should open all doors for you."

"Then I shall do it," she said. "I'll stop by the bank first and then go on to the jail."

"I hope you may gain something from it," Dr. Gregory said in his kindly way, now that he saw she was determined. "I could be completely wrong."

"And you will meanwhile look after Ian's patients," she said.

"To the best of my ability," he promised.

When lunch was over she rushed upstairs and changed into a gray dress and bonnet she felt subdued and suitable for a visit to the jail. Then she had Charles bring the carriage to the side door for her. By the time she left, Dr. Gregory's prediction had been fulfilled. An enormous crowd of patients, mostly on foot, had shown up and were clustered on the stairs and drive. News of Ian's predicament had spread rapidly, and the curious had come out in droves.

Charles lost no time driving along Princess Street. They passed by historic Edinburgh Castle so much associated with Mary, Queen of Scots, and her son, James VI of Scotland, and James I of England who was born there. They drove along the Royal Mile where in 1561, Mary, young widowed ex-Queen of France and Queen of Scotland, made her entry into the city. One hundred and eighty-four years later her great-great-grandson, Charles Edward Stuart, the Young Pretender, at the head of his fierce Highlanders, entered the city on his way to Holyrood.

She was too lost in her own problems to recall any of the historic associations about the route on which they went. At last the carriage halted before the bank, and she got out and made her way to its impressive entrance. Just as she was about to go in a young man came hurrying out and almost bumped into her. He removed his hat to apologize and she found herself looking into the face of Samuel Todd.

"So we meet again," the young lawyer said, a somewhat sneering look on his broad face. "I ask your pardon for my haste."

"It did not matter," she said.

"So what I predicted has come true," Samuel Todd lorded over her. "Your husband now finds himself in grievous trouble."

She met the shifty brown eyes of the lawyer with a direct glance of her own. "I have no doubt his name will be cleared."

"He and Marsh are deep into it," Samuel Todd warned her. "I much doubt that they can escape punishment."

"I did not ask for your opinion."

"But I have given it," the lawyer said. "An example of my too generous nature."

"That is the last thing I would ever accuse you of having," she told him sharply as she brushed by him to enter the bank and leave him standing there with his hat still in hand.

It was not a happy coincidence that the first person she should meet on entering the bank was Ian's younger brother, Walter. The usually amiable Walter seemed to be in a nervous state.

His first question was, "Has Ian returned?"

"No," she said.

"Blast," the handsomely-dressed young banker fretted. "He has doused us all in a cesspool."

"I hardly think it that bad," she protested.

"Ian has tarnished the name of Stewart."

"The name has survived a good deal in the past," was her reminder to him.

Walter continued to appear unhappy. "Not of this sort. This is a public scandal, not one within the family. Ian has already been questioned, and I fully expect he will be named as the head of the resurrectionist gang!"

"And I look for the opposite," she said, forcing herself to sound lightly optimistic in a manner which even surprised herself.

Walter, the serious-minded banker, was thrown off by her manner. His mouth gaped and he said, "I wish I could find foundation for your hopefulness."

"I wish to see your father," she said.

"It is a bad time," Walter faltered. "He has been busy."

"It is a bad day for all of us, and I am also busy. That is why I must see him at once."

"Very well," Walter said, beaten down by her firmness. "I will take you to him."

He did and she found the elder Ian Stewart seated at his desk looking extremely depressed. Lines of fatigue were plain on his aristocratic face. But he kept his manners and

rose to see her safely seated and Walter out of the room before he encouraged her to tell him the purpose of her visit.

"You wonder why I am here?" she opened with.

He stared at her. "I had hoped you'd come with good
news of Ian. But that is not so. He is still missing."

"Still missing," she said. "But I think I may be able to
make some progress to helping him in his absence."

"Indeed?" His father sounded skeptical.

"Yes. I hope to prove his innocence. But I must have a
pass to visit that woman, Sadie Scott, at the jail."

"You want to visit that woman?"

"Yes."

"What on earth for?"

"I have the hope that talking with her on a woman-to-
woman basis may bring about some results. I hope to
somehow get the truth from her."

"She is a polished liar," Ian's father warned her.

"I'd like to try her."

Ian's father gazed at his desk top in a mood of despair.
"I had some hope until you found that girl's clothing in the
house and Ian ran off in the face of it."

She said, "We may be convicting him too easily."

He glanced at her. "You honestly think that?"

"Yes."

"What do you want me to do?"

"Give me a letter that will provide me with entry to the
jail. I wish to question Sadie Scott."

He said, "I can get you in there, but I can't make her
talk."

"I will attend to that," she promised.

He gazed at her with new wonder. "I am amazed at your
sudden resurgence of confidence."

"I have to believe," she said. "And I do."

186

His sigh was deep. "I have to hope you are right," he said. "I'll give you the note." And he at once wrote it for her and sealed it in an envelope with his sealing-wax and stamp.

He escorted her to the door. "Be careful, Ann."

"I will be."

"You are visiting a tiger of a woman."

"I know."

"You have no guess of how vicious their sort can be."

"Dr. Gregory warned me."

"He has had some experience with her sort. I believe the university has provided a service for treating jail patients. I can't honestly expect much from your expedition, Ann. But do it if it gives you any comfort."

"Thank you," she said, taking the letter. She appreciated the tolerance of her father-in-law. Ian had been blessed with good parents. But now that she had the means to act she began to be uneasy. Would she succeed? She was dreadfully uncertain.

When she went out and gave Charles the address of the jail she saw that he was startled. But she got in the carriage and let him drive her there. When they reached the imposing old edifice she was still wrestling with her doubts. Because there was a walled courtyard before the jail building, Charles had to wait with the carriage on the other side of it.

She left the carriage and went through the gate to the courtyard. It was a large square, cobblestoned and with great stone buildings on two sides of it and high stone walls on the other two sides. To her distress she saw a rough gibbet erected in the center of the courtyard. This meant that an execution was to take place soon. One did not have to be a murderer to hang. It was enough for an apprentice

187

to be caught tapping his master's cash box for a few shillings!

Ann averted her eyes from the gallows and went inside. She climbed steep stairs to the first floor and the office of the chief jailer. An ancient in black with a bald head was sourly writing entries with a quill pen in an immense ledger. She stood before the old clerk in the outer office and waited for him to raise his head from the ledger. It seemed an age before he deigned to lift his rheumy eyes and glare at her.

"Yes?" he asked tartly.

"I have a letter for the jailer," she said.

The old clerk put down his quill pen and took the letter in a sullen manner. Then he limped across to a door and in to the inner office.

Ann waited alone in the chill atmosphere for several minutes before a large man with a huge black beard appeared. The beard was made more prominent due to his bald pate. He had a friendly face as he halted before her.

"You are Mrs. Stewart," he said.

"Dr. Ian Stewart's wife," she said, spelling it out for him.

"Yes, I gather that from your father-in-law's note," the jailkeeper said. "This is a rather unusual request. Are you sure you want to go through with it?"

"I'm sure."

The man with the black beard showed interest. "What do you hope to gain? She's told us a dozen different stories. The woman is an inveterate liar!"

"I think I will know when she lies."

He raised his eyebrows. "Womanly intuition?"

"Something like that."

The big man hesitated. "There is something else. She isn't a pleasant person."

"I hardly expected her to be."

"You are clearly a lady of refinement. She may shock you."

Ann shook her head. "It is difficult to shock a doctor's wife. We see all sorts. I have often helped my husband with his patients."

The jailer looked impressed. "Very well, then. I see no reason why you should not talk with Sadie Scott. I shall send a guard with you, and he'll stand by to remove you at any time. He will wait in the corridor outside her cell."

"Thank you," she said, secretly wondering whether it was going to be worth all this struggle.

The guard, an elderly man, came and took her along a narrow hallway to a different building. He marched ahead solemnly and they finally came to several padlocked doors. There were guards at the various doors and she began to feel that she had entered a heavily guarded fortress. Which, in fact, was not all that far from describing the place.

"We have set her apart," the guard explained as they went along another corridor. "She was in the main section with the other prisoners, but it was decided we might get more information from her if we kept her alone."

"She'd normally be with other prisoners?"

"A hundred or more down in the main cells, all fallen women like herself," the guard said virtuously. "I tell you, I'd hesitate to take you down there."

"Do such places reform?"

"Reform, ma'am?" the guard said with disgust. "There's not one in a hundred of them have anything like that in mind. I've been a guard these many years and I can swear to that."

"Too bad," she said, as they came to a final padlocked door.

On the other side of this door was a short corridor with a row of cells on one wall. The guard halted before the first cell in which a woman stood staring up at the barred window above her. Her back was to them and she paid no attention to them.

"You have a visitor, Sadie," the guard said and let Ann in the cell. Then he locked the door hastily after her.

The woman in drab gray had long, straw-colored, stringy hair which hung forlornly. She slowly turned around to stare at Ann. Ann was surprised that the woman was so youthful, likely younger than herself. But this was a face prematurely aged with great dark circles under haggard eyes and a sickly, pasty skin color. The woman was so gaunt it seemed that she might never have had enough to eat.

She gave Ann a hostile look. "Well?"

"I'm Ann Stewart," she said. "Dr. Ian Stewart's wife!"

The gaunt face took on a jeering look. "The fine lady!"

"I'm not here to lord it over you," Ann told her, "I'm here because I need your help."

Sadie Scott raised her eyebrows. "What sort of help can the likes of me give to you?"

"You can save my husband!"

Sadie Scott's eyes became hard. "What about my man, Scott, and Hannigan. Who will save them?"

"I'll do all I can to see they get a fair trial if you will but be fair about my husband. I'm sure he's innocent and I think you indicted him because you were paid to!"

The woman smiled at her nastily. "You say I'm lying for money?"

"For some reason. But please change your mind. Tell me the truth. Save my husband and I will try and save you."

"No one can help me now," the Scott woman said harshly. "You know that and so do I. But maybe Scott and

Hannigan will get away. They were the ones who dealt with your fine doctor!"

"I think you made up that story."

"The price he offered was ten pounds and the price of the whiskey to keep her body in. And we gave him her clothes in the bargain. I had thought to sell them, but he spoiled that!"

Ann gasped. "You gave him Nancy's clothing?"

"Yes," the bleak-faced Sadie Scott said. "Though I don't know why he wanted them. He left with them in a cotton bag which he'd carried."

Ann could not reply. She was too shocked. She had come to the jail in the hope of proving her husband's innocence, but this first statement from the woman opposite her seemed to only prove him more guilty.

Ten

There was no mercy in the gaunt Sadie Scott's face. She stood glaring at Ann in a hostile manner and apparently enjoying her despair. Then she said, "You'll get no more out of me! You had better be on your way!"

Ann hesitated, trying to recover from the blow the woman's words had given her. Then she forced herself to go on asking more questions. "Did my husband know Hannigan and Scott well? Had he done business with them before?"

"He bought bodies before," the other woman said sullenly. "They met in a bar one night."

"Are you sure the doctor was Dr. Ian Stewart?"

"I had the name and his address written down," Sadie Scott said. "Scott gave it to me so I could go to him in case there was ever any trouble."

"How many times did you see him?" she asked.

The gaunt woman looked wary. She ran her boney fingers through her thin hair and then said, "He must have been at our place a half-dozen times."

"Did you talk with him?"

"Hannigan did all the talking," Sadie Scott said. "It was Hannigan's doing. He roped Scott into it because he was bad with the drink. Scott always stayed with me in the room back by the kitchen when the doctor came."

Ann felt she was getting some valuable information despite the woman's hostile attitude. She said, "Then you didn't ever actually see this doctor?"

"I listened to him through the doorway. Such a fine, educated man!" the woman sneered. "But he didn't mind where the bodies came from!"

"When did you first meet Nancy?" Ann asked. She was now convinced that Sadie Scott had never seen the mysterious doctor. So how could she be sure it was Ian? Why not someone else posing as him?

The woman turned her back on her. "I don't have to answer your questions!"

"It could help you. I will tell my friends, who are powerful, if you try to help. And they will do what they can for you."

The gaunt Sadie slowly turned to her again. "You expect me to believe that?"

"I mean it sincerely."

There was another pause. Then Sadie said, "It was the doctor brought Nancy to us. According to him, they'd been meeting in Mercy Cemetery. Meeting there regularly! That's the sort of fine husband you had!"

"Go on," she said tautly.

"The night he brought her to us she was already dizzy with drink and trying to put on airs, if you please! And she was no more than a backstairs maid! Then she came and sat with Scott and rolled her eyes at him as if she were a true beauty. And she and Scott finished the bottle of gin on the table before she fell forward, her head in her arms!"

"What then?"

Sadie licked her dry lips as if what she was about to go over was a grim recollection, even for her. She said, "Hannigan came in then. The doctor had gone away somewhere. Hannigan gave me a wink and said, 'I'll see she gets properly to sleep.' And he lifted her up in his arms and took her into the bedroom. Scott was too far gone with drink to pay any attention, and there was nothing I could do to stop him."

"What happened next?"

"Hannigan was gone for a while. Then he came back and told me, 'She's done for! I expect the drink was too much for her! All that's left now is to see her body is delivered to Dr. Stewart.' I knew that had been the plan all along and that he'd murdered her. But I didn't say anything."

"Did he say the body was going to Dr. Stewart?"

"Yes. It was Stewart who brought her to us. It was all a game!"

Ann said, "Nancy worked for us. It would have been madness for my husband to bring her here and have you murder her to sell her body. He would realize he'd be bound to be questioned."

The Scott woman's expression was cold. "He was seeing her outside the house. Perhaps she was with child and he had to be rid of her!"

This shocking reply made the kind of sense which Ann would have preferred not to hear. But it didn't really matter now, since she was convinced the man in the case had not been her husband but someone pretending to be him. Sadie Scott had never actually seen the doctor and so could not identify him. Hannigan and Scott, who were still at large, would be the only ones who could do that. And they might never be found. In that case, Ian would be safe. But his reputation would be irreparably damaged by the woman's testimony. And if she lied and pretended to have seen him, then she might point him out as guilty even though this wasn't so.

It was a bad mess which might end up in any way. Ann was only encouraged by the thought that the nefarious trio of grave robbers had been dealing with an impostor. She said to the woman in the cell, "I will go now. You have helped me. And I will not be ungrateful! I promise you!"

Sadie Scott regarded her uncertainly. Then in a quick, desperate outburst, she declared, "It was Hannigan! He's the villain! It was him who killed her! And he made Scott and me help him with the body! He'd have killed us too if we hadn't helped!" She began to sob.

She was moved by the sudden show of fear on the part of the gaunt Sadie. She said, "I'll remember all that. I will do what I can!" And she turned and left the cell.

The jailer had been waiting for her and hearing it all. He gave her a grim look as he locked the cell door. "She's a foxy one, ma'am. You can't tell anything about her."

They started down the corridor on their way out. "Still, you can't help feeling some sympathy for her," Ann said. "She's a battered drab, used by those two men."

"To hear her tell it," the jailer said. "But for all we know she may have been the brains behind it all."

Astonished, she said, "You think so."

"I've known stranger cases," the big man said as they came to the first of the padlocked doors along the corridor.

At last she reached the stairway and was free to leave. It had been a strange experience and one which had left her with a feeling of exhaustion. She was drained emotionally. Yet she knew the visit had been profitable. She had new facts to help defend Ian.

She felt there was a better than even chance that someone had posed as Ian. But there were other things which still bothered her and made her worry whether her husband were guilty or not. The woman's account of having to give the doctor the clothing when she had counted on selling the various items, for example. This fitted in with her finding the bag with Nancy's clothing in the surgery.

As she reached the lower hallway she was aware of a loud murmuring of voices from outside. And when she opened the door and went out into the big, square, cobblestoned courtyard, she found that a startling change had taken place there since she went through it on her way in. Now the entire space was filled with men and women, all gazing at the gallows set up in the middle of the area.

She pushed her way by two burly men and came to an old woman with a battered straw bonnet and a brown face covered with warts. She asked the old woman, "What is going to happen?"

The old woman gave a shrill of laughter. "What's to happen, me darlin'? It is a hanging that is to take place!"

"Now?"

"Any minute! You may as well stand here! You'll have as fine a view as from anywhere!"

"I don't want a view!" Ann said in a panic, and she pushed past the old woman whose derisive laughter trailed after her.

She was shoved back and around. People jostled by her and paid no attention to her. Her bonnet tumbled back off her head and only remained with her because of the strings around her neck. She was panting, pushing and not making any progress in escaping from the courtyard. The bodies were pressed too tight and all eyes were focused on the gibbet! At last she stopped trying to get away. It was a decision arrived at through sheer exhaustion.

She saw a stern-looking man go up the stairs of the temporary gallows and check the rope. He turned and gave a nod. There was a low murmur from the crowd. It seemed to roll up in one voice. Then she saw a thin, middle-aged man with bent head and shirt open at the neck slowly make his way up the steps of the scaffold. He stumbled on the last step and almost fell. A hush came over the crowd as two guards came quickly to his assistance and helped him to his place by the rope.

Ann stared at the man and felt she might faint. She had a weird experience as she studied his lined, worn face. The features began to twist and change and then it was Ian she saw standing there. Ian, looking so old and weary! Tears sprung to her eyes and she pressed a hand to her mouth to keep from sobbing out.

She bent her head and heard the prison chaplain say a prayer for the man. The crowd seemed to be waiting for something and then down close to the scaffold some hard, female voice cried out, "Speak your piece! Utter your repentance! Do not cheat us!"

Ann listened to the words in shock. So this was how it went. They expected the doomed man to put on a show for them. There were cheers from the crowd in reply to the woman's shouts and she thought the man waiting to be hung would collapse. He had shut his eyes and he was swaying a little.

The stout chaplain came forward and raised a hand for silence. Then he announced, "There will be no speech, though the prisoner is duly repentant. He is a mute!"

Having delivered this news, the chaplain stepped back. The information was passed along through the crowd. There were rumbling murmurs of disapproval, and Ann feared for a moment that in their disappointment the viewers might rush the scaffold and tear the prisoner to bits. But the situation was saved by a new diversion—the hanging itself. She saw the noose being placed about the doomed man's neck and bent her head.

There was an eerie silence in the courtyard now. She clenched her teeth and fought to breathe in the hotly-pressed mass of human bodies. She heard the rope creak, the gallows snap open, and the dry, swaying sound as the rope swung back and forth with its weight. There was what seemed like a long universal sigh from the crowd and then the murmuring resumed.

Terrified, she raised her eyes and caught a glimpse of the thin body hanging there, neck stretched weirdly and head to one side. With a gasp, she turned away from the sight!

"You mustn't faint!" The words were spoken by a voice familiar to her. She took her hankie from her eyes to look up into the solemn face of young Dr. Harry Turner.

"You! Here!" she said.

"On official business," the young doctor said. "This body is to be turned over to us by the prison officials for dissection. The proper means of securing bodies."

She leaned on his arm. "It was so horrible!"

"What did you come here for?" he asked.

"I was in the prison. I didn't know what was going on out here. I was caught in the crowd. I couldn't escape."

"Not likely," he said. "Hangings are rare shows for these folk. But you will notice they are scattering quickly enough now."

She glanced around the gray courtyard and saw that he was right. She said, "I must leave."

"Have you a carriage?"

"Outside."

"I'll see you safely to it."

"Thank you," she said. "I think I can manage."

"I wouldn't think of allowing you to go alone," he said, leading her along by the arm. "All manner of rogues and thieves mingle in these crowds. You could come to harm."

"Thank you," she said.

"What word of Ian?" he wanted to know.

"None."

"I can't understand it," Dr. Harry Turner said. "This is not like him."

"I know. I fear some harm may have come to him."

"Let us hope not. He is in enough trouble as it stands," the young doctor said.

They had reached the street and she indicated, "My carriage is waiting down there."

"Fine," he said, taking her down the street towards where Charles was waiting. "What were you doing in the jail?"

"I went to see that woman."

"Sadie Scott?"

"Yes."

"What for?"

"I thought she might talk to me. Tell me things she hadn't told the others."

"I'd say you were optimistic," the young doctor said.

"I was. Too much so. She said very little."

"I would expect that. She is a hardened criminal."

Ann said, "But I did gain one bit of information."

"What?"

"I don't think she ever actually saw Ian."

"Is that what she said?"

"More or less."

Dr. Harry Turner gave her a warning glance. "You know she has changed her story several times as it is."

"So I've been told."

"She probably told you what she expected you wanted to hear. Be wary that she doesn't play on your emotions."

"I thought her unyielding and independent until the last when she softened a little," Ann said.

They had reached the carriage and the young doctor halted and said, "I think you wasted your time with her. I wouldn't bother seeing her again. Bad enough that Ian mixed with such scum. You should spare yourself."

"But I must help him somehow!" she insisted.

"He can best help himself by putting in an appearance. This running off has only prejudiced things against him."

"I know," she said. "Thank you for seeing me to my carriage. Now you can go about your business."

The young doctor sighed. "I know dealing in the bodies of the dead is not anything to be proud of. I dislike my task today. But at least I am doing it differently from Ian. The law delivers these bodies to us."

"I understand," she said quietly.

The young doctor hesitated rather awkwardly for a moment. Then he said, "Do not think I am happy at Ian's plight. As you know, I consider him my best friend. We were students together. If anything happens I shall miss him sorely."

"Yes, of course you will," she said, turning to enter the carriage. Charles was standing with the door open for her.

"If there is anything I can do please send me a message," Dr. Harry Turner begged her.

"You are kind," she said.

"I will call on you soon," the young doctor told her. Then he stepped back and waited until she was seated in the carriage. He waved to her as they drove off. She sat back against the seat and closed her eyes.

The journey back to Mercy House seemed to be intolerably long. Once again they had to traverse the busy section of the ancient city, where all seemed noise and confusion. The sounds of venders chanting their wares mixed with the rumblings of wagons and the shouts of the wagon drivers.

They passed an organ grinder with his monkey surrounded by a group of bedraggled children. At another corner a vender of roasted chestnuts extolled his wares. Highlanders in their kilts walked in front of the carriage slowly, glaring at Charles and sending him into curses. All Edinburgh was alive on this afternoon and belligerent.

There were still quite a few patients waiting for Dr. Gregory to see them when she arrived at Mercy House. The front steps were still filled with waiting people. She went in by the side door. She was completely weary even though she had sat back and rested during the long carriage ride. Mrs. McQuoid was there to greet her.

"You have a visitor," the cook said.

"Who?"

"Miss Todd," the cook said. "She is waiting for you in the parlor. I have taken the liberty of serving her tea. May I bring in some extra for you, ma'am?"

"Please do," she said. "No other word?"

"Nothing, ma'am," the cook said sadly, knowing that Ann was asking if there had been any news of Ian.

Ann went on into the parlor, bracing herself to be as casual as possible. It wasn't easy after her experiences of the afternoon and with her mind still in a turmoil. But she did not wish to reveal the full extent of her concern to Martha Todd. She knew the girl would simply rush back with any information to tell her brother.

Martha was seated at the tea table. When she saw Ann enter the room she got up and rushed over and kissed her on the cheek. "How glad I am you have returned," the girl said. "I was so afraid I might have to leave without seeing you."

Ann said, "Well, now I am here. And Mrs. McQuoid is bringing some extra tea in for me."

"She's a gem!" Martha Todd said. "She has taken such good care of me."

"I'm glad," Ann said. "Let us sit down. I'm weary." They sat together and Martha turned to her and said, "How is it with Ian? Have you any idea where he has gone?"

"No."

"How awful for you!"

She looked down. "It is not exactly the happiest hour of my life."

"Samuel says your husband has probably sailed off on some ship. That he's gone to Australia or some other outlandish place and will never be heard of again."

Ann said, "I don't think that."

"I hope he returns for your sake, dear Ann," Martha said with a sympathetic look on her pretty face. "And I also hope he is cleared of all those dreadful charges against him."

"I have faith he will be."

The petite girl looked impressed. "I think you are very brave. But then I'm sure love makes one have extra courage. I know it has worked that way with me."

Ann managed a wan smile as she inquired, "And how is your romance developing?"

"Perfect!" the petite Martha said, with ecstasy. "Almost every night I meet him in the cemetery. And I vow I would never go there alone if I did not know he was waiting."

Ann said, "It is a desolate, lonely place. Nancy was last seen there. I don't think you should venture into the cemetery at all."

"I won't after our engagement is revealed," Martha said. "And that will be within a few days. I'm so happy I can't begin to tell you about it."

"I'm happy for you," Ann said. "Yet I do think you

should have your meetings with this young man somewhere beside the cemetery. It is far too dangerous a place."

"He is always waiting. And I never feel alone with him," Martha said. "I will soon be able to reveal his name. He has had to be discreet, but soon we can tell all the world about us."

Ann said, "Can't you tell me who it is?"

"I must wait," Martha told her. And she at once became silent.

They had more tea and then the petite girl left. Ann again offered her a warning against the rendezvous she was keeping in the cemetery but felt sure the pretty, rather simple girl had paid no attention to her. Martha had barely left when Dr. Jock Gregory came from the office after seeing the last of the day's patients.

He told Ann, "Just as I expected. A lot showed up out of curiosity. They were sorely tried to make up some specific illness. I paid them back in their own coin by prescribing a sharp purgative whenever there was any suspicion."

"You are so kind to do this for us," she said.

"It is a small thing," Dr. Gregory said. "I courted Ian's mother before she was married. I feel like an uncle, at least. How did you make out at the jail?"

"I met with dubious results and had a dreadful experience," she said, and she recounted the afternoon's events for him.

When she finished, he said, "Too bad you had to witness the hanging. It's a grisly business. It often makes me wonder if our methods of dealing with law breakers are not primitive. But if the law is less than perfect so is medicine. I cannot very well criticize."

"It is over with," she said. "I will try and forget it. But for a moment I thought I could see Ian standing on the gallows."

"Do not allow yourself to think such things," the kindly doctor told her.

"What do I do now?" she said. "I have reason to believe that this woman never did see Ian. How can I go about proving that these criminals were dealing with an impostor?"

He frowned. "That is difficult to say. It would be better if Ian were here. In his absence it is hard to prove anything."

"That is what distresses me most," she agreed. "Where has he gone and why?"

"As to the why, the majority of people will assume it is because he is guilty," her friend said. "You and I do not think so, but many people will."

"So we can only wait and hope for his return?"

"Barring no other developments, I would say so," Dr. Gregory sighed. "Do you feel like remaining alone in this house with only two elderly servants as companions? I'm sure Ian's parents would make you most welcome at Stormhaven."

She shook her head. "I have no wish to involve them more than I must. I will make out somehow."

"I know you have always found this old house frightening."

"I have. But facing this problem of proving Ian to be innocent has relegated my fears to second place."

"I have attended to the office calls," he said. "If there are any emergency calls you will simply have to tell them Ian is away and send them elsewhere."

"I will. And thank you for what you have done."

"I would like to do more," he said. "But I have just returned from my long stay in America. There is much work to be caught up with at the university."

"I realize that," she said. "You ought not to be penalized because Ian chose to run off as he did."

"I'm anxious to help as much as I can," the doctor said. "I'll do his hospital rounds again in the morning and be here for his office calls."

"You're sure this is not too much for you?" she worried.

"No. I can catch up with my own affairs in the evenings," he said. And, as he prepared to go, he gave her a final, solemn look. "Do take care!"

"Of course," she said. Both of them knew there was little she could do to protect herself. She was caught in a vicious trap until Ian returned.

After the doctor left she ate a solitary dinner. Mrs. McQuoid was depressed and showed it by the silence she offered when serving her. Usually the older woman talked a good deal, but now she was silent and tense. The atmosphere of the old house seemed to be charged with a strange electricity, a tautness born of their waiting. Ann began to condemn her husband in her mind for what he had done.

Pacing up and down in the parlor, she reviewed all that had transpired between herself and the woman in the prison. And she felt that if only Ian hadn't fled they would have been able to battle this thing and win out over it. But there were grimly accusing circumstances also. The mysterious doctor had insisted on having Nancy's clothes. This seemed to link the crime directly to Ian. She had found Nancy's things in the closet off his surgery. But they could have been planted there by some other person determined to bring ruin to her husband.

She went to the window and gazed out towards the gates of Mercy Cemetery. Dusk was falling and a single black crow soared by above the window and then, uttering a melancholy cry, vanished in the direction of the cemetery. She thought of Martha Todd's story about meeting some young man there and again it bothered her. True, Martha lived on the other fringe of the cemetery and no doubt met her friend close by the gates on that side.

Yet she did not consider the cemetery safe as a meeting place. Not after what had happened to Nancy. And the grave robbers were still at work. Hannigan and Scott would not be the only ones engaged in that grisly enterprise. The hazards of being alone in a cemetery at night had grown with the surge of body stealing. She wished she had been more critical of Martha when she had told of her many visits to the cemetery. But she was almost certain the petite girl would have ignored any warnings she might have given her.

And if Martha's brother, Samuel, should turn out to be the evil genius behind this plot against Ian, the girl would be perfectly safe. Her brother would not harm her. Ann felt this was reasonably certain. Whatever else he might be, Samuel Todd had always struck her as being a devoted brother.

Once again she had the feeling that she couldn't bear the old house. So she found a hooded cloak and, placing it on, went outside. She was standing in the driveway when a carriage turned off the street and came in. Her heart gave a great leap of hope as she looked to see if it might be Ian returning. But she was doomed to disappointment when the carriage came to a stop and Dr. Clinton Marsh emerged from it.

The ugly old doctor came to her and said, "Madam, I am here to deliver a message."

"What sort of message?"

The heavy-lidded eyes were fixed on her with a sort of contempt. "It is from your husband."

206

"From Ian? What can you tell me about him?" she demanded. "Where is he?"

"Pray, do not be so excited," the evil-looking Marsh said. "He is safe and in Glasgow."

"What is he doing in Glasgow?"

"He has an important mission there," Dr. Clinton Marsh said. "That is all I can tell you."

"Why did he send this message through you?"

"I am his best friend," Dr. Marsh said.

"I am his wife," she replied. "He should confide in me before trusting you with such messages."

The doctor showed no more emotion than he had during their previous meetings. He said, "I am not here to argue that point. I have simply delivered my message as your husband requested."

"When will he return?"

"I cannot say."

"Will it be soon?"

"I do not know," the university professor said coldly. "I should think you'd be pleased at knowing he is alive and well and so ask no other questions."

"Then you are wrong!"

He shrugged. "Accept it as you will. I must be on my way now."

"You have nothing else to tell me?"

"No."

"But you have only tortured me!" she protested.

"I came here thinking I was doing you a favor," Dr. Marsh told her.

"You are holding back the important things from me," she accused him. "You have used my husband as your scapegoat in your mad need for dead bodies. He acted as your agent and now he takes all the blame."

"If that is what you prefer to think, madam," Dr. Marsh said in his arrogant way. "I wish you goodnight." He bowed and returned to the somber, black carriage and it drove off.

Ann stood there in a troubled state as she considered what the man in the fast-vanishing carriage had told her. She wasn't even sure that he'd told her the truth but somehow she felt it might be. Ian was in Glasgow for some reason which the old doctor knew but wouldn't divulge. Perhaps he had gone there to take passage on a ship to Australia, as Martha had suggested, and she would never see him again. The thought sent a flood of fear and desolation through her! She might never see Ian again!

The mournful night closed in around her. The gates of Mercy Cemetery were hardly visible now. She would walk no further on this night. Turning, she made her way up the front steps and into the house which had always made her so uneasy. She wearily discarded the cloak and was about to go upstairs when Mrs. McQuoid appeared from the shadows of the hall.

The old woman looked nervous. She said, "Charles has gone to visit his sister for a while."

"Oh?"

"She has been poorly lately," the old woman went on. "He will be back later."

"That is all right. Thank you for telling me," she said.

A shadow crossed the old woman's face. "I don't like being here alone."

"I know."

"It's been worse with Nancy gone and the doctor not here," Mrs. McQuoid said. "The ghosts have always been here and now they want to have the place for themselves!"

"Why do you say that?"

Mrs. McQuoid glanced about her apprehensively. "Because I can feel it, ma'am. They're waiting there in the shadows, the whole sorry lot of them!"

Ann said, "You're allowing your nerves to rule you. You mustn't do that!"

"No, ma'am, it's more than that," the old woman said. "I sometimes see figures in the shadows. The man without his head and that other one, his chest covered with blood!"

"Please!" she protested. It was bad enough without the old woman making things worse.

"I can't help it, ma'am."

"You've never complained about the house being haunted before," she said.

"Not that I haven't worried about it," the cook replied. "On winter nights when the wind whistles about us I've heard them moving about."

"I know what happened to Nancy was a shock to you," she said. "But you mustn't lose your courage. Soon the doctor will return and everything will be like it was again."

"I thought I heard him downstairs a little while ago," the cook said.

"You what?"

"I did," the woman insisted. "I heard someone in the cellar and it sounded like his step. I know it from hearing him moving about in his surgery down there. It's directly below the kitchen."

She was upset by the woman's words and tried to cover this up by saying, "You just thought you heard something. You know the doctor isn't down there."

Mrs. McQuoid gave her a pleading look. "When will he return? I heard a carriage. I thought it might be him."

"So did I. But it wasn't. It was someone with a message from him."

"Then he is safe?"

"Apparently. But I have no idea how soon he will return," she said.

"He wasn't mixed up with the thieving of bodies, was he, ma'am?"

"No. You needn't worry yourself about that."

"The doctor would never have harmed Nancy," Mrs. McQuoid complained. "Those others have to be telling lies about it all!"

"I'm sure they are," she said. "Now I advise you to go to your bed and forget all about it."

"I'll go," the cook said dismally. "But that's not saying I will sleep."

The cook vanished down the dark hall which led to the rear of the house. The exchange had not done anything to strengthen Ann's morale. She had her own grim fears of the old mansion to contend with and preferred not to hear the laments of others. Never before had she seen Mrs. McQuoid in such a tense state.

Not that there was much wonder about it. The old woman's world was falling apart. With Nancy murdered and the doctor missing the old woman found it difficult to cope. Ann could hardly blame her since she didn't know how long she could last in the situation.

What had particularly bothered her was Mrs. McQuoid's reference to hearing Ian in the cellar. The old woman had seemed sure she'd heard his familiar step. And yet he was not down there. All at once a throbbing question presented itself in Ann's mind! Was it possible her husband were back and hiding in the cellar? This hadn't struck her before, but now she began to wonder.

The more she wondered the more it seemed that she must go down and investigate the cellar for herself. She had made a vow that she would not go down there alone again, but this was a new situation. Mrs. McQuoid had been serious when she'd said she thought she'd heard Ian's step. It was entirely possible that he was down there.

It would do no harm to give the surgery a quick look. She could avoid the other dark recesses of the cellar and just check on the big room. If he were not there she would put it aside as wild imagination on the cook's part and forget about it.

Once she had made up her mind she decided to go down and do the investigating at once. Waiting would not make it any easier. And if Ian should be lurking down there without telling her she wanted to lose no time getting in touch with him.

Spurred on by this thought and by the curiosity instilled in her by the older woman's words she found a candle and lit it. Then she headed for the operating room.

On her way down the stairs she heard the sound with great clarity. It sounded exactly as if someone had walked across the floor of the room. She remained part-way down the steps with the candle in her hand, staring through the cellar shadows at the door of the room, hoping it might open and Ian emerge.

She even called out, "Ian, is that you in there?"

The words echoed across the room, mocking her. She was angry and frustrated, but she was certain she had heard some footsteps and they had sounded as if it were Ian. Mrs. McQuoid had been quite right in that.

Not receiving an answer, she went on down the steps and slowly made her way across the uneven earthen floor of the cellar. Now all the ghosts began to plague her; her fears came teeming out of the darkness to torment her. All this while she was just an inch away from hysteria, but she didn't dare give way to it.

She reached the door and stood there listening, and once again she heard footsteps plainly, as if Ian were busy at some project in there.

She opened the door and lifted the candle high to take the best advantage of its light. And there standing at the table was a figure, but it wasn't Ian! She shrieked out in terror!

Eleven

It was the headless phantom again! Standing in the very spot where Ian usually stood when busy at his operating table. As Ann shrieked out in fear, the grotesque thing came groping through the shadows towards her. The candle fell from her hand, plunging the place into darkness, as she turned and fled towards the stairway.

She reached the ground floor corridor in a state of utter shock. She had closed the door leading to the cellar and was leaning weakly against it as Mrs. McQuoid came hurriedly to her. The older woman had on her nightgown with a robe thrown hastily over it. An ample nightcap with a pink ribbon strung through it was on her head.

"What is it, ma'am?" she cried.

Ann gave her a weary look. "I was a fool again. I went down into the cellar alone. I listened after you said you'd heard Ian's footsteps and it seemed I heard him. But when I went down there I saw the ghost!"

"The Lord save us!" the old woman exclaimed in dismay. "I told you the ghosts were restless!"

"I should never have gone down there," Ann said. "My nerves are in no fit state for that sort of thing."

"Was it the headless one?"

She nodded. "Yes."

"This house is cursed, ma'am," the cook said. "No one ought to try and live here. It should be torn down!"

"I've always been uneasy here," Ann admitted. Before

they could go on, there was a loud pounding on the front door which made them exchange frightened glances. The knocking on the door was repeated again.

Mrs. McQuoid gasped. "Who could it be?"

"It is late!" Ann said. Then a thought struck her. "It may be the doctor returned."

"Would he not let himself in?"

"He might not have his key," Ann said. "We'll have to find out who it is!"

"It could be those villains! The grave robbers!" Mrs. McQuoid lamented.

"No, I think not," she said. She led the way to the door. And she told the cook, "You stand close by to help me if I should need help!"

The old woman whispered hoarsely, "What can we two poor defenseless women do?"

Ann pulled back the bolt on the door and opened it to find her husband's father standing outside. The elder Ian Stewart looked embarrassed as he said, "I hope I didn't frighten you."

"Do come in," Ann said. "We had no idea who it might be."

The white-haired man came inside and removed his hat. "I did not intend to be this late. But I did not wish to leave Stormhaven until my wife, Flora, was asleep. She is taking this business very badly."

"I know how fond she is of Ian," Ann said. "Mrs. McQuoid will get us some tea."

"Yes, ma'am," the cook said and went to look after this chore.

Ann took her father-in-law into the parlor and lit several candles. She sat down then and he paced slowly back and forth before her.

He said, "I had to find out how you made out at the jail this afternoon."

"I was only partly successful," she said. "Sadie Scott is a very difficult person to reason with."

The banker nodded. "I can imagine."

"Still, I think I did reach her in the end. I'm almost positive she never actually saw Ian. And I have an idea someone else used his name."

"That is what I would give everything to know," Ian's father said.

"If Ian were here we might be able to prove it."

"What made him run away?"

"He is in Glasgow."

"Glasgow?" the banker exclaimed in amazement. "What is he doing in Glasgow?"

"I don't know," she said. "That was the message brought me."

"By whom?"

"Dr. Marsh."

"He had the nerve to show himself here! All of Edinburgh is talking about his being behind the grave robberies! And he has dragged my son into the mire with him!"

"I feel very much as you do about him," she said. "But I had to listen to what he had to say."

"Did he tell you why Ian was in Glasgow?"

"No."

"Probably he has sent him there so it would seem that Ian is wholly to blame," Ian's father lamented. "It was a sorry day when my son came under his influence."

"That was in medical college."

"I did not want Ian to be a doctor," her father-in-law said. "He would have been excellent at the bank. But he would not listen. And not only did he want to practice medicine, he had to be a surgeon! Better to leave it to the barbers!"

"Ian doesn't think so!"

"It is an unhappy profession. Most surgeons are not given the use of the prefix of doctor to their names. There is no honor in it! If he must remain a doctor let him specialize in something else!"

"If he returns to his practice I doubt that he will wish to change in any way," she said.

Ian's father halted his pacing as Mrs. McQuoid came in with tea and cakes for them. He apologized, "I'm keeping you up. You both could be having your rest."

She poured his tea for him. "That is not true. We have just had a bad scare. Your arrival is well-timed."

He stared at her. "A bad scare?"

She told him about it, ending with, "I don't expect you to understand. But if you lived here for a few weeks you might also be discussing the ghost. I vow that it exists."

Ian's father looked uncomfortable. "You could be right. I can only say it is not proper that you and that elderly woman should be alone in this house."

"Charles, the coachman, will be here shortly," she said. "He is dependable. I do not worry when I know he is at home."

"Good," Ian's father said. "I think you should have come to stay at Stormhaven directly after Ian left."

"I think I should remain here. He might come back in the night, or at short notice, and find me not here. He may need my support when he returns."

Her father-in-law stared down at his steaming cup of tea and said, "He surely will, unless we can clear him of his supposed involvement with these grave robbers!"

"So I feel I must stay here. Dr. Gregory has been attending to his patients."

"Gregory is a fine man," Ian's father said. "I would that Ian had patterned himself after Jock rather than after that Marsh."

She sipped her tea. "We cannot arrange these things as we wish."

The old man sighed. "I thought when I had a family I would direct it as I have the affairs of the bank. I would plan out the sort of career I wished each son or daughter to have and guide them in it. But it hasn't worked out that way. I have a family of rebels who wish to go their own way and pay no heed to me."

"Yet Ian is truly fond of you."

"Then he might have spared me this disgrace," his father said bitterly.

She said, "I have heard that in your youth you were also something of a rebel."

Her father-in-law gave her a shame-faced glance. "It is true," he said. "I was always one to want my own way."

"So what you deplore in your family you thought fine for yourself," she suggested.

"Probably. The hour is late. I do not want to argue about it. Not with Ian in Glasgow and things in the state they are."

"I understand," she said.

"We have the finest lawyers in the city ready to work for him," Ian's father went on. "I will spare no expense to clear his name if it can be cleared."

"I still have faith in my husband," she said.

"Good girl," Ian's father said approvingly. "I think you should talk to the lawyers tomorrow. Tell them what you found out from this Scott woman. Perhaps they can arrange to see her and make further progress."

She said, "Hannigan and Scott are still at large. If

they were captured they might talk."

"Agreed."

"Every effort should be made to find them."

"I have been assured the authorities are on the lookout for them. But they are wily scoundrels and may be hard to catch."

They talked along these lines for almost an hour. During this period Charles returned from his visit to his sick sister. Only then did Ian's father leave. And, before he left he arranged with her to visit the offices of his lawyers the following day. She saw him safely on his way and then went up to bed. The worst of the shock of seeing the ghost had left her by the time she was ready to seek sleep. Still, it was not surprising that when she did sleep she was tormented by a series of nightmares.

In her nightmares she was usually walking in the cemetery. She was afraid without knowing just what it was she feared. Then from behind a giant gray tomb there sprang the phantom without a head. He seized her in his arms and tormented her! She would scream and struggle to escape only to move on to another nightmare!

Still in the cemetery, she would suddenly come upon an open grave. Stretched out in it with his hands neatly folded on his lap was the grave digger, Angus McCrae. She would bend over the side of the grave to speak with him when suddenly she realized she was not alone. There was someone standing behind her. Whirling around, she would be confronted by the lawyer, Samuel Todd. An evil smile on his face, the lawyer would shove her backwards into the grave!

Again she woke up with a cry of fear, aware that she'd been suffering from dreams induced by the tormented state of her mind. She sat up and gazed into the shadows, then glanced at the empty bed beside her and wondered where

Ian was on this dark night. If only he would return from Glasgow!

Sleeping, dreaming and waking brought her to a gray, foggy morning. She rose with a feeling of gloom in the knowledge that she was facing another day of tension without Ian. She had promised to make a visit to the lawyers and would do so though she had little heart in it. She supposed there would be much legal talk with very little done. This had been her experience with lawyers in the past. Great talkers but hardly men of action. And she needed strong support at this time.

She was having breakfast when Mrs. McQuoid came in and told her, "He's out there!"

"Who?" she asked.

"The grave digger!"

"Angus McCrae? What is he doing here this morning?" she asked.

"Come for some vittles as he often does," the cook said. "And he's full of his crazy talk today!"

"Oh?"

The cook nodded. "Yes. Says he saw the grave robbers again last night!"

She sprung up from her chair. "I must talk with him."

"You can try," Mrs. McQuoid said. "I promise you that you won't get much sense out of him."

Ann went out to the kitchen and discovered the scarecrow figure of Angus McCrae seated at the long kitchen table. He had removed his floppy black hat to reveal a shining bald head fringed with gray hair. He was voraciously attacking a beef bone, the remains of a roast, on which a good deal of meat had been left. He was fast finishing the meat.

On seeing her he cut short his eating and stood up. "A

good morning to you, ma'am," he said. "And thank you for your gift of food."

"That is all right," she said. "What about your seeing the grave robbers last night?"

A sly look crossed the old man's face and he chuckled. "I came out of my tomb. I don't often do that. But last night the moon was full and I wanted to enjoy it."

"Go on," she said.

The mad old man was obviously happy to have her interest. He said, "Have you ever watched a full moon, ma'am? It is a kind of magical experience."

"I'm sure it is," she said impatiently. "But I want to hear about the grave robbers, not the moon."

"They were there again," the old man said. "There were three of them."

"Three? All men?"

"If you'd call them that! I'd name them vultures," the old grave digger said. "I hid behind a tombstone when I saw them coming. And, because of the moonlight, I had a good look at them."

"And?" she said, tensely, anxious to hear all he knew.

"There were two older ones and a young one not unlike the doctor. I mean, like him in size and sounding like him. But I couldn't see his face."

"Then what makes you think it might have been my husband?"

"I can't exactly say," the old grave digger replied. "Maybe it was mostly because he sounded like him. I heard him talking. The tallest one was carrying a sack over his shoulder. A big sack. I could tell by what they were saying there was a body in it."

Ann was shocked by what he had to say. It seemed all too likely that it might have been Ian with the thugs,

Hannigan and Scott. And the man carrying the sack with the body could well have been Hannigan. She said, "What did you do?"

"Do? Why nothing, ma'am," the grave digger said. "I didn't want any trouble."

"But those three were there robbing graves!"

"None of my business, ma'am," Angus McCrae said. "I dig the graves. I don't care what happens to them afterwards. And that's a funny thing."

She frowned. "What are you talking about?"

"About the stolen body. This morning I made a search to find out which grave was open. Whose body they had robbed. And what do you think?"

"I have no idea."

"Nary a grave was open. They had a body, but it didn't come from a grave. Now I call that a puzzle. And afterwards I thought it might have been the moonlight and that I just fancied the whole thing!"

"And you're sure they were carrying a body?"

"Yes. And talking about it among them. Arguing where they should take it."

She said, "Then it couldn't have been merely a fancy on your part."

"I guess not, ma'am," the scarecrow figure in grubby black said. "Can I finish the meat, ma'am?"

"Yes. Please do," she said.

"Thank you, ma'am," he said, sitting down and once again attacking the bone.

She watched him with a feeling of despair. And then she said, "Will you do me a favor?"

He looked up. "Of course, ma'am."

"Don't tell your story to anyone else. I mean about seeing the grave robbers."

221

"You're the only one I ever speak with, ma'am," the ancient grave digger said. "I don't look for trouble."

"Thank you," she said. "It might hurt my husband to have a story like that spread."

"Don't you worry about me, ma'am," Angus McCrae said. "I'll be as silent as the tomb!" And then he chuckled at his own joke.

She had Charles bring the carriage around and drive her to the lawyers. They were in a pretentious brick building off High Street and very much as she had expected. The elderly partner who received her in his office was hard of hearing and wore a brown wig which was slightly askew. His name was Dudley Milton.

In a cracked voice, Lawyer Milton warned her, "Unless your husband shows himself, the appearances are all against him."

"I know that," she replied loudly.

The old lawyer nodded and gave her the impression he hadn't heard her at all. He rubbed his thin chin and went on, "His father feels that you may have found some valuable information from this Scott female."

"I found a little," she shouted. "I don't think she ever saw my husband during the various transactions. She heard him referred to as the doctor."

The old lawyer had been watching her intently as if he'd been trying to read her lips, and now he cleared his throat and said, "That is bad if she knew him as the doctor."

"She didn't know him as the doctor!" Ann protested loudly. "She didn't actually see him at all!"

"All," Lawyer Milton said catching her last word. "Well, if they all knew him as the doctor that makes a strong case against him."

Ann felt the situation had all the elements of farce. She

knew she was wasting her time and the old lawyer's as well. She shouted, "I think I'd better write it all down!"

The ancient Dudley Milton nodded solemnly. "A good deal does depend on who acts for the Crown. If this comes to court they will try hard for a conviction! A dastardly crime!"

Ann was too weary of it all to do more than merely say, "Yes."

The old man went on, "The Stewarts are a fine family. Your husband's father has done much for Edinburgh. It is a great tragedy. But then every family sooner or later faces something like this. You must bear up, my dear young lady. Bear up!"

"Thank you," she said rising.

The old man rose arthritically to see her out. "I will have my junior partner talk with Mr. Stewart again. And we will be ready to prepare the best case possible for your husband as soon as he returns."

She left the lawyer's office with a feeling of utter hopelessness. She had not been able to make herself understood and this was the person charged with preparing Ian's defense. Poor Ian! Perhaps he was better off in Glasgow. But if he were in the cemetery last night he must have returned. This hurt her deeply to think that he might have returned and not tried to get in touch with her.

Charles was seated on the carriage waiting for her. She was about to get into it when she heard her name shouted above the tumult of the street sounds. She turned to look down the busy street and see who it might be. Suddenly she spotted Samuel Todd hurrying towards her.

Samuel Todd had beads of perspiration streaming down his broad face. He was breathless and took a moment to blurt out, "Have you seen Martha?"

"A day or two ago," she said. "Why?"

"She is missing!" The young man said in an upset voice.

"Missing?" Fear began to gather at the back of her mind.

"Yes. She went out somewhere last night without a word to me and she didn't come back."

"That doesn't sound like Martha," she said.

Samuel Todd looked troubled. "She has been behaving most strangely lately. The maid tells me that more than once she has gone to Mercy Cemetery to meet someone."

"That is true," she agreed. "She told me about it herself. She had meetings there with some young man whom she met at the party at Stormhaven."

"Blast Stormhaven and damn the Stewarts!" Samuel Todd cried angrily. "They have brought me nothing but trouble."

She felt for him and was frightened for Martha. But it didn't seem fair that he should place the blame on her husband's family. She said, "I'm sure the Stewarts have meant you no harm!"

"You don't need to defend them or your grave-robbing husband," Samuel Todd raged on. "If anything has happened to Martha somebody will pay dearly."

"I'm truly concerned," Ann said. "Martha is a good girl. I hope she is safe."

Samuel Todd, having vented his rage, now seemed to lapse into despair. "I don't know what to do! I have searched for her everywhere."

"Let us hope she is with a friend," Ann said. "I will be returning to Mercy House, and if she should come there I will send her straight home."

The lawyer showed gratitude on his broad face. "Thank you, Ann. I didn't mean to rail at you. But I am at my wit's end!"

"You do not have to apologize," she said.

"I am now making the rounds of her friends' houses. Seeing you will save me one visit."

"Good luck, Samuel," she said.

He nodded mutely and stood there in a sort of daze as she got into the carriage and was driven away. He presented a tragic figure standing there bemused. And she was terribly worried about Martha, especially in the light of what she'd heard from Angus McCrae. Could the sack which the three were carrying have contained Martha's body?

She closed her eyes as the carriage creaked over the cobblestones of the crowded streets. Ignoring the noise around her, she tried to concentrate. Martha had met someone at the party and was continuing to meet him in the cemetery. She tried to narrow down who it might be and almost at once found herself coming up with the name of Dr. Harry Turner.

How like Martha to seek out a doctor to have a romance with. She had told her that she wouldn't be able to divulge his name or their marriage plans until he gave consent. She had always wondered about the young doctor. He had shown a keen interest in Nancy. And it wasn't too much later that Nancy had been murdered and her body sold by the grave robbers. Had he made Martha the same sort of victim? Had that been his reason for making love to her? Aware all the time that soon he would betray her to her killers! Could anyone be so cruel?

Had he cleverly pretended to be another doctor, her own Ian, in order to throw suspicion on a rival who was doing too well? It all fitted in so perfectly that she didn't know why she hadn't thought about it before. But it was only with Martha's disappearance that she'd really become extremely suspicious of Dr. Harry Turner!

Perhaps the fact that the pieces of the puzzle fitted so neatly made this solution too easy. But she could not get the possibility out of her mind. She was anxious to get back to Mercy House and discuss this with the family's good friend, Dr. Jock Gregory, before he began to see the afternoon patients.

When she arrived back at the vine-covered, ancient red brick house the fog was lifting. She could see the cemetery clearly with its forest of gravestones. A few patients were already on the steps, waiting. She went in by the side door and found, to her relief, that Dr. Gregory was already there.

The pleasant family friend came to greet her. "What is the latest?"

"I have been to see the lawyers," she told him. "I'm shattered! Old Dudley Milton is deaf and probably senile! How can he help my husband?"

Dr. Gregory said, "Don't fret. His son is in the firm with him and he is most competent. So is the old man, despite his deafness. Once he gets the facts clear he has an astute mind."

"You'd never guess it," she complained.

"Trust Ian's father to pick the right men," he said.

They were standing facing each other in the hall. She said, "And there is worse news."

"Tell me," the doctor urged her.

"Martha is missing," she said, going on to explain it along with her dark suspicions of Dr. Harry Turner. And as she recounted the story for him it seemed all the more reasonable that her theory was correct.

The older doctor listened with sober concern. Then he said, "You are being hasty in your judgment, I fear."

She was surprised. "You think I'm wrong in blaming Dr. Turner?"

"I do," he said. "Especially when we aren't sure that anything truly bad has happened to Martha yet."

"I'm sure she was murdered by the grave robbers. And it seems to me they have been dealing with Harry Turner."

"It's possible," Dr. Gregory said with a sigh. "Turner was a wild lad at the university. But brilliant, mind you! I'd hate to think he has become so twisted as to do the things you suggest."

"Perhaps he is mad?"

"He would have to be, to commit such crimes," the doctor agreed grimly. "But I refuse to indict him on such flimsy evidence."

"Folk seem willing enough to indict my Ian on a good deal less," she said.

"Ian is still very much in the shadow," he pointed out. "I dislike having to say it but, in the face of all I have heard, your husband must still be thought of as the one most liable to be guilty."

"How can you say that?" she asked in anguish. "You are supposed to be a family friend!"

"And I am. I'm not accusing Ian myself. I don't think him guilty. But I'm pointing out what most other people are liable to think. His name along with that of Marsh is being repeated all over the city! The public has already tagged them as the moving spirit behind the grave robbers!"

"Unfair!" she protested.

"I agree," he said. "But easy. So don't let us too easily accuse someone else who may be just as innocent as your husband."

She was determined. She said, "I think Harry Turner is guilty, and I believe it is a plot designed to ruin my husband. I shall go to his office and accuse him of having assignations with Martha in the cemetery. If he admits it

227

then we know he has to be the guilty one."

"Dare you go to him in such a fashion?"

"Yes. At this point, I will dare anything. It is to save Ian and avenge Martha."

"Be wary," was the old doctor's final advice.

Early in the afternoon she had Charles drive her to the fine old house in the center of the city where the Turners, father and son, had their practice. She saw to her satisfaction that the line at their front door did not match that at Mercy House. And she went directly to the door and caught the attention of a tall, dour servant who stood inside to see the line was orderly.

She said, "I must see young Dr. Turner at once."

"Do you have an appointment, ma'am?" he asked.

"No," she said.

"Then you must take your place in line," was his reply as he turned his back on her importantly.

She snatched at his sleeve. "Wait," she said, "I am the wife of his friend Dr. Ian Stewart. I'm sure he'll admit me at once if you tell him I'm here."

The dour one eyed her sourly. "You're Dr. Stewart's wife?"

"Yes."

He said, "I'll ask him." And he vanished inside.

She waited on the steps, conscious of the stares she was getting from the others. A few were murmuring about her brazen manner. She felt her cheeks burn as she listened to the rude comments voiced about her.

After what seemed like an age the servant came back and said, "He'll see you. Come with me."

Ann followed him inside. The hall smelled of sweating human flesh and carbolic. He led her to a door on the left of the hall and opened it for her. When she went in, she found young Dr. Harry Turner waiting by his desk. His pleasant face took on a satisfied smile.

"I knew that one day you would come to me."

"Did you?" she said.

"Of course," he replied. And he came to her. "Forgive me, it was my idea of being funny. And I can see that you have not come here in the mood for humor."

"I have not."

"What is it? Bad news about Ian?"

"No," she said.

The young doctor eyed her warily. "You have surely come here for some reason. What is it? How can I help you?"

She looked at him directly and with a taut voice, she said, "You can help me by telling me the truth about Martha and you."

His mouth gaped open. "Martha and me?"

"I'm waiting," she said.

"I don't know what you're talking about," he protested. Her eyes met his and she decided to take a great gamble. It seemed certain that otherwise she was going to get nowhere with him. "Would it surprise you to hear that Martha told me she was meeting you secretly?"

"It would," he said.

"I can even tell you where she met you. In the cemetery."

Harry Turner had gone pale. He said, "Who I meet is none of your business!"

"I think it is," she replied much more calmly than she felt inside. "Martha is missing."

"Missing?"

"Yes," she said. "And I think you know all about it."

Harry Turner stared at her in silence for a moment, then he snapped, "What do you want to do, ruin me? Because

Ian was silly enough to get mixed up with Marsh and destroy his career, are you out to destroy mine?"

"No, I only want the truth. If you don't tell me I'm going straight to Samuel Todd. You'll find him harder to deal with than me."

"You are a little fool!" Harry Turner said angrily.

"So be it," she said, and she turned to leave.

"Wait!" Harry called after her in a faltering voice.

She turned, certain that at last he was ready to reveal at least part of it. She said, "What for?"

He came several steps towards her. "I'll admit it. I have been seeing Martha. Now are you satisfied?"

"So you were the romantic hero of whom she boasted?"

Harry said wryly, "You find that amusing?"

"Not really," she said. "Why did you have her meet you in the cemetery and in secret?"

"My father doesn't want me to become engaged or marry until I'm better established in my profession," he said. "It's a strictly private matter and Martha understands."

"Where is she now?"

"I don't know."

"Didn't you meet her last night?"

He looked like an animal at bay. His hands clenched and unclenched. He said, "She was to meet me. She didn't appear."

"Didn't you think that odd?"

"No. I thought she was probably ill. She'd complained of having a slight chill."

"But you didn't go to her cottage to inquire after her?"

"I couldn't. No one was to know about us. I can't think why she told you."

"She didn't," Ann said. "I tricked you into telling me!"

230

He came close to her, his hands tightly fisted and raised as if he meant to strike her. "You vixen!"

"I'll go now," she said. "But you will hear of this later. And I only hope, for your sake, that poor Martha is safe."

She left him standing there looking more guilty than she had expected. She was glad to escape the room and his lies. It made her feel ill. And she remembered that often, when he came to spend the evening with Ian, she had complained to Ian, warning her husband that this was no true friend. But she had not guessed then the full extent of his villainy.

Pushing her way down the steps to the accompaniment of jeers from the waiting patients, she rushed to her carriage. Not until she was in it and on her way back to Mercy House did she feel safe. And even then she realized she had placed herself in added danger. By allowing Harry to know that she believed he was a murderer, she had made herself a target. The one thing he would feel he must do would be to silence her.

She had not expected to so readily get an admission from him that he'd been seeing Martha. But he had stumbled into her trap. Once she knew about this she was easily able to put the rest of the puzzle together. She could barely wait to get back home and tell Dr. Jock Gregory.

Happily, the line of patients was shorter that day and so she did not have to wait long before the older doctor was free to join her. He listened to her account of her meeting with Harry Turner with grave attention, hearing her out until she was finished.

She gave him an anxious look. "What do you think?"

"Perhaps you are right about Dr. Harry Turner," he said.

"Oh, I'm sure of it," she told him. "What should we do next?"

Dr. Jock Gregory did not hesitate in replying, "I think the brother must be told."

"I agree."

He asked, "Do you wish me to take this information to Samuel Todd?"

She nodded. "I think so. It would be hard for me."

"Very well," the veteran doctor said grimly. "It is not a pleasant task, but I see plainly that it must be done."

"Thank you," she said. "I feel sure now that Dr. Harry Turner was the one who pretended to be Ian. If only Ian would return."

Dr. Gregory said, "It seems I must also see Marsh."

"Yes," she agreed. "He claimed he knew where Ian was, but he wouldn't tell me anything else."

"He must be made to tell all," Dr. Jock Gregory said with a stern air. "As his colleague, I think I can challenge him on this."

"You will let me know what happens?" she asked.

"Depend on that," he said. "But be patient. It may take until morning. And I advise you not to leave this house. There is no telling to what lengths Turner will go if he is guilty."

"I know that," she said, shuddering at the memory of his face when she'd left him in his office.

Dr. Gregory left and she began the vigil she was destined never to forget. The dinner hour came and went. She went to the parlor and stared out the window. Darkness began to descend so that she could no longer see the cemetery gates. Then she suddenly was aware of a distant murmuring of voices—a murmuring of voices which grew louder!

Then she was amazed to see a group of perhaps twenty or thirty approaching the house. It was hard to count them or make them out clearly in the near darkness. They came to a halt at the edge of the driveway, but she could plainly hear their angry murmuring. She stood there, trembling, wondering what it meant!

Suddenly a jeering voice cried out, "Ghoul!"

Another voice shouted, "Grave robber!" This was followed by a rock coming in through the window above her head and shattering several of the small glass panes!

Twelve

There were more ugly shouts from the unruly crowd who had gathered out there in the darkness and then another rock was thrown. It hurtled through the air to crash through several more window panes. Ann gazed at the damage in stunned dismay. It was her first experience with rioting of this sort.

Mrs. McQuoid came running out to join her as she cried, "What is happening, ma'am?"

She gave her a frightened glance. "An unruly crowd. They seem to be making some sort of demonstration!"

Mrs. McQuoid went close to the windows where the shouts of "Body thieves! Resurrectionists and grave robbers!" could be plainly heard. The elderly woman gasped, "They're mad! What will we do?"

"I don't know," Ann said. "Perhaps if we remain very quiet they will go away."

At that instant Charles appeared in the room. His lined, old face took on a look of anger as he saw the broken windows and the glass scattered over the rug. He said, "I have a good musket, ma'am. I'll go out there and let them know they can't threaten decent folk!"

"No, Charles," she said. "You could never stand them off alone. If you go out there it will only make them worse!"

There were jeers and additional derisive shouts from the crowd which had gathered outside, and it seemed likely that all they needed was a leader to encourage them to storm the house.

"They'll kill us all! Burn us down!" Mrs. McQuoid said in despair.

"Cowards! All of them!" Charles said with disgust as he eyed the rioters at the end of the driveway.

Ann debated what to do. She was about to send Charles out the side door in an attempt to get help when something quite unexpected happened. An imposing carriage appeared in the driveway, and the rioters had to split their ranks and stand back to let it pass. It had no sooner gone by the sullen crowd than the carriage halted and a slender woman emerged from it. It was Flora Stewart, Ian's mother.

The pleasant-faced woman confronted the mob and told them sternly, "You have no right here! Your actions are completely illegal!"

"What about your son?" someone in the crowd shouted back at her. "He steals bodies from their graves!"

"That has not been proven," Flora cried, standing up to the rabble in a sturdy fashion which Ann and the others watching from the house could not but admire.

"Stewart is a resurrectionist!" someone else cried, and the mob took it up, chanting and moving closer in a semicircle around Flora Stewart.

Old Charles was at the window watching. He said to Ann, "I'd best get out there and defend Mrs. Stewart!"

"No," Ann halted him with a gesture. "Wait! I think she can manage this herself!"

"That lone old woman!" Mrs. McQuoid said in disbelief.

"Watch and see," Ann advised, caught up in the drama of it all.

"My son is innocent! You have been lied to! Go back to wherever you have come from before you get yourselves into serious trouble!" Flora Stewart told the irate mob. It made some impression; there was a murmuring among themselves and then a miracle occurred. The mob began to melt away. Within a few minutes they had vanished. All during this vital period, Flora Stewart fiercely stood her ground outside the carriage. When she was sure the danger was over, she said something to her coachman and then came walking towards Mercy House.

Ann rushed to open the front door and greet her personally. "You were so brave!" she told her mother-in-law as she embraced her. "I never would have found such courage."

Flora entered the hall and asked, "Was anyone hurt? I know they threw some rocks."

"A few windows broken," she said. "Mrs. McQuoid can stuff them with something for the night and tomorrow we can have Charles get the needed glass cut and replace the broken panes."

"What an ordeal for you!" her mother-in-law said with sympathy.

"You were the heroine of it all," Ann insisted. "The way you stood up to those vandals was wonderful!"

Flora gave a rueful smile. "I couldn't bear their talk about my son. Ian is a young man of character. I would not let them tear his good name to shreds!"

"I ought to have been out there with you!" she said. Charles and Mrs. McQuoid had gone about fixing up the damage as best they could while she and her mother-in-law discussed it all.

"No. It was best that I defied them alone. And I'm an old woman while you are still young. It worked out as well as we could expect. If only they don't decide to return!"

"I doubt that they will," she said. "At least not tonight. How did you come to arrive at such an opportune moment?"

"Ian's father told me of your distress," Flora said. "I could not bear to think of you here alone. My husband wasn't able to come with me, but I ordered the carriage myself. I had a strong feeling you might need me!"

"And I did!" Ann said. "Do come in and sit down."

"I must hear all that has happened," Ian's mother said.

Ann took the woman to the divan at the far end of the room, away from the broken windows. They sat down and she told her about her meeting with young Dr. Harry Turner and her grave suspicions about him. She ended by saying, "Not only may he have been responsible for Nancy's death but also for the death of Martha."

"If she is dead," Flora Stewart said. "We must hope that she is not until we hear otherwise."

"I'm dreadfully afraid for her."

Her mother-in-law said, "You made a good choice in asking Jock Gregory to deliver the information to her brother. And I hope he will also be able to get the information we need about Ian from that awful Dr. Marsh."

"He is going to confront Marsh," Ann said.

"If Ian were only here," his mother worried.

"I know."

"I find it wrong of him to desert you at this time and not even leave you a message."

Ann said, "I did get a sort of message from Dr. Marsh."

"A strange message!" Flora Stewart said with derision.

Ann said, "I think Ian had to leave in a hurry. The circumstances prevented him from giving me a warning."

"What was his mood when he left?" Ian's mother asked.

She sighed. "I had said some harsh things to him. He was angry. I understand now I should have been more tolerant."

"You were taunted into complaining," Flora said. "No one could blame you."

Ann gave a small shudder. "It's this old house. We have had nothing but bad luck since we came here."

"I know," the older woman agreed.

She gave Ian's mother an earnest look. "And I don't think the bad luck is at an end yet."

"Let us hope it is."

"Every morning when I rise I see that cemetery. It is a grim, desolate place. And it reminds me daily of all that has happened."

"My husband said you visited the lawyers?"

"I saw Mr. Dudley Milton," she said. "And I found him old and uncomprehending."

"You did?"

"His hearing is gone and I doubt that he has any genuine interest in Ian's predicament."

Flora said, "I must speak to my husband about that. Your feeling is that we should find someone more suitable?"

"Unless the young Mr. Milton is a lot more energetic," she said. "Dr. Gregory seems to think that he is."

"That must be it," her mother-in-law said. "My husband is generally careful about whom he employs."

Their conversation was interrupted by the appearance of Mrs. McQuoid, looking more upset than ever. The cook said, "I don't like to intrude, ma'am, but me and Charles think there is someone in the cellar again!"

Ann got up quickly. "In my husband's surgery room?"

"Yes," the cook said. "There were footsteps down there again. We both heard them!"

Flora Stewart had also risen. "What does this mean?"

Ann explained to her, "Ian has a room for surgery in the cellar. The other night there were mysterious footsteps down there. And now it seems they have returned."

"Perhaps it is Ian come back?" Flora Stewart suggested hopefully.

"I doubt it," she said.

"Shouldn't we investigate?" his mother urged.

Ann was reluctant. "It might be dangerous. It is not a pleasant place down there."

"And I'm not easily scared," Ian's mother reminded her. "Let us go down and see what we find."

Mrs. McQuoid said, "Charles could go down."

Ann said, "I think perhaps we should all of us make a search of the cellars. Mrs. Stewart and I will lead the way, and you and Charles can back us up. In that way we shall have lots of support."

"I'll tell him," the cook said, and went off to get him.

"This is probably a waste of time," Ann apologized. "Mrs. McQuoid is so nervous she probably just imagined she heard something."

"Even so, we should investigate down there," the older woman said.

So that was how the four of them came to venture into the cellar. They were all carrying lighted candles and Charles had his musket with him for good measure. Ann led the way as they approached the door to the cellar room which Ian had called his surgery. A thrill of fear rippled through her as she reached for the doorknob and tried the door.

It opened easily. What they saw caused gasps from all of them. Candles were burning at the head and foot of the long surgical table, and on the table under a white cloth there was a body!

Flora Stewart asked in a taut whisper, "Has there been a body on that table?"

"No!" Ann said tautly.

Mrs. McQuoid in the rear uttered a murmur of dismay. "I knew I heard footsteps! Someone has lit the candles!"

Old Charles advanced aggressively with his musket ready. "What now, ma'am?" he asked.

"I don't know," Ann said in a low voice, staring at the figure on the table. "There must be some secret passage into this house!"

Ian's mother said, "No doubt there is! Mystery and scandal have continually dogged this place!"

Ann continued to stare at the table. She knew what she must do, but she couldn't bring herself to take those few steps towards the table and lift the sheet. Finally, trembling and on the verge of fainting, she forced herself to do it.

All the ghosts in the old house seemed to press in on her as she raised the sheet. It took only a single, brief look to tell her it was Martha! The wan face had beauty in death, even with the wildly staring eyes which told of the horror of her last moments alive. Worst of all, someone had begun dissecting the body! An arm had been detached and the surgical knife lay there, bloodied from its task!

Ann hastily covered the body again and turned away in a state of near collapse. As her mother-in-law placed an arm around her for support, she murmured, "Martha! It is Martha!"

"Then she has been murdered!" Flora Stewart said.

"Butchered! The scalpel there!" Ann said. And her rage making her stronger again, she added, "So it had to be Harry Turner! Her body shows the marks of a trained surgeon's knife!"

Mrs. McQuoid and old Charles were standing in open-mouthed horror at all this. The door to the cellar was open and there was the possibility that the murderer might be still lurking out there.

Ann told Charles, "Make a quick survey of the cellar proper. See if you find anything."

"Yes, ma'am," the old man said and started out.

Then Ann told Mrs. McQuoid, "You had better follow him and call out at the first sign of danger."

"I'll do that," the cook agreed, following the old coachman out.

Flora Stewart gave her a distressed glance as soon as they were left alone in the room. "What will we do now?"

Ann was battling to keep her thoughts clear. She said, "This could make things worse! The body wasn't left here just to terrify us! It was done to implicate Ian more!"

His mother nodded. "I believe it! And if the body has been partly dissected it will point to Ian all the more!"

"Harry Turner has done his work well," Ann said grimly. "You must go back to Stormhaven and bring Ian's father here!"

"I agree," Flora Stewart said. "We need someone to take this situation and report what has happened. And we can only pray that they will not think Ian had a hand in this."

"I now want him to be in Glasgow," Ann said. "That could be his salvation."

"I will lose no time," her mother-in-law said. They left the room just as the two servants were returning from their search of the cellars.

"We found no one," Charles told Ann.

"I didn't expect you would," she said bitterly. "He has safely escaped."

She sent her mother-in-law off in her coach to fetch Ian's father. And then she had Charles go out and get the carriage and go to Dr. Jock Gregory's with the news of this latest terrifying development. This left only she and Mrs. McQuoid in the house. But they would not be alone for long, and she did not think that the murderer was likely to return.

Mrs. McQuoid hovered near her after the others had gone and after a little, asked, "Is there anything I can do, ma'am?"

Trying to keep her busy, she told the old woman, "Make me some strong black tea! I need something!"

"I will, ma'am," Mrs. McQuoid promised and hurried down the long, dark hallway to the kitchen.

Now Ann was alone with the full agony of her doubts and fears. It seemed to her almost certain that Dr. Harry Turner was the murderer. And this would mean it was also Turner who'd been mixed up with the grave robbing! But all the time he had plotted to place the blame on her husband, and there was a chance he might yet succeed. The mob of angry citizens who had stoned the house earlier had shown the temper of the people. Once it became known that Martha had been murdered and her body dissected in the cellar of Mercy House, it was all too likely the mob would return and this time finish their work!

Earlier, she'd been hoping that Ian would return. Now she was equally anxious that he should not. It seemed to her his only bleak hope of escaping blame lay in his being in that other city on this night of horror. Soon Ian's father would return and take hold of things. He would know exactly what to do and who to summon.

If Charles found Dr. Gregory at home she had no doubt that he would come to her aid as soon as possible. So with these two men to direct things, the best possible judgment should be shown. There could be no errors now. Not with Ian under the shadow he was.

And what about Samuel Todd? What would his reaction be when he learned that Martha had been a victim of the body thieves? His anger and sorrow would be impossible to measure, and he would lash out at everyone. Worse, he was firmly of the opinion that Ian headed the ring of grave robbers!

She was standing in the shadowed hallway debating all these things when she heard what she thought was a cry from the kitchen. Thinking Mrs. McQuoid might have had some kind of accident, she rushed down the dark hall to the kitchen. When she threw the door open and burst in, she saw no sign of the old woman for a moment.

Then she spotted her stretched out on the flagstone floor by the stove. There was blood trickling from her temple where someone had given her a blow on the head!

"Mrs. McQuoid!" she exclaimed. And she ran over to the prostrate woman and knelt by her. The injured woman was breathing but unconscious.

Ann remained at her side a moment. Then, hoping that Ian's father and mother might be arriving within a short space, she hurried back to the hallway to look for them. It was hard to say whether Mrs. McQuoid was badly hurt or not. But what really terrified her was the knowledge that someone had been in the kitchen and attacked her.

Now Ann knew that she was not alone in the house! The murderer was somewhere lurking in the shadows! But where?

She hesitated by the front door, ready to rush out into the night and worrying that whoever it was might be expecting that. He might be waiting for her out there in the darkness, ready to spring on her.

So she remained there, frozen with fear. And then, as her terror seemed to have reached the breaking point, she noticed that the front door was slowly opening. She watched it with a shocked fascination.

The door handle was turning and the door opening, inch by inch. She was about to shriek out her terror when she suddenly saw who it was. The door had opened sufficiently to reveal a pale and gaunt Ian, hatless and looking as if he'd been in some kind of scuffle!

"Ian!" she cried.

"Ann," he said in a dull voice and took a step towards her.

All at once fresh fears surged through her. Ian was here! This changed everything! It meant the body in the cellar could have been his work. He could be the killer after all!

Tautly, she asked, "How long have you been here?"

"Not long." There was a strangeness in his eyes.

"Have you been in the cellar?"

"No."

"Did you strike down Mrs. McQuoid?"

He shook his head. "No."

"When did you get back from Glasgow?"

"Tonight! Listen to me, Ann," he begged her and he came closer to her.

She backed away from him, on the edge of hysteria now. She said, "I can't believe you! Not anymore!"

"You must!" he implored her.

"There is a secret passage into this house, isn't there?"

"Yes," he said. "There's a tunnel from the cellar to a fake tomb in the cemetery. Mercy had it built as a means to escape if robbers hit the house. He had a mania about it!"

Accusingly, she said, "You didn't tell me about it!"

"I didn't want to make you afraid!"

Scornfully, she said, "Afraid! I've been afraid ever since I set foot here! And you didn't mind because it suited you!"

"Ann, please," he begged.

"You used that tunnel," she said excitedly. "Used it for

your trade in bodies. You and that Mad Marsh! And you were in the house earlier tonight. You brought Martha's body here and struck down Mrs. McQuoid!"

He looked at her oddly. "Martha's body!"

"You killed her, just as you killed Nancy! You are mad! I should have guessed it long ago! But I didn't want to accept it!"

"Ann!" He came to take her in his arms.

"No!" she screamed, and she turned and ran down the hall to the door leading to the cellar. She quickly went in to the steps and closed the door after her. Then she bolted it. She heard Ian pounding on the door and pleading with her to open it.

But she knew that she daren't. He was violent and ready to deal with her next. Sick with despair, she made her way down the cellar steps. How long before his father and mother would come to rescue her? What would be their feeling when they knew that Ian was there and insane?

She moved towards the candlelit study. She was caught between two horrors. The lesser one seemed the dead body of Martha in there on the operating table. Slowly she made her way to the open doorway of the room. The fluttering candles gave a weird, soft glow of light over the sheet-covered body and made her think of the old mansion's ghosts.

Now there would be a new tale of horror to add to the history of the grim old house. Somewhere down here was the passage to the cemetery and freedom. If she could only find it she might escape. But then there was the chance that Ian might be waiting for her in the cemetery at the other end of the tunnel—waiting to kill her!

She had not listened to him! She'd not been able to. And what about poor Mrs. McQuoid? She was torn by all these different thoughts as she stood there waiting.

Waiting for what? She asked herself the question, and she knew the answer might be death! If Ian could get to her he would surely add her to his list of victims!

The rustling came from the other end of the surgery. The end which was all in darkness. She did not locate where it came from at first. And then, as she turned to stare in the direction of the eerie sound, she was stunned to see a figure gradually shaping in the darkness!

The figure of the headless man!

"No!" she screamed and stumbled back.

But the man without a head sprang forward and his hands gripped her throat. She screamed and fought to free herself. But it was to no avail. She soon knew she would be defeated. The hands closed off her screams and gradually were shutting off her breathing!

Her eyes were wide and filled with terror! Her lovely face was turning purple, and she knew that very soon she must lose consciousness. The creature without a head loomed over her, gradually throttling her!

From somewhere, a vast distance away, her name was called. And she felt a glow of hope. She had recognized the voice. It was Ian who had shouted out to her. All her fear and hatred of him had vanished in this moment when she was so near death. She only heard his voice and was satisfied.

After that, things happened with a startling rapidity. She was first conscious of being released from the stranglehold which had been finishing her. Now she lay on her side on the floor and vaguely was aware of a struggle between Ian and the headless ghost. It seemed a long and fierce struggle to her. But everything was very mixed-up in her mind.

Then the struggle suddenly ended and a battered Ian was standing over his adversary, breathing heavily. He stood there a moment before he turned and came over to her. Kneeling by her, he asked, "How are you?"

"All right," she whispered hoarsely, her throat aching.

"He nearly had you."

"Yes."

"After you locked the door on me, I had to go to the cemetery and come back by the tunnel. I was almost too late!"

"I know," she said, staring at him, still dazed. Tears came into her eyes. "I blamed you!"

"That doesn't matter!"

"I should have known better!"

"You had a right to believe anything," her husband said wearily. "Can you stand up?"

"Yes," she said.

He helped her to her feet and said, "I'll take you upstairs."

"The ghost?"

Ian's face was grim. "He won't give us any trouble for a while. He's unconscious."

"Who?" she asked.

"See for yourself," her husband said.

She slowly turned to gaze at the unconscious figure on the floor. The disguise which had made him seem headless had been torn away so that his face was revealed. And she felt stunned as she recognized the ruined, creased face of Angus McCrae!

"Angus!" she said in disbelief.

"We'll talk about this later," Ian told her, and then he guided her out of the room and they went upstairs.

Hours had passed. Ian's father and mother had arrived and Ian's father had taken control of the situation. The stern banker was at his best in this sort of crisis. The proper authorities were summoned and Angus McCrae turned over to them. Martha's body was also removed from the premises.

Dr. Jock Gregory had arrived shortly after Ian's parents and surprisingly had brought along with him his colleague, Dr. Clinton Marsh. Mrs. McQuoid had recovered from her faint. She had been only slightly injured by the blow which she'd received on her head.

But her indignation knew no bounds. "To think that Angus would harm me after all the meals I gave him!" This was what she could not forget.

It was long after midnight as they all gathered in the parlor of the red brick house. Ann herself prepared the hot tea which everyone seemed to need. And then Ian's father took over.

He called on Ian, saying, "I think we are entitled to an explanation and it had best come from you."

Ian gave Ann a warm glance, and then he went over and conferred with Dr. Marsh who was seated at the opposite side of the room. After this brief discussion he came to the middle of the room.

Ian said, "First, let me say that Dr. Marsh and I have been dealing in bodies for dissection. But in a strictly legal manner. The bodies were mostly brought by vessel from England and were those of criminals who had died on the gallows."

Ian's father asked, "Were these the caskets which Ann saw in the cellar here?"

"Yes," Ian said. "They were later moved to the university. Dr. Marsh and I knew an illegal trade had been going on in bodies, but we had nothing to do with it."

Ian's father frowned. "What about Nancy?"

"It was with the murder of Nancy and the attempt to place the blame on me and Dr. Marsh that we became suspicious. Dr. Marsh knew the captain of the vessel which had brought us the bodies from England was in Glasgow. He sent me there to get him and bring him back. He also asked me to find out something else."

"What else?" Ian's father wanted to know.

"Many years ago," Ian said, "Dr. Marsh had an associate whom he had to dismiss. His name was Dr. Andrew Coombs. He had fallen into drinking to the point where he could no longer look after his duties."

Dr. Jock Gregory spoke up. "I remember Coombs! Clever surgeon but a little mad! And when he was in his cups, all mad!"

Ian nodded. "That's the man. He left Edinburgh and was lost track of for a long while. Then he got himself in trouble in England with grave robbing. He somehow passed the blame to someone else and returned to Glasgow. After that, he dropped out of sight."

Dr. Gregory said, "But you found him?"

"Yes," Ian said. "I located people who knew him in Glasgow and learned he'd taken the name of Angus Mc-Crae. I at once recalled that Ann had spoken of a drunk and derelict grave digger who lived in a tomb in the cemetery. And this derelict bore that same name."

"I can see that," Ian's father exclaimed. "Clever of him to set himself up as a harmless, drunken grave digger when he was actually heading a gang of grave robbers. What better place for him to be?"

"Mercy Cemetery suited him perfectly," Ian said. "And he might well have gotten away with robbing the graves and murdering poor Nancy, had he not been so madly anxious to even the score with Dr. Marsh. And when he involved Dr. Marsh he had to involve me, since Marsh and I have been working together."

Dr. Marsh spoke for the first time, saying, "I began to suspect it was the work of someone with a grudge against me."

"Someone who was a doctor," Ian said. "It didn't take Dr. Marsh long to think about Andrew Coombs and to ask me to try and locate him in Glasgow."

Ian's father said, "So you went to Glasgow on a double mission?"

"Yes. The captain is here to substantiate our story about receiving bodies from England on his ship. And I brought back what I needed to know about the missing Andrew Coombs. Only I didn't return soon enough to save Martha Todd."

"You should have confided in Ann," his father told him.

"I suppose I should have," the young man agreed. "But at that moment things were very mixed-up."

Dr. Jock Gregory rose and said, "I think we can be thankful. We have our murderer and the leader of the grave-robbing ring. There need be no more of the grisly business."

The harsh voice of Dr. Clinton Marsh interrupted him, "It will continue! Make no mistake about that!" The old surgeon had risen. "As long as the profession is denied the use of bodies for dissection there will be a market for stolen cadavers."

Dr. Jock Gregory listened with a serious expression on his pleasant face. "I am forced to agree with you. Until the situation is dealt with properly, the evil trade will go on. But not here in Glasgow. At least not for a while."

"Amen to that," Ian's father said. "Enough tragedy has been caused by it."

Flora told her husband, "And now we must go back to Stormhaven. We can do no more here." She went over and kissed first Ann, then Ian, good night. It was a signal for the gathering to break up.

Ian's father came to them and said, "I know Ian will have to see his patients here until he can find another place. But there is no need for you to go on living here. There is plenty of room at Stormhaven. I want you to stay with us until you have found another, more suitable home."

Ann brightened. "Thank you," she said. "I'll pack and come tomorrow."

They saw everyone on their way. Ann made a special check on Mrs. McQuoid to see that she was all right. The old woman was sleeping peacefully.

Rejoining Ian, she said, "Mrs. McQuoid seems fine now. She's having a sound sleep."

"I'm glad," her husband said. "She and Charles can remain here and keep the place in order until I locate another property."

"This will be our last night here," she said, gazing around her.

Ian nodded. "At least we'll be together."

Her eyes met his. "Can you forgive me for doubting you?"

"You had every reason to doubt me," he assured her. "It is I who should ask your forgiveness. Dr. Marsh insisted that we operate in strict secrecy and that wasn't fair to you."

"In the end, I was blaming Harry Turner," she told him.

"Poor Harry! He'd never be capable of such things," Ian said. "You should know that!"

"I don't know him as well as you do," she said.

"That's obvious. It had to be someone completely unscrupulous and a good bit mad. Your Angus McCrae fit the bill."

She gave a tiny shudder. "I should have known he was mad from the start."

"Don't think about it," Ian said gently, and he drew her to him for a long embrace. Then they went upstairs.

More than three months had passed and already summer was ending and the first signs of autumn were in the air. The brief stay which Ian and Ann had expected to make at Stormhaven had extended into more than a quarter of a year. Ann did not mind, as she enjoyed the imposing mansion with its fine gardens and she was able to get to know Ian's family better.

Ian's father and mother were gracious and charming. And even their son, Walter, and his wife, Heather Rae, were pleasant enough. Ann enjoyed minding their children. And the two youngsters seemed to take an instant liking to her.

Ian's practice returned to normal. With his vindication his popularity increased. He and Dr. Harry Turner continued to be rivals for the pick of the city's patients. Martha's tragic end made a change in Harry. He became a much more serious person.

Hannigan and Scott, the grave robbers, were finally caught and hung along with the mad Andrew Coombs. It was ironic that in death they provided legal bodies for dissection. Dr. Marsh, for all his grim qualities, politely refused the bodies and they went to other doctors.

Samuel Todd was grieved to an extent none of them had expected by the tragic fate of his sister. He shortly after abandoned his law practice in Edinburgh and went to England. Rumor had it that he hoped to be active in the criminal courts as a prosecutor.

Ann enjoyed the company of her young sister-in-law, Sophie, who was in a temporarily depressed state because her Italian music teacher had run off with another wealthy Edinburgh girl.

"I shall never trust a man again!" The eighteen-year-old had exclaimed with indignation.

"I don't believe that," Ann smiled at her, "and neither do you!"

Roger, Ann's sixteen-year-old brother-in-law worshipped her. His calf love was amusing to the others but pitiful to Ann. She tried to be kind to him and encouraged him in his plans to one day be a famous builder of bridges.

"Let the rest of the Stewarts gather dust in their banks," Roger said scornfully. "I'll have a real life!"

"Ian also has his career," she reminded the boy. "He made the first break by deciding to be a doctor."

"I don't count him," Roger said. "He's so much older."

Ann smiled. She and Ian were close to the same age.

Dr. Jock Gregory was a regular visitor to Stormhaven. And one fine evening in the early autumn he sought Ann out in the garden. She had gone out to gather some flowers for the tables before the frost killed them. When the sturdy little bald man approached her she was on her knees by a rose bed.

"Good evening," he said. "Have you heard the news?"

She rose and faced him. "What news?"

"Ian hasn't told you?" Dr. Gregory asked.

"He hasn't been home yet," she replied.

Dr. Gregory looked pleased. "He's been appointed to take Marsh's place at the university. Marsh is retiring."

Ann was only slightly surprised at the news. She said, "We have discussed his teaching medicine. I think he wants to do it. I'm glad he's accepted the post."

"And you know what goes with it?" Dr. Gregory said. "A

delightful cottage on Rock Street near the university. Your search for a house is over."

"I'm glad," she said. "I've enjoyed being at Stormhaven. But I do want a home of my own."

Dr. Gregory turned and said, "I'm afraid I've spoiled things. Here comes Ian now. And he'll want to give you the news himself."

She laughed. "It doesn't matter all that much!"

Ian came up to them. He smiled at the doctor and then turned to her. "I can tell by your face. You've heard!"

"Yes," she said. "I've heard. A new life and a new house."

"And this time it will be all right," Ian said confidently as he took her in his arms.